THE HIUNTING OF HOLLOW PIRK

By Evelyn Cross

Copyright © 2025 Evelyn Cross
All rights reserved.

No part of this book may be reproduced, distributed, or transmitted in any form or by any means, including photocopying, recording, or other electronic or mechanical methods, without the prior written permission of the publisher, except in the case of brief quotations embodied in critical reviews and certain other noncommercial uses permitted by copyright law.

For information, address:
@realevelyncross

Cover Design by Evelyn Cross
Edited by Evelyn Cross

For K.T. Carlisle,
 Your writing opened my eyes to the beauty of suspense, the thrill of mystery, and the deep, lingering fear that comes from a well-crafted story. Your work inspired me to push boundaries and embrace the darker corners of the imagination. Thank you for being a guiding light in my journey as a writer.

Table of Contents

Prologue…4

Chapter 1…5

Chapter 2…26

Chapter 3…41

Chapter 4…55

Chapter 5…69

Chapter 6…105

Chapter 7…116

Chapter 8…138

Chapter 9…157

Chapter 10…169

Chapter 11…177

Chapter 12…188

Chapter 13…198

Chapter 14…219

Epilogue…231

Prologue

Hollow Park was once a place of laughter and light, a thriving amusement park that drew families from all over the country. During its prime in the early 2000s, it was a beacon of joy—bright lights, towering roller coasters, the scent of popcorn and fried dough filling the air. The echoes of children's laughter and the distant melody of carnival music wove together into a symphony of happiness. It was a place where memories were made, where summer nights stretched long, and where the world outside seemed to disappear, if only for a little while.

Then, in 2010, the first strange occurrences began. Rides would malfunction without explanation, whirring to life long after closing hours. Ferris wheel gondolas swayed on windless nights. Carousel horses twisted and jerked in slow, unnatural movements, their painted eyes seeming to follow guests as they walked by. Employees brushed it off at first—faulty wiring, mechanical failures, the wear and tear of time. But the problems grew worse. Entire attractions refused to power down, remaining illuminated and running in the dead of night, even when disconnected from their circuits.

A year later, in 2011, the first children went missing. Families would turn their backs for mere seconds, only to find their sons and daughters gone without a trace. Security footage captured nothing unusual—just children stepping out of sight, never to be seen again. Then, in 2012, it wasn't just children. Adults vanished, too. Parents. Employees. Tourists. Their disappearances were swift, unexplained, and left no evidence behind.

Rumors spread like wildfire. Guests whispered that some of the animatronics looked too real, their movements too fluid, their eyes too knowing. Others complained about an awful stench lingering near the rides, a smell that no amount of cleaning could erase. Employees reported hearing voices long after the park had emptied, whispers woven into the hum of the machinery. Shadows stretched too far, moving in ways they shouldn't.

By 2015, Hollow Park was shut down, the official report citing a gas leak as the cause. But no one believed it. The people who lived near the park claimed that, even years later, they could still hear it—the distant music playing on the wind, the rusted rides creaking as if still in motion. Some swore they saw figures moving between the stalls and coasters, flickering shapes that disappeared when approached.

The legend took on a life of its own. The ghosts of the missing, trapped in an endless loop, doomed to ride the attractions for eternity. The cursed theme park, forever holding onto the souls it had taken.

But those were just stories.

No one really knows what happened to the missing people.

Chapter One

The halls of Westbrook High buzzed with the usual end-of-day energy—lockers slamming shut, voices overlapping in conversation, the occasional burst of laughter echoing down the corridor. The late afternoon sunlight filtered through the windows, casting long streaks across the worn linoleum floors.

Dakota Jones adjusted the strap of his backpack as he walked alongside Lane Williams, weaving through the crowd of students heading in different directions. Their last class of the day was just around the corner, but Dakota's mind was elsewhere.

"Alright," Dakota said, nudging Lane with his elbow. "After school, we check out the place on Maple Street."

Lane smirked, running a hand through his already messy brown hair. "You sure it's not just another busted-up shack? The last one barely even had a roof."

"That's what makes it fun," Dakota countered. "Besides, this one's supposed to be a little different. My brother said it was abandoned for years, but no one's ever really gone inside. The doors are still boarded up."

Lane raised an eyebrow. "So... breaking and entering?"

"More like creative exploring," Dakota said with a grin.

As they reached the classroom, Dakota let out a sigh, leaning against the doorframe. "I can't wait until we graduate, man. No more curfews, no more school schedules. We can finally go further—bigger places, real abandoned spots, not just these old houses in town."

Lane gave a small laugh. "Yeah, yeah. Just don't get ahead of yourself. We've still got a month left of this place."

But Dakota's mind was already past that. He could see it—road trips, forgotten buildings, history waiting to be uncovered. They were just getting started.

Dakota leaned back in his chair, half-listening to the teacher drone on about something he was sure wouldn't matter after graduation. His gaze drifted toward the window, where the early April sun cast a warm glow over the parking lot. Just one more month, and he'd be free.

A hushed conversation a few desks over caught his attention. Two classmates, Tyler and Marcus, whispered back and forth, their voices just low enough to make eavesdropping feel unintentional.

"I'm telling you, they just disappeared," Tyler murmured.

Marcus scoffed. "People don't just vanish, dude."

"Then explain Hollow Park," Tyler shot back. "Those people—poof. Gone. No bodies, no clues, nothing."

At the mention of the old theme park, Dakota's attention sharpened. He hadn't thought about Hollow Park in years. He'd only been once, back in the summer when it first opened, but he didn't remember much—just flashes of bright lights, the smell of popcorn, the distant screams from roller coasters twisting through the sky. It had been just another theme park. Or so he thought.

Marcus leaned in, lowering his voice even more. "Isn't it some big investigation now?"

"Yeah," Tyler nodded. "A couple of adults and a bunch of kids. Gone without a trace. No one knows what happened."

Dakota frowned, shifting in his seat. He hadn't heard much about the disappearances, but the way Tyler spoke about them sent an uneasy chill down his spine.

Tyler leaned in, his voice just above a whisper. "They've been looking into it for almost a year now. The park isn't even allowed to open again until they figure out what happened."

Marcus let out a low whistle. "Damn. So what, if they don't solve it, the place just stays shut down forever?"

Tyler shrugged. "Pretty much. Owners are losing money every day it stays closed. If this drags on much longer, they'll probably just shut it down for good."

Marcus shook his head. "Man, that sucks. Hollow Park was sick. I went there a couple of times before all the weird shit started happening."

Tyler scoffed. "Yeah? Would you go back now?"

Marcus hesitated for a second too long. "I mean… maybe not at night."

Dakota stayed quiet, pretending to be focused on his notes, but his mind lingered on what he'd just heard. A year-long investigation, people missing without a trace, a theme park on the verge of permanent closure. He hadn't really thought about Hollow Park since that one summer, but now, he couldn't help but wonder—what the hell happened there?

The final bell rang, and the usual flood of students spilled into the hallways, eager to escape another day of high school. Dakota weaved through the crowd, spotting Lane near his locker.

"You ready?" Dakota asked, leaning against the metal doors.

Lane smirked. "For what? Sitting on a bus for twenty minutes?"

"For later," Dakota clarified. "Grab the flashlights, I'll bring the camera. Meet me at my place after dinner."

Lane nodded as they made their way outside and climbed onto the bus, slipping into their usual seats near the middle. The ride home was the same as always—background chatter, the hum of the engine, the occasional burst of laughter from the back.

"So, how are we getting in?" Lane asked, stretching his legs out in the narrow space between the seats.

Dakota shrugged. "Windows are boarded up, but the back door might be loose. Worst case, we find another way."

Lane smirked. "You mean I find another way while you supervise?"

Dakota chuckled. "Exactly."

The bus slowed as it approached Dakota's stop. He stood up, slinging his backpack over one shoulder. "See you after dinner," he said over his shoulder before stepping off.

The warm scent of something cooking greeted him as he walked through the front door. From the kitchen, his mom's voice called out, "Hey, honey! How was school?"

"Fine," Dakota replied, kicking off his shoes. "Lane and I are gonna hit the library after dinner to study."

"Alright," she said. "Just don't stay out too late."

Dakota smiled to himself as he headed to his room. If only she knew.

Dakota sat on the edge of his bed, flipping absentmindedly through his phone. The soft hum of the house surrounded him—the faint clatter of dishes from the kitchen, the distant murmur of the TV from the living room. The air was warm, carrying the comforting scent of roasted chicken and spices, a familiar staple in their house. His mom always had dinner ready around the same time every night, like clockwork.

Just as he started to relax, his bedroom door creaked open.

Bryan, his older brother by two years, leaned against the frame, arms crossed. His dark eyes studied Dakota for a moment before he smirked. "You remember Hollow Park?"

Dakota glanced up, raising an eyebrow. "Yeah, why?"

Bryan stepped inside, leaving the door half-open behind him. He had the same lazy confidence he always carried, but there was something different in his tone—something more serious. "I overheard some guys at work talking about it. Apparently, there's a whole investigation going on. People missing, weird shit happening."

Dakota frowned, sitting up straighter. "Yeah, I heard some guys at school talking about it too. Something about how no one knows what happened to the missing people."

Bryan nodded, dropping onto the chair at Dakota's desk, spinning it slightly side to side with his foot. "It's been a year, and they still don't have answers. I remember when that place first opened—place was packed, people came from all over. Now? It's just sitting there, rotting."

Dakota thought back to the one time he'd gone. His memories of Hollow Park were faint—flashes of neon lights, the distant sound of music, the metallic tang of greasy amusement park food in the air. It had felt normal back then. Just another theme park.

"I don't get it," Dakota said after a moment. "It was just a park. What the hell happened to make people disappear?"

Bryan shrugged. "That's the thing—nobody knows. Some people say it's haunted. Some say it was a serial killer. Others think the owners knew more than they let on." He leaned forward, resting his elbows on his knees. "But one thing's for sure—something isn't right with that place."

A heavy silence settled between them. Dakota wasn't the kind to buy into ghost stories, but something about the way people talked about Hollow Park made his skin crawl.

"Anyway," Bryan finally said, pushing himself up from the chair. "Figured you'd wanna know. You and Lane are always messing around in creepy places. Just… stay the hell away from that one."

Dakota smirked. "What, worried about me?"

Bryan scoffed, already halfway out the door. "Worried about Mom having to put up missing posters."

The door clicked shut behind him, leaving Dakota alone with his thoughts.

For the first time, he wondered—if he and Lane ever did visit Hollow Park, would they be the ones to finally figure out the truth?

Or would they just become another story?

Dakota shook his head, forcing the thought away. It was just rumors—stories passed around like urban legends, growing more elaborate with every retelling. The investigation was still ongoing, and sooner or later, they'd find something. A logical explanation. The disappearances had only happened last year. He was sure Hollow Park would reopen in a few months, running like nothing ever happened.

His stomach rumbled, pulling him from his thoughts. Right on cue, his mom's voice rang from the kitchen.

"Dinner's ready!"

Dakota stretched, pushing himself off the bed and heading down the hall. The warmth from the kitchen was immediate, wrapping around him like a familiar blanket. The house smelled of roasted chicken and buttery mashed potatoes, a comforting aroma that reminded him of childhood. The wooden table in the center of the room had already been set, plates stacked in the middle, steam rising from the food.

Bryan was already seated, hunched over his plate, fork in hand, barely acknowledging Dakota as he walked in. Dakota grabbed a plate, scooped up some chicken, mashed potatoes, and green beans, then took a seat across from his brother.

Their mother sat down moments later, brushing a few strands of graying hair from her face before reaching for her own plate. She always carried herself with quiet warmth, her eyes filled with that ever-present mix of concern and pride only a mother could have.

With graduation looming, it didn't take long for the conversation to turn to the future.

"So," she began, cutting into her chicken. "Have you put any more thought into what you're going to do after graduation?"

Bryan barely looked up from his plate. "Get a job, I guess."

Dakota raised an eyebrow. "That's specific."

Bryan smirked. "What, is that not what you're going to do? Fine. Get a warehouse job, drive a forklift or something." He popped a green bean into his mouth and shrugged. "Pays good, easy enough."

Their mom sighed. "Bryan, you've got good grades, you could go to college—"

"Not for me," Bryan said, shaking his head. "I'm not built to sit in a classroom for another four years."

She turned to Dakota, hope in her eyes. "What do you think?"

Dakota leaned back slightly, twirling his fork between his fingers. "Something exciting. Maybe video or content creation."

Bryan snorted, nearly choking on his drink. "Oh yeah, because that's a real job."

Dakota shot him a glare. "People make money off it. You just have to be creative."

Bryan smirked. "Right. And in the meantime, you're living off ramen in some dingy apartment."

Their mother sighed, giving Bryan a pointed look before turning back to Dakota. "It's your life, sweetheart. Just make sure you have a plan. Something solid."

Dakota nodded, but in his head, he already had a plan—one that involved cameras, adventure, and exploring places most people were too scared to step foot in.

And he wasn't going to let anyone tell him otherwise.

Dakota let out a satisfied sigh as he pushed his empty plate aside. The meal had been good—warm, filling, the kind of home-cooked dinner he knew he'd miss once he was out on his own. He stood, gathering his plate and silverware before rinsing them off in the sink. The water was warm against his fingers, and the scent of dish soap filled the air as he quickly washed away the remnants of mashed potatoes.

His mom looked up from her own plate, giving him a soft smile as he walked over. "Leaving already?"

Dakota wrapped his arms around her in a quick hug. "Yeah. Gotta meet Lane."

She squeezed him gently before letting go. "Be careful, okay?"

"I always am."

Bryan scoffed from the table. "That's debatable."

Dakota rolled his eyes but didn't bother responding. He grabbed his backpack from the corner of the kitchen and slung it over one shoulder before heading toward the front door. As soon as he opened it, the cool evening air rushed in, a welcome contrast to the warmth of the house.

Lane was already outside, leaning casually against the porch railing, hands stuffed into the pockets of his hoodie. The streetlights were just beginning to flicker on, casting long shadows across the pavement. The sky had deepened into a rich navy blue, the last streaks of sunset barely visible on the horizon.

Dakota stepped out, letting the door swing shut behind him. From inside, his mom's voice called out one last time. "Be careful!"

He glanced at Lane, who grinned. "You ready?"

Dakota smirked, reaching into his bag. "Always."

He pulled out the camera—an old, cheap video recorder he'd had for years. The dark blue plastic casing was covered in scratches, the edges scuffed from being dropped one too many times. It wasn't the best, but it got the job done.

As they walked down the street, the fading sunlight casting eerie shadows on the cracked sidewalk, Dakota flipped open the camera. The familiar start-up jingle played, a sound he'd heard a hundred times before.

He turned it toward himself, pressing record.

"Uh… hey guys, welcome back to another exploration video," Dakota started, voice slightly awkward.

Lane chuckled beside him. "Dude, you suck at intros."

Dakota groaned. "I know, I know. I never get these right."

Lane smirked. "Good thing no one watches them."

Dakota laughed, shaking his head. He turned the camera toward the road ahead as they neared the abandoned house, its dark silhouette looming against the twilight sky.

Their adventure was just beginning.

Lane reached into his backpack, rummaging around before pulling out two flashlights. He clicked one on, casting a beam of light across the cracked pavement, illuminating patches of overgrown grass creeping through the sidewalk. The other, he handed to Dakota, who took it without a word, focusing on his camera instead.

With a quick tap of the buttons, Dakota switched the camera to night vision mode. The dull greens and blacks filled the tiny screen, giving the world an eerie, otherworldly look. The abandoned house ahead of them came into clearer view, its sagging roof and boarded-up windows standing like a relic of the past.

He turned the camera toward Lane. "Alright, man. What's the count? How many places have we hit so far?"

Lane smirked, adjusting the strap of his backpack. "Let's see… there was the old train station, the mill on the outskirts of town, that busted-up motel by the highway—"

Dakota groaned. "Oh yeah, the motel. That place was nasty."

Lane laughed. "Dude, I told you not to touch anything, but you had to go sticking your hands in random drawers."

"I was looking for cool stuff," Dakota defended. "Not my fault all I found were rat droppings and a dead cockroach."

Lane shook his head, grinning. "Alright, so this is, what, number… eight?"

"Nine," Dakota corrected, angling the camera toward the house ahead. "And this one's different. The last few were just run-down buildings. This place? No one's been inside in years. Still boarded up."

Lane turned his flashlight toward the house, its dim beam barely cutting through the growing darkness. "Which means, best case, we're the first ones to check it out. Worst case…" He trailed off, glancing at Dakota with a smirk.

Dakota turned the camera back toward himself. "Worst case, we find something we shouldn't."

Lane chuckled. "As long as it's not another cockroach nest, I'm good."

The house loomed in front of them now, the cool night air settling heavily around them. Dakota could already feel the anticipation creeping in—this was why they did this. The rush, the mystery, the thrill of stepping into the unknown.

He pointed the camera toward the front door.

"Let's see what's inside."

The wooden porch groaned beneath their weight as Dakota and Lane stepped up to the front door, their footsteps crunching on the brittle, overgrown leaves scattered across the worn planks. The air smelled of dust and dry rot, the scent of something long abandoned, left to decay.

Dakota reached for the rusted handle, curling his fingers around the metal and giving it a twist. The knob barely budged. He pressed his shoulder into the door and tried again, harder this time, but it refused to give.

"Guess we're not getting in that way," Lane muttered, sweeping his flashlight over the faded, peeling paint and cracked windows. The glass was so caked in grime it was impossible to see inside.

Dakota exhaled through his nose, stepping back. "Let's check the back."

Without another word, they moved along the side of the house, stepping carefully over uneven ground. The grass had long since died, leaving patches of dirt and tangled weeds in its place. The air felt heavier back here, thicker somehow, like the house itself was holding its breath.

The flashlight beam flickered across the backyard, revealing remnants of a life once lived—rusted playground equipment half-swallowed by the earth, a deflated basketball resting near a crumbling patio, the skeletal remains of a long-dead tree casting claw-like shadows against the house.

Then, there it was—the back door.

It wasn't much, just a warped sheet of plywood hanging loosely on rusted hinges, a simple latch lock keeping it in place. Dakota adjusted the camera in his grip, zooming in slightly. The plywood was weathered, speckled with black mold, its edges curling from years of exposure to the elements.

Lane crouched down, running his fingers along the latch. "This should be easy enough."

A quiet click sounded as the lock gave way, and with a cautious push, Lane eased the door open.

The creak that followed was long and drawn out, the kind of sound that made the hairs on the back of Dakota's neck stand up. It wasn't just the noise—it was the way it echoed, stretching out into the silence like a breath finally exhaled after years of stillness.

Lane turned his flashlight toward the opening, the beam barely cutting through the darkness inside. Dust particles drifted in the stagnant air, illuminated like tiny floating embers in the glow.

Dakota lifted the camera, focusing the lens on the entrance. "Looks safe enough," he muttered, though he wasn't entirely sure he believed it.

Still, he stepped forward.

His boots scuffed against the wooden floor as he crossed the threshold, the scent of mildew and stale air hitting him instantly. The air inside felt different, colder somehow, as if the temperature had dropped the moment they entered.

Lane followed close behind, nudging the door until it rested slightly ajar. The house swallowed them whole, the last sliver of the outside world disappearing behind them.

For a moment, neither of them spoke. The silence pressed in from all sides, thick and absolute.

Dakota tightened his grip on the camera, panning the lens across the shadowed room.

They were inside now.

The hunt for the unknown had begun.

The floorboards groaned beneath their feet as Dakota and Lane ventured deeper into the old house. The air was thick with dust, making each breath feel heavy, almost stale. Shadows stretched long across the peeling wallpaper as Dakota lifted his camera, the night vision casting an eerie green hue over everything.

"Alright," Dakota murmured, angling the camera toward the hallway ahead. "Looks like we're in the living room… or what's left of it. Walls are cracked, ceiling's sagging. No furniture, just a bunch of debris." He panned the camera toward the floor, where broken glass and chunks of plaster were scattered across the warped wooden boards. "Definitely abandoned for years. No signs of squatters, no graffiti… this place is the real deal."

Lane trailed slightly behind him, sweeping his flashlight across the adjacent rooms, checking every darkened corner. He muttered, "Damn, it smells in here."

Dakota smirked, keeping the camera rolling. "Well, yeah. Pretty sure no one's opened a window in decades."

The smell was bad—stale, damp, with a faint, underlying musk of decay. Not fresh, but old, lingering in the very bones of the house.

He turned the camera toward Lane, who wrinkled his nose as he aimed his flashlight down what looked like a hallway leading deeper into the house. "Yeah, but this is next level, man. Like, something died in here years ago and just… stayed."

"Adds to the charm," Dakota quipped, stepping forward. He turned the camera back to himself, adjusting his grip. "So, from what I read, this house belonged to an old couple—"

A sudden, blood-curdling scream ripped through the silence.

Dakota's breath caught in his throat, his entire body locking up as the sound echoed through the house. His pulse slammed into his ears, heart hammering against his ribs.

Lane.

Without thinking, he bolted toward the sound, camera shaking in his grip as he sprinted down the hall. His flashlight beam bounced wildly, casting frantic shadows along the walls.

"Lane?!" Dakota's voice cracked slightly, but he didn't care. His mind raced with possibilities—had something fallen? Had Lane fallen? Or—

He burst into the doorway of what looked like an old bathroom, skidding to a stop.

Lane stood frozen near the bathtub, his flashlight locked onto something inside. His breathing was uneven, his posture rigid.

Dakota hesitated at the threshold, his pulse still pounding. "Dude, what—"

Lane slowly lifted a hand, palm out. "Shut up."

Dakota swallowed hard, stepping closer. The camera was still rolling, capturing every shaky movement as he inched toward the tub. He had no idea what to expect—something dead, something alive? His mind conjured every horror it could.

Finally, he peered over the edge.

His stomach twisted.

The bathtub was filled with a giant, thickly woven spider nest. Layers upon layers of webbing stretched over the porcelain like a cocoon, dark with dust and time. The sheer size of it was grotesque, stretching up the sides like a pulsating mass. The thought of how many spiders had built it—how many still lurked inside—made Dakota's skin crawl.

Lane stood stiffly beside him, jaw clenched, staring at the monstrosity.

Dakota barely turned his head before Lane cut him off.

"Don't. Say. A word."

Dakota bit back a grin, but his wide-eyed horror was still genuine. He kept the camera trained on the nest.

"Jesus," he whispered.

Lane exhaled sharply, still not looking at him. "We're burning this house down when we leave."

They moved through the bottom floor with practiced ease, sweeping their flashlights across every inch of the decayed house. The walls, once painted in warm colors, had faded into dull, cracked remnants of their former selves. The wooden floors creaked under their careful steps, the air thick with the scent of dust, mildew, and something faintly sour—like wood rotting from the inside out.

Dakota kept the camera rolling, narrating in a low voice. "So far, just your standard abandoned house. Dust, decay, questionable smells. But I think we can all agree…" He turned the camera toward Lane with a smirk. "That nest in the tub was a work of nightmares."

Lane scoffed but kept his eyes on the flashlight beam sweeping over an old fireplace. "That was enough spiders to take over a whole town."

"Good thing this isn't some children's horror story," Lane muttered, pausing to peer into an old cabinet.

Dakota grinned. "Yeah, because we'd definitely be dead already."

Lane let out a small laugh, shaking his head.

Dakota turned the camera back toward himself. "Alright, so—this house. Here's what we know. Or, what we're saying we know." He gave the camera a pointed look. "Real or not, doesn't really matter as long as we keep you guys hooked."

His voice took on a storyteller's tone as he walked, panning the camera across the room. "This place supposedly belonged to an older couple who up and vanished. No moving trucks, no goodbye letters—just gone. Some say they died right here in the house. Others say they were never real to begin with. Either way, this place has been sitting here, untouched, ever since."

Lane rolled his eyes. "Very convincing."

"Thank you." Dakota smirked.

They wandered in silence for a few more moments, their footsteps the only sound in the hollowed-out house. Then, they reached the base of the staircase.

Dakota tilted the camera upward, the night vision casting an eerie glow over the warped wooden steps. The second floor loomed above, wrapped in shadows.

Lane hesitated, shining his flashlight over the staircase. "You think this is a good idea?"

Dakota glanced at him. "Getting cold feet?"

Lane shook his head. "Not worried about what's up there. Worried about these stairs. I mean, look at them." He pointed his flashlight at the warped wood. "What if they don't hold? What if we get stuck up there?"

Dakota shrugged. "Only one way to find out."

Lane sighed. "You're an idiot."

Dakota smirked before turning the camera to himself. "Alright, moment of truth. Will I plummet to my death? Stay tuned."

Slowly, he placed a foot on the first step. It groaned under his weight but didn't shift. He took another step. Then another. Each one was deliberate, his breath steady as he tested the stability. Every so often, he turned the camera back toward Lane, who watched from the bottom with a skeptical expression.

When Dakota finally reached the top, he turned the camera down toward Lane. "We're good. Just don't jump up and down when you get up here."

Lane let out an exaggerated sigh. "Fantastic."

He climbed up next, careful but not as hesitant as Dakota had been. When he reached the landing, they exchanged a glance before turning their attention to the hallway ahead.

They checked the first few rooms, sweeping their flashlights inside. All of them were empty—just dust and forgotten memories. Nothing unusual.

Then, a sound.

A sharp, distinct noise—like something shifting.

Both of them froze.

The noise had come from the end of the hall. From behind the only door they hadn't opened yet.

Slowly, they turned their flashlights toward it, the beams converging on the dark wood. The door was intact, closed, unlike the others.

Dakota swallowed, steadying his grip on the camera. He glanced at Lane, who arched an eyebrow before smirking.

Lane turned to both Dakota and the camera. "Alright. Let's take bets. What's behind the door?"

Dakota exhaled. "Giant spider that made the nest in the tub."

Lane hummed in thought. "Good guess. I'm going with escaped asylum patient."

Dakota snorted. "Classic."

Lane smirked. "You know me."

They turned back toward the door.

The air felt heavier now.

And then, without warning, the door creaked.

Their breath caught in their throats as they stared at the door, uncertain whether to step forward or back away. The once-abandoned house now felt different—less like an empty relic and more like something alive, aware of their presence.

Dakota tightened his grip on the camera, keeping it locked on the door. The faintest sliver of darkness was visible through the small opening, the wood cracked just enough to suggest something had shifted on the other side.

Lane's flashlight beam wobbled slightly. He adjusted his hold, clearing his throat in a failed attempt to mask the nerves creeping in. "So… what's the move?"

Dakota inhaled, steadying himself. "Only one way to find out."

Slowly, they inched forward, every step amplifying the eerie silence surrounding them. The floor creaked under their weight, the old wood groaning in protest.

They stopped just a few feet from the door, standing side by side. The air was thick, heavy.

Then, without warning—

The door swung open.

A blur of movement shot past them, followed by a sharp, earsplitting hiss.

Both of them jolted, Dakota stumbling back a step as Lane instinctively raised his flashlight like it was a weapon. The sound of claws skittering against wood echoed down the hallway before disappearing completely.

Silence returned.

It took them both a second to register what had just happened.

"A… a cat?" Dakota muttered, lowering the camera slightly.

Lane exhaled loudly, rubbing a hand down his face. "A goddamn cat."

For a beat, they just stood there, processing. Then—laughter.

It started slow, a chuckle from Dakota, before Lane doubled over, hands on his knees, laughing so hard his breath came in gasps. Dakota couldn't help it—he joined in, the weight of their nerves melting into exhaustion and relief.

"We almost died," Lane wheezed between laughs.

"By a cat." Dakota wiped at his eyes, still grinning. "Legendary explorers, scared shitless by a stray cat."

Lane shook his head, still grinning. "We're never telling anyone about this."

With the tension finally broken, they made their way downstairs, stepping a little lighter than before. The house no longer felt quite as ominous—just another old, forgotten place left behind by time.

As they stepped out the back door, Dakota turned the camera toward himself, composing the final shot. Lane pulled the plywood door shut behind them, securing the latch.

"Alright," Dakota said, angling the lens to capture both of them. "That's it for tonight. Another successful adventure—well, as successful as nearly getting murdered by a cat can be."

Lane snorted, shaking his head.

"We'll be back with another one soon," Dakota continued, glancing at Lane. "Maybe something bigger next time."

Lane smirked. "As long as it's cat-free."

Dakota grinned. "You guys know the drill. Like, subscribe, and drop a comment. Tell us—what's the scariest thing you've ever found in an abandoned place? Let us know, and maybe we'll check it out."

He gave a final wave before cutting the recording. The small beep of the camera shutting off felt like the official end to the night.

As they walked back toward their neighborhood, the streetlights buzzed faintly overhead, casting long, stretching shadows against the pavement. The cool night air was refreshing after the stale, suffocating atmosphere of the house.

They fell into an easy conversation, talking about the night, the footage, and, most importantly, their future.

"Man, I can't wait to get out of here," Dakota admitted, stuffing his hands into his jacket pockets. "Once we graduate, we can go anywhere. Find bigger places, abandoned asylums, entire ghost towns."

Lane nodded. "Yeah. No more school, no more schedules. Just us, the road, and a bunch of creepy-ass buildings."

Dakota smirked. "Living the dream."

Eventually, they reached the point where their paths split.

Lane gave a lazy salute. "Later, man."

"Later."

Dakota watched him go for a moment before turning toward his house, stepping up onto the porch. The warm glow from inside spilled through the living room window, a stark contrast to the darkness they had just returned from.

He pushed the door open and stepped inside.

His mom was sitting on the couch, book in hand, but the moment she saw him, she lowered it slightly. "There you are," she said, relief evident in her voice. "Where have you been? I was starting to get worried."

Dakota forced an easy smile. "Sorry, Mom. Lane and I went to his house after the library closed."

She glanced at the clock on the wall. 10:30 PM.

She didn't say anything right away, just sighed softly before shaking her head. "I just don't like you wandering around so late."

Dakota dropped his backpack onto the floor near the stairs. "I know. I get it. But, Mom… I'm eighteen. I can take care of myself."

She gave him a look, one that said *you'll always be my kid, I'll always worry*.

He softened. "I appreciate you caring, though. Really."

She studied him for a second, then smiled gently. "Just don't do anything stupid."

Dakota chuckled. "Too late for that."

She rolled her eyes but let it go.

He hesitated for a second before speaking again. "Love you, Mom."

Her expression warmed. "Love you too, sweetheart."

With that, Dakota turned and made his way upstairs.

As he shut his bedroom door behind him, he let out a long breath.

Tonight had been fun.

But soon, he and Lane would be going after something much bigger.

Something real.

Something dangerous.

And they had no idea what was waiting for them.

The smell of breakfast drifted through the air, warm and inviting, coaxing Dakota from the last remnants of sleep. The rich scent of bacon mixed with the sweetness of waffles, and somewhere beneath it all was the comforting aroma of fresh coffee brewing.

Yawning, he sat up, rubbing the sleep from his eyes before swinging his legs over the side of the bed. The cool floor sent a brief shiver up his spine as he stood, stretching his arms over his head. The morning light filtered through the blinds, casting faint golden lines across his walls.

Another school day. One step closer to graduation. One step closer to freedom.

After pulling on a pair of jeans and a hoodie, Dakota grabbed his backpack and made his way to the kitchen. The sizzle of bacon filled the space, his mother standing at the stove, focused on finishing up the last bit of food. The table was already set—plates stacked with eggs, waffles, and crispy bacon. A glass pitcher of orange juice sat in the middle, droplets of condensation sliding down its sides.

Dakota slid into his usual seat, grabbing the pitcher and pouring himself a glass. The cold citrus hit his throat, refreshing and sharp.

"Morning," he said, voice still laced with sleep.

His mother turned her head slightly, offering him a warm smile. "Morning, sweetheart." She set a full plate down in front of him before returning to the stove. "Eat up before it gets cold."

Dakota didn't need to be told twice. He picked up his fork, cutting into the eggs as he took his first bite. The familiar comfort of home-cooked breakfast settled in his stomach, and for a brief moment, everything felt calm, routine.

That calm was interrupted by the sound of shuffling footsteps.

Bryan appeared in the kitchen, his hair a complete mess, eyes barely open. He was still dressed in a wrinkled T-shirt and plaid pajama pants, dragging his feet across the tile floor. He let out a long yawn, stretching before dropping into the chair across from Dakota.

No good morning. No greeting. Just a lazy, half-mumbled, "What's for breakfast?" as he rubbed his face.

Dakota smirked, taking another bite of his eggs.

Their mother, still tending to the stove, didn't even bother turning around. Instead, she answered with an exaggeratedly sweet, "Good morning to you too."

Bryan grunted in response, reaching for the orange juice and pouring himself a glass. Dakota held back a laugh.

The next several minutes were filled with the quiet sounds of breakfast—plates clinking, forks scraping, the distant hum of the refrigerator. Dakota ate quickly, finishing off his plate before standing and stretching. He walked over to his mother, wrapping his arms around her in a quick hug.

"Thanks, Mom."

She patted his arm gently. "Have a good day, honey."

With that, Dakota grabbed his backpack and headed for the front door. The morning air was crisp as he stepped outside, the sun still low in the sky. At the end of the driveway, Lane was already waiting at the bus stop, hands tucked into the pockets of his hoodie.

Dakota jogged over, adjusting the strap of his backpack.

"How'd the footage turn out?" Lane asked as soon as Dakota reached him.

Dakota exhaled, still waking up. "Pretty good. I just need to edit it and upload it."

Lane nodded. "Think it'll get some views?"

Dakota shrugged. "Hopefully. We need to start gaining traction if we want to do this full-time after graduation."

The distant rumble of an engine signaled the approach of the bus. It slowed as it neared them, tires hissing against the pavement.

Just as the doors creaked open, Bryan came stumbling out of the house, still moving at half-speed, lazily making his way toward his car.

Lane watched him for a second before shaking his head. As he and Dakota climbed onto the bus and took their usual seats, Lane leaned in slightly, voice low with amusement.

"Man, your brother really just doesn't care, huh?"

Dakota huffed a laugh, glancing out the window as Bryan sluggishly slid into the driver seat. "Not even a little."

As the bus pulled away from the stop, the hum of conversation filled the air, the routine of another school day settling in.

But in the back of Dakota's mind, he was already thinking about their next adventure.

The cafeteria was alive with the usual lunchtime chaos—students chatting over their meals, trays clattering, the occasional burst of laughter cutting through the noise. The scent of pizza, fries, and mystery meat filled the air, blending into something that was strangely nostalgic yet vaguely unappetizing.

Dakota and Lane sat at their usual table near the back, away from most of the crowd. Dakota pushed around the last of his fries with a half-interested look before glancing up at Lane.

"So, what about that old apartment building downtown?" Dakota asked, leaning forward slightly. "You know, the one that got shut down after the city condemned it."

Lane raised an eyebrow. "You wanna check it out?"

"Why not?" Dakota shrugged. "It's been empty for years. Place was ruled unsafe, people had to move out overnight. I bet there's still furniture and personal stuff inside."

Lane took a sip of his soda, considering it. "Could be cool. But, like… how unsafe are we talking? Because I'm not trying to fall through a floor."

Dakota smirked. "Guess we'll find out."

They kept talking, their voices drowning in the sea of cafeteria noise, their words meant only for them. The apartment building had potential—tall, looming, with plenty of rooms to explore. It was the kind of place that told a story without saying a word.

Then, out of nowhere, Tyler slid into the seat across from them.

It was… odd. Dakota and Lane didn't have anything against Tyler, but they didn't really talk much, either. They weren't friends, just people who existed in the same space.

Tyler leaned in slightly, resting his elbows on the table like he was about to share classified information. His sharp brown eyes flicked between them before he spoke in a hushed tone.

"You guys run that YouTube channel, right?"

Dakota blinked, caught off guard. "What?"

"The exploration videos," Tyler clarified. "That's you two, isn't it?"

Dakota glanced at Lane before nodding. "Yeah, that's us. We've been all over the city looking for cool places."

A smirk tugged at the corner of Tyler's lips. He wasn't just some curious classmate—he was a known conspiracy theorist, the kind of guy who questioned everything and never took anything at face value.

Tyler stayed leaned forward, voice low. "You guys heard about the Hollow Park incident?"

Dakota exchanged a glance with Lane before nodding. "Yeah, I've heard some things. A couple of guys were talking about it in class. Missing people, big investigation. But honestly?" He shook his head. "I don't buy it."

Tyler tapped his fingers on the table, his expression unreadable. "You don't find anything weird about it?"

Dakota shrugged. "I mean, yeah, it's weird, but that doesn't mean it's some big mystery. People go missing all the time."

Tyler tilted his head slightly, studying them like he was trying to gauge just how deep their curiosity ran. Then, with a smirk, he said, "If it ever fully shuts down, you guys should check it out. Find the truth. Put the rumors to rest if it's all talk."

With that, he stood, pushing his tray forward as he turned to leave.

Dakota and Lane barely had time to process what had just happened before Tyler disappeared back into the crowd.

Lane exhaled, leaning back in his chair. "Okay… that was random."

Dakota nodded, staring at the empty space where Tyler had just been. "Yeah."

Lane chuckled, shaking his head. "But you gotta admit… that does sound like one hell of a video."

Dakota smirked. "No doubt." But then, his expression turned more serious. "Problem is, we can't do much right now. Everything we do is trespassing, but this? This is an active crime scene. And technically, the park isn't even abandoned yet."

Lane sighed. "Yeah. We'd be in way deeper shit if we got caught sneaking into Hollow Park."

Dakota nodded. "Not to mention, we aren't ready for something like that. We don't have the means or the equipment to explore an entire amusement park."

Lane twirled his straw in his drink, thinking. "So… we wait?"

"For now," Dakota agreed. "But if that place ever shuts down for good…"

Lane smirked. "We'll be the first ones through the gate."

And with that, they let the conversation drift to something else, but the idea lingered in the back of their minds—restless, waiting.

Because deep down, they both knew it wasn't a question of *if* Hollow Park would shut down.

It was *when*.

Chapter Two

The summer sun was relentless, hanging high in the sky, beating down on the stretch of highway ahead. Waves of heat shimmered off the blacktop, making the road look like it was melting into the horizon. The steady hum of tires rolling over asphalt mixed with the faint sound of music playing from the van's speakers.

Dakota kept one hand on the wheel, his sunglasses shielding his eyes as he focused on the road ahead. The **Ford Transit**, their prized van, rumbled steadily along, packed with equipment in the back. A year ago, they had barely scraped by with a cheap camera and unreliable flashlights. Now, thanks to their viral success, they had everything they needed—high-quality gear, better funding, and, most importantly, the freedom to explore wherever they wanted.

Lane sat in the passenger seat, camera in hand, recording the passing scenery. The rolling fields soon gave way to distant buildings as they neared their destination, the familiar excitement creeping in. He panned the camera across the dashboard, catching the faint glint of sweat on Dakota's temple before focusing in on him.

Dakota glanced at the camera, smirking. His intro came effortlessly now—smooth, confident, almost rehearsed.

"What's up, guys? Welcome back to another exploration," he began, his voice steady, no trace of the awkwardness that had once plagued his early videos. "Today, we've got something special for you. We're heading out to an **abandoned school**, one that shut down about ten years ago after budget cuts forced the district to close it down. Since then, it's been left to rot, but—" he grinned, "—thanks to one of our awesome viewers, **@LostAndWandering**, we've got the inside scoop on how to get in."

Lane chuckled off-camera, shaking his head.

Dakota continued, "This place is **huge**—three floors, a gym, an auditorium, and supposedly, some rooms that still have desks, books, and old lesson plans left behind. Should be a solid explore, so stick with us."

He flashed a quick thumbs-up before Lane cut the camera. The small beep confirmed it was off.

For a moment, neither of them spoke. Just the open road, the soft hum of the van, and the knowledge of how far they had come.

Lane leaned back in his seat, stretching. "Man… we really did it, huh?"

Dakota smirked, keeping his eyes on the road. "Hell yeah, we did."

A year ago, this had been nothing more than a dream—long talks about traveling, exploring, making videos. Now? They were living it. They weren't rich, but they were making enough. Enough to travel, to keep the dream going, to **not** be stuck in some dead-end job wasting away behind a desk or in a warehouse.

They didn't need to say it out loud, but the feeling was there. A silent celebration.

Another adventure waited ahead.

And they were ready.

Dakota reached for the bottle of water sitting snugly in the cupholder, twisting the cap open with one hand while keeping the other steady on the wheel. He took a small sip, the cool liquid refreshing against the heat of the afternoon. The road stretched ahead of them, the hum of the tires rolling over the asphalt filling the silence.

Then Lane spoke, breaking the quiet.

Dakota glanced over, watching as Lane aimed the camera out the window, capturing the sight of passing buildings and signs.

"Well, there it is," Lane said, his voice casual but carrying a hint of excitement. "Goodbye, Westbrook. Hello, Graystone."

The city was noticeably different—larger, busier, with taller buildings and older streets lined with businesses, some thriving, others forgotten. It wasn't their first time traveling to a new city for an exploration, but every time still felt like an adventure.

Dakota spotted a gas station up ahead and flipped on his turn signal, pulling off the highway and into the lot. He eased the Transit next to a pump, shifting the van into park before looking at the camera.

"Alright," he said, smirking. "We're not getting anywhere if we don't make a quick stop first."

With that, he unbuckled, grabbed his wallet, and stepped out into the sweltering heat. The air smelled of gasoline and hot pavement as he slid his card into the reader, selected the fuel grade, and began pumping.

Lane stayed inside, keeping the camera rolling for a moment before flipping the screen toward himself. "We'll be stopping at a little motel in town—just like always. You guys know the drill. The exploration's going down **tonight**."

He gave the camera a quick nod. "See you guys soon."

With a press of a button, the camera beeped as he shut it off.

By the time Dakota finished fueling up, he climbed back into the driver's seat, put the van in gear, and pulled back onto the road. The GPS led them further into the heart of Graystone, weaving through its old streets before guiding them to their temporary stop—a small roadside motel, the kind of place that didn't ask questions as long as you had the cash.

Dakota eased the van into the lot, parking near the front office. The neon **VACANCY** sign buzzed faintly in the window, the sun casting long shadows over the cracked pavement.

Lane stretched in his seat, glancing at Dakota. "Ready for another one?"

Dakota smirked, shutting off the engine. "Always."

The motel room wasn't anything special—beige walls with water stains near the ceiling, an old TV mounted on the wall that probably hadn't been updated in decades, and a janky desk bolted to the wall with a wobbly chair that had seen better days. The place smelled faintly of stale air conditioning and cheap cleaning supplies, but it was enough for what they needed: a place to crash before the night's exploration.

Dakota and Lane moved around the room, setting up their gear with the practiced efficiency of two people who had done this a hundred times before. Chargers were plugged in, camera batteries lined up neatly on the desk, and flashlights laid out in a row like weapons before battle.

"Make sure the batteries are actually charging," Dakota called over his shoulder, adjusting the cords tangled near the wall outlet.

Lane checked, pressing a button on one of the chargers. A tiny red light blinked to life. He gave Dakota a thumbs-up. "We're good."

Dakota, satisfied, dropped into the rickety chair at the desk, the wood creaking beneath him. In front of him sat the latest addition to their arsenal—a brand-new drone they had picked up just a few days earlier. The sleek black device sat on the desk, its propellers folded in neatly. The instruction manual was open beside it, pages creased as Dakota skimmed through them.

He pressed a button. The drone beeped, lights flickering to life along its body. Another press, and the propellers spun momentarily before shutting off.

Lane walked over, leaning in to get a better look. "Damn. These things have really improved over the years."

Dakota grinned, picking up the controller. "Yeah, and now we can finally get some real overhead shots. No more shaky GoPro-on-a-pole bullshit."

Lane chuckled. "RIP to the homemade 'drone' setup."

Dakota flicked a few switches, then moved the control sticks. The drone gave a soft mechanical whir before lifting off the desk, hovering a few feet in the air. Its tiny camera lens adjusted automatically, tilting slightly as it stabilized.

Dakota guided it around the room, weaving between the motel's dim lighting. The soft hum of the propellers filled the space as the drone floated past Lane's head, then over the bed, before circling back toward Dakota.

He smirked, handing the controller to Lane. "Here, your turn."

Lane took the controls, adjusting his grip before experimenting with the levers. The drone responded smoothly, banking left and right, rising slightly before dipping back down.

Meanwhile, Dakota flipped open his laptop, clicking through a few settings before opening the drone's live-feed app. The loading screen flickered before the video feed snapped into place, showing a perfect bird's-eye view of the room.

Lane hovered the drone above them, and Dakota grinned as he saw himself on the screen, looking up.

"This is sick," Dakota said, excitement clear in his voice. "We can get way better shots now. A real bird's-eye view."

Lane maneuvered the drone a bit more before slowly bringing it back down for a soft landing on the desk. He let out a satisfied breath, setting the controller down. "Yeah, this is gonna change everything."

Dakota nodded, still staring at the laptop screen. He could already picture it—wide aerial shots of abandoned places, overhead views of decayed buildings swallowed by nature. Their videos were about to level up in a big way.

And tonight? Tonight would be the first real test.

Dakota grabbed the camera, flipping it on with a practiced motion. The familiar beep signaled it was recording, and he adjusted the grip before panning it around the motel room. The dim lighting gave everything a slightly yellowish tint, but it didn't matter—this wasn't about aesthetics.

"What's up, guys?" Dakota started, his voice steady and confident. "We're getting ready for tonight's exploration, but before we head out, we've got something new to show you."

He turned the camera toward the desk, where the drone sat, its sleek black frame reflecting the dull glow of the bedside lamp. He zoomed in slightly, emphasizing the small but powerful machine.

"This," Dakota continued, "is our newest piece of equipment. A drone. That's right—we're stepping it up. No more shaky shots, no more low angles. We're talking full aerial views, full perspective." He reached out, tapping the side of the drone. "This little guy is gonna give us footage like never before."

Lane, who had been leaning against the wall, crossed his arms and smirked at the camera. "And we won't have to climb on top of questionable buildings just to get a cool shot."

Dakota chuckled, turning the camera toward him. "Yeah, that's a plus."

Lane pushed off the wall, stepping into frame. "Not much longer now. We're just charging up our gear, and then we'll be heading out."

Dakota nodded before turning the camera back toward himself. His expression became slightly more serious as he addressed the viewers.

"Real quick—just a reminder," he said. "Don't try this at home. What we do is dangerous, sometimes illegal, and we've been doing this for a long time. We know what we're doing." He pointed at the camera. "You don't. So sit back, enjoy the video, and leave the exploring to us."

With that, he reached over and clicked the camera off. The small beep echoed in the room, signaling the recording had ended.

He pulled out the battery, swapping it onto the charger with the others. The red indicator light blinked to life, joining the small collection of batteries lined up on the desk.

Lane sat on the edge of the bed, stretching his arms over his head before glancing at Dakota. "So, what do you think? Any bad vibes from this one?"

Dakota smirked. "Dude, every place has bad vibes. That's half the fun."

Lane rolled his eyes. "Yeah, but an abandoned school? Feels different, you know? It's one thing to explore an old house or a factory, but a school… people spent their lives there. Kids. Teachers. It's weird."

Dakota leaned back in the rickety chair, folding his arms. "That's what makes it interesting. Every place we go tells a story." He paused, glancing at the clock. "And tonight? We get to hear this one."

Lane nodded, running a hand through his hair. "Well, let's just hope it's a story and not a horror movie."

Dakota chuckled. "Guess we'll find out soon enough."

They sat there for a few moments, the hum of the motel's air conditioning filling the silence. The anticipation was setting in. The waiting was always the hardest part—because once they were out there, once the camera was rolling and the unknown stretched out before them, there was no turning back.

Night had finally come.

The heat of the day had faded, leaving the air cooler, tinged with the scent of asphalt and distant pine. The streetlights barely reached this far, casting only faint patches of light along the empty road. The school stood in the distance, a massive silhouette against the dark sky—its windows hollow, its walls scarred by time and neglect.

Dakota pulled the **Ford Transit** off to the side, easing the van into a clearing just down the street from the school. He killed the headlights, letting the darkness swallow them whole.

Lane unbuckled his seatbelt, stretching slightly before stepping into the back of the van. The night air greeted him with a crisp bite as he moved to the back, flipping open the storage compartment. His fingers found the black case, lifting it carefully. The drone.

A few moments later, Dakota joined him, pulling his laptop from one of the shelves. He crouched on the van floor, flipping it open, the screen casting a faint blue glow across his face as he brought up the **live feed software.** Lane, kneeling beside him, set the drone on the floor, flipping its switches. A low, mechanical chime sounded as the lights flickered on, illuminating the van interior with tiny flashes of red and green.

"Alright, setting up the live feed," Dakota muttered, fingers flying across the keyboard as he linked the drone's camera to the laptop. The screen flickered, and then—there it was. A grainy black-and-white aerial view of the van's interior, waiting to stretch its view beyond.

Lane opened the side door, gripping the drone's frame. He powered it up, and the propellers whirred softly, picking up speed. The hum deepened as the drone lifted off the van floor, floating smoothly out the open door and into the night.

Dakota kept his eyes on the screen, adjusting settings—night vision, camera stabilization, angle rotation—his movements precise. "Alright," he said, voice steady. "Fly it over the school. Let's see what we're working with."

Lane nodded, taking a seat in the passenger chair, fingers gripping the controller. He maneuvered the drone forward, its small frame cutting through the night as it gained altitude.

Dakota tracked the feed, the school coming into view—dark rooftops, overgrown courtyards, shattered windows that gaped like empty eye sockets. The place was completely lifeless.

Lane glanced at him. "What do you see?"

Dakota scanned the screen. "Looks clear. No vehicles, no people. Doesn't look like security patrols the place." He adjusted the zoom, sweeping the perimeter. "The viewer who sent this in said cops don't come back here. City doesn't want to waste resources on it."

Lane smirked slightly. "So, free real estate?"

Dakota nodded. "Pretty much."

For another minute, they let the drone hover, watching for any sign of movement—anything unusual. But there was nothing. Just an empty husk of a building, waiting.

"Alright, bring it back," Dakota said.

Lane guided the drone back toward the van, the soft buzzing growing louder as it descended. Within moments, it hovered just inside the open door before touching down gently on the floor. The propellers slowed, then stilled.

Dakota reached forward, carefully placing it back in the case. Lane handed him the controller, which he tucked inside before snapping the case shut. With practiced efficiency, Dakota closed his laptop, sliding it back onto the shelf.

With everything secured, he climbed back into the driver's seat. Lane shut the side door and strapped in.

Dakota turned the key, the van rumbling back to life.

This time, he drove forward, pulling into the school's abandoned parking lot, easing the van into the darkest corner he could find.

The night stretched before them, and the real work was about to begin.

Lane and Dakota moved to the back of the van, flipping open the storage compartment where their gear was neatly packed. The night air had settled into a heavy silence, broken only by the distant hum of crickets and the occasional rustle of wind against the trees lining the lot.

Dakota unzipped his backpack, double-checking the contents. **Extra batteries, spare SD cards, backup lights.** Everything had to be accounted for—nothing was worse than running out of power in the middle of an exploration. Lane did the same, shifting through his own bag before giving Dakota a nod.

"We're set," Lane murmured.

Dakota grabbed the **body mount**, strapping it securely to his chest. The rig extended outward, the adjustable arm locking into place as he took the camera and clipped it on. A small click confirmed it was secure, and with a press of a button, the familiar beep of the camera turning on echoed in the quiet van.

Lane grabbed two flashlights, tossing one to Dakota before clicking his on. The bright beam cut through the darkness, casting long shadows across the cracked pavement.

"Alright," Dakota said, voice steady. He tapped the camera mount, adjusting the angle before glancing at Lane. "Let's do this."

They stepped out into the night.

The school loomed ahead, its massive frame silhouetted against the dark sky. The once-proud structure had become nothing more than a forgotten husk, its **brick walls streaked with years of neglect**. Vines had begun to creep up the sides, curling over shattered windows and broken signage. The main entrance—**a set of glass double doors—had been completely destroyed**. The shards glittered in the light of their flashlights, scattered across the cracked pavement like tiny mirrors reflecting a forgotten past.

Dakota looked at the camera, adjusting the focus. "Alright, guys. We've made it. This is **Ridgeway High**—shut down over a decade ago when the city pulled its funding. Since then, it's been left to rot." He panned the camera across the building. "From what we've heard, there's still stuff inside—desks, books, maybe even old lesson plans. So, let's see what's left."

Lane stepped ahead, shining his light over the **graffiti-covered walls** near the entrance. "People have definitely been here," he muttered, kicking aside an old beer can.

Dakota turned the camera toward him. "Think we'll find anything good?"

Lane smirked. "Hopefully not another giant spider nest."

Dakota snorted. "Yeah, one of those is enough for a lifetime."

They approached the entrance cautiously. The doors were gone, the frame bent inward, leaving behind a gaping hole where students once walked in and out every day.

Lane crouched down, inspecting the shards of glass that still clung to the frame. "Watch your step," he muttered, carefully navigating through.

Dakota followed, keeping the camera trained on the entrance as they slipped inside. The moment they crossed the threshold, the temperature seemed to drop slightly, the stagnant air thick with the **scent of mildew, old paper, and decay.**

Their flashlight beams sliced through the darkness, illuminating the **main lobby**—or what remained of it. The **front desk was covered in dust**, the wood warped from years of exposure. A few overturned chairs lay scattered near the entrance, and the walls were lined with **old posters, their edges curling and faded beyond recognition.**

Dakota turned the camera slightly, speaking in a hushed voice. "Alright, we're inside. So far, everything looks untouched, aside from the graffiti. Looks like people come here to drink, maybe party, but… otherwise, this place still has its bones."

Lane stepped further in, sweeping his flashlight across the **hallway ahead**. Rows of **lockers lined the walls**, their doors dented and rusted. Some were hanging open, revealing **forgotten books and old papers left behind.** The quietness of it all was unsettling—like the building itself was waiting.

Dakota kept the camera rolling, his voice barely above a whisper. "Let's see what's inside."

And with that, they moved deeper into the school, into the unknown.

The halls stretched out before them, long and empty, their footsteps echoing off the cracked tile floors. The faint smell of mildew and dust lingered in the air, mixing with something stale—**the scent of time settling in a place long forgotten.**

Lane trailed his flashlight along the **rows of dented, rust-covered lockers**, pausing to tug on a few as they passed. Most of them were jammed shut, their locks rusted beyond saving. Dakota, keeping the camera steady, moved beside him, occasionally pulling at random lockers, hoping to find something left behind.

With a screech of metal, one finally gave way. The door creaked open, revealing **a stack of crumpled papers**, an old textbook with torn pages, and a faded school ID, too scratched to make out the photo.

Dakota zoomed in with the camera. "What do we have here?"

Lane picked up one of the papers, shaking off the dust. "Chemistry homework," he muttered, squinting at the faded writing. "Some kid half-assed their answers. Probably cheated off someone else."

Dakota smirked. "That, or they just sucked at science."

They continued down the hallway, trying door after door, but most were locked tight.

Then, Lane's flashlight landed on a door that was slightly ajar.

"The science lab," he murmured.

Dakota turned the camera toward it. The **faded plaque** above the door read *Lab 201*, though most of the numbers had been scratched off. Lane pushed against the door, and with a soft creak, it swung open.

They stepped inside.

The air in the lab was heavier, thicker with the scent of **rotting wood and aged chemicals**. Papers were **scattered across the floor, desks and chairs flipped and tossed haphazardly** like someone had ransacked the place in a hurry.

The **teacher's desk**, still standing in the corner, was coated in dust. **Broken beakers and Bunsen burners littered the countertops, glass shards reflecting their flashlight beams like tiny stars.**

Dakota moved the camera around, letting it capture every detail. "Looks like this place got trashed," he murmured.

Lane walked over to the teacher's desk, tugging at the drawers. The first one stuck, but after a sharp pull, it came loose with a loud snap.

Dakota leaned in, focusing the camera on the papers inside. "Let's see what the good old science teacher left behind."

Lane reached in, pulling out a **dust-covered binder**. The grime clung to his fingers, and he made a face, wiping his hand on his jeans. "Gross."

He flipped it open, revealing **old assignments, graded tests, and printed answer keys**—the kind teachers probably weren't supposed to leave lying around.

Dakota zoomed in. "Damn, someone could've **aced** their finals if they found this back in the day."

Lane smirked, pulling out a random test sheet. The name at the top was **Carmen Houston.** Her final score? A tragic **42%.**

Lane burst out laughing. "Oh man, Carmen did not study."

Dakota grinned at the camera. "Carmen Houston, if you're watching this... *pay attention in class!*"

They both laughed, shaking their heads before setting the binder back in the drawer.

"Well," Lane said, stretching his arms, "this place is cool and all, but let's check out the next floor."

Dakota nodded, turning the camera toward the door. "Up we go."

They stepped back into the hall and made their way to the stairs, the creaking steps leading them further into the unknown.

They wandered the **second-floor halls**, their flashlight beams flickering over **empty classrooms, overturned desks, and lockers already picked clean.** The deeper they went, the more it became apparent—there was nothing here.

Dakota sighed, his footsteps echoing against the tiled floor. "Man... this is kind of boring."

Lane, scanning the rooms as they passed, gave a small nod. "Yeah. Feels like we got here a few years too late. Looks like people have already taken anything worth seeing."

They pressed on, moving through the corridors, checking inside every open door, but **each room was the same—empty, forgotten, stripped of anything interesting.** There were no eerie remnants of the past, no strange finds, no sense of mystery. Just another abandoned place left to decay.

By the time they reached the **third and final floor,** their excitement had drained. They swept the halls quickly, but it was the same story—nothing worth recording, nothing worth remembering.

Dakota let out a long breath, shaking his head. "Welp... that's that."

Lane smirked. "Not every place can be gold."

With that, they made their way back downstairs, stepping through the shattered entrance one last time. The cool night air hit them as they walked toward the van, the quiet settling in around them.

Dakota lifted the camera, turning it toward himself for the outro. "Alright, guys, that's it for tonight. Not much to see here, but hey—**they can't all be winners.**"

Lane leaned into the frame, smirking. "Shoutout to **@LostAndWandering** for sending this one in. Not the most exciting, but still worth checking out."

Dakota nodded. "Thanks for watching. You know the drill—like, subscribe, and let us know where we should go next."

With that, he shut the camera off.

They packed up their gear, returning everything to its rightful place in the van**.** Dakota placed the camera in its case, securing the batteries and SD cards, while Lane slid into the driver's seat. Dakota dropped into the passenger seat, rubbing his eyes briefly before letting out a sigh.

"Well," Dakota muttered, "at least the footage is still usable. Just nothing crazy."

Lane nodded, adjusting the mirrors before starting the van. "Yeah. Hopefully, the next one's better."

The engine rumbled to life, and with one last glance at the abandoned school, they pulled away, disappearing into the night.

The motel room was dimly lit, the soft glow of Dakota's laptop screen casting faint blue hues across the wall. The faint hum of the air conditioner filled the otherwise silent space, a steady background noise against the occasional click of Dakota's mouse as he sifted through footage.

Sitting at the **rickety motel desk,** Dakota leaned in, focused, piecing together the night's exploration. He cut clips, adjusted brightness, trimmed the dull moments, and added the **intro sequence and music.** Even though the school had been a bust, he still wanted to make the video as engaging as possible.

Lane lay sprawled on one of the beds, staring at the ceiling, his hands resting on his stomach. He hadn't moved in a while, just **blinking slowly, lost in thought.** The bed's thin mattress creaked slightly as he shifted his weight.

"So," Lane muttered, his voice breaking the quiet, "what are we doing next?"

Dakota didn't look up, his fingers still moving across the trackpad. "Dunno," he murmured. "I'll check the comments tomorrow while you drive home. See if anyone's got a solid lead."

Lane exhaled through his nose, still staring at the ceiling. "Cool."

The **minutes stretched on,** filled only with the soft sounds of Dakota finishing up his work. The video **processed and uploaded,** the familiar **uploading bar slowly crawling forward** before finally completing.

With a tired sigh, Dakota **shut his laptop,** rubbing his eyes as he stood up. He flicked off the **main light,** plunging the room into darkness except for the dull orange glow from the neon motel sign outside.

He collapsed onto the **other bed,** stretching briefly before settling into the worn-out mattress. "We should probably crash," he muttered. "Long drive back tomorrow."

Lane didn't answer right away. Then, after a moment, "Yeah."

The motel room fell into silence once more.

Another trip done. Another location crossed off the list.

But something bigger was still waiting for them.

They just didn't know it yet.

The TV droned on in the background, its soft glow casting shifting patterns of light across the dimly lit living room. Dakota sat slouched on the couch, phone in hand, scrolling through **the endless stream of comments** on their latest YouTube video. Some were praising their work, others were offering suggestions for new locations, and a few—like always—were just trolls looking for attention.

Lane sat beside him, feet propped up on the coffee table, half-watching the screen while absentmindedly tossing a stress ball in the air.

"Anything good?" Lane asked, not taking his eyes off the ceiling as he caught the ball and threw it again.

Dakota shrugged, still scrolling. "A few leads. Someone mentioned an old hospital a couple of cities over. Another guy swears there's some underground bunker near the train yard, but that sounds like total BS."

Lane caught the ball and sat up, grabbing the remote. "Bunker could be cool."

"If it's real," Dakota muttered.

Lane smirked and flicked through the channels, stopping when he landed on the local news.

"This just in—Hollow Park has officially shut down."

The words snapped them both to attention. Dakota lowered his phone, Lane leaning forward slightly as the broadcast continued.

"The once-thriving theme park has met its bitter end today as the owner has officially declared bankruptcy. After years of speculation, legal troubles, and its inability to reopen, Hollow Park is no more."

The screen cut to a **pre-recorded interview** with the park's owner, a middle-aged man in a suit who looked exhausted, as if the years of trying to save his business had finally broken him.

"I've lost too much money," he admitted, shaking his head. "The park's been shut down for too long. There's a **major gas leak** that's been **causing hallucinations—people seeing things, hearing things that weren't there.** The cost of repairs? I just can't afford it."

Dakota and Lane exchanged a look but stayed silent, watching.

The reporter, standing across from the owner, tilted her head slightly. "And what about the **missing people**? Some still claim—"

The owner **waved her off,** visibly annoyed. "No one has ever gone missing in my park. Hollow Park was **one of the safest places around**. My security team reviewed **hours upon hours of footage**—there was no **evidence** of foul play, no strange occurrences, nothing."

The clip ended, cutting back to the news anchors, who continued their discussion about the park's final days, but Dakota and Lane weren't listening anymore.

Dakota slowly set his phone down on the couch. Lane exhaled through his nose, staring at the screen before finally turning to Dakota.

They didn't say it.

They didn't have to.

Because they both knew—**this was it.**

Chapter Three

This was it.

The **big score.** The one that would set them apart from every other explorer, from every **wannabe ghost hunter and urban legend chaser** trying to make a name for themselves.

Hollow Park.

Everyone wanted to see it. Everyone wanted answers.

And Dakota and Lane were going to be the first ones inside.

The **kitchen light buzzed softly**, barely illuminating the small table where they stood. Spread out in front of them was a **full map of Hollow Park**, slightly worn, creased from years of folding and unfolding. Dakota had spent the last hour **marking key locations, tracing possible entry points, and noting anything that could help them navigate the park safely.**

Because this wasn't just some **abandoned school or rundown motel.** This was an **entire amusement park. Fenced off. Patrolled.** And if there really was a **gas leak**, that added a whole new level of danger.

Lane crossed his arms, scanning the map. "So, what's the move?"

Dakota tapped a **section near the back of the park**, where the service roads once ran. "We could fly the drone over first—get a layout before we go in. If security's still making rounds, we'll see it from the feed."

Lane nodded, but his focus drifted, his fingers tapping idly against the table. His gaze lingered over the **faded outlines of roller coasters and attractions**, as if picturing them in their former glory—lights flashing, rides roaring, the distant sound of children laughing. But now? The place was **dead. Silent. Rotting.**

After a moment, Lane glanced at Dakota. "What do you think really happened?"

Dakota exhaled, resting his hands on the table, staring down at the **map like it held the answers.**

"I don't know," he admitted. "But I hope we figure it out."

A heavy silence settled between them.

Because whatever had happened in Hollow Park—whatever had caused the shutdown, the disappearances, the rumors—**they were about to find out.**

And they had no idea what was waiting for them inside.

Dakota and Lane **moved quickly through the apartment,** their energy buzzing with adrenaline and anticipation. Notebooks and loose papers covered the kitchen table—scribbled notes, rough sketches of the park layout, supply lists, everything they needed to make this happen.

This was **the biggest exploration of their lives.**

And they had **no clue what they were walking into.**

Lane grabbed a **clipboard**, flipping through their notes while Dakota sorted through the gear. "Alright," Lane muttered, "so we've got three main objectives before we even step foot in that place. One—figure out the layout and patrol routes. Two—find a way in that doesn't get us arrested. Three—don't die from some supposed gas leak."

Dakota snorted as he double-checked the **camera batteries, extra SD cards, and backup flashlights.** "Yeah, that last one's kind of important."

Hollow Park wasn't just **some local urban legend.** This was **big.** Everyone wanted to know what happened—**what really happened.** And if they could be the first ones inside, get real, undeniable footage, **this would put them on the map.**

Lane tossed the clipboard onto the table and stretched, rolling his shoulders. "I say we dedicate an entire day just to scoping it out. No going in yet—just seeing what we're up against."

Dakota nodded, tightening a strap on one of the equipment bags. "Agreed. We don't know what kind of security is still there, if any. And with the gas leak stuff…" He trailed off, grabbing his laptop from the counter. "We should see if we can get our hands on old maintenance records. If we can find out where the supposed leak is, we can avoid those areas."

Lane grabbed his **duffel bag,** tossing in **a few essentials—extra clothes, a pocket knife, their small first-aid kit.** "Smart. Last thing we need is to pass out from inhaling something toxic."

They moved **through the apartment like a well-oiled machine**, gathering everything they needed, making last-minute adjustments to their plan. Every so often, Dakota would add something to the running **checklist** taped to the fridge.

- **Cameras?** ■
- **Flashlights & Batteries?** ■
- **Maps & Blueprints?** ■
- **Food & Water?** ■

- **Crowbar (just in case)?**

The list went on.

By late afternoon, the **van was packed.**

Dakota wiped the sweat from his forehead as he leaned against the open back doors, surveying their supplies. Cameras, drones, tripods, spare gear—everything meticulously organized into compartments. Lane stood beside him, arms crossed, nodding in approval.

"This is it," Lane said.

Dakota exhaled, the weight of the moment settling in. "Six-hour drive. Probably a week in town, minimum."

Lane smirked. "You think we're gonna find anything?"

Dakota glanced at him, then back at the van.

"I don't know," he admitted. "But I hope we do."

Because Hollow Park wasn't **just another abandoned place.**

This was **the one.**

And whatever waited for them inside—it was waiting.

The van rumbled down the highway, the tires humming against the pavement as the distant glow of the city faded into the rearview mirror. The soft sound of the radio played in the background, a faint melody filling the space between them. The air smelled faintly of **coffee, worn leather, and the plastic scent of their equipment cases stacked in the back.**

This was it.

This was the expedition they had been waiting for.

Lane tapped his fingers against the armrest, his restless energy obvious. "Dude, this is the big one," he said, half in disbelief. "This is our *magnum opus.*"

Dakota nodded, adjusting his grip on the wheel. "Yeah." His voice was steady, but his mind was running a mile a minute.

They had done plenty of **urban explorations before.** Abandoned schools, forgotten hospitals, places left behind by time. But **this wasn't just another dead building.**

This was Hollow Park.

The place was still **fresh**—it hadn't been rotting away for decades, it hadn't been forgotten. It was still on the **forefront of everyone's minds,** wrapped in **conspiracy theories and unanswered questions.** And now, it was finally shut down for good.

For the first time, they weren't just breaking into a **forgotten relic.** They were stepping directly into the **biggest mystery in Hollow Creek.**

But what the hell were they supposed to do if they actually found answers?

Lane must've been thinking the same thing because he glanced at Dakota, brow furrowed. "Let's say we do find something," he said. "Like—*actual* proof that something weird went down there. Then what?"

Dakota exhaled through his nose, staring at the road. "I don't know."

"Who do we even tell? How do we even upload this without getting ourselves screwed?"

That was the real problem.

This wasn't **some forgotten school or an abandoned motel where the owners had long since stopped caring.** This was a **major amusement park** that still had an **active legal team.** If Hollow Park's owners caught wind of what they were doing, they could be in **serious trouble.**

Not just for **trespassing.**

But for **whatever it was they weren't supposed to see.**

Dakota tightened his grip on the wheel. "We have to be careful. If we screw this up, it's not just a deleted video or a fine. It could cost us everything."

Lane looked out the window, watching the **rolling hills and open roads blur past.** "Yeah…" He shook his head slightly. "This is the biggest thing we've ever done."

For a few moments, neither of them spoke. The reality of what they were doing was **starting to sink in.**

Lane reached for the camera, flipping it on. The small screen flickered to life, casting a faint glow in the dim van. He lifted it toward Dakota.

"Alright," Lane said, his voice calmer now, more focused.

Dakota barely hesitated before slipping into the routine.

"What's up, guys," he said, his tone practiced but charged with real energy. "Tonight's the night. We're on our way to **Hollow Creek** to check out **Hollow Park.** The place has officially shut down, and you guys have been *begging* us to go check it out. So, that's exactly what we're gonna do."

He kept his eyes on the road, but there was an edge to his words. "This one's different, though. We don't know what we're walking into. There's security, there's **gas leaks,** and we don't even know if it's safe to be there."

Lane turned the camera toward himself. "But that's not stopping us."

The weight of their decision settled between them.

After a beat, Lane shut the camera off and set it down on the dashboard.

They weren't scared.

They had never been **scared** of finding anything paranormal. They had never been the type to jump to conclusions, to assume ghosts and demons were lurking in the shadows.

But that wasn't what had their stomachs twisted.

It was the **real-world dangers** that unnerved them. **Squatters. Rabid animals. Security. Police.**

But even more than that—

It was the weight of this being the **biggest urban exploration they had ever attempted.**

And if they screwed this up…

It could cost them **everything.**

The answers to the questions.

Their careers.

Their freedom.

Maybe even their lives.

Dakota swallowed hard, pushing the thought away as he **drove them further into the unknown.**

The highway stretched endlessly ahead, dark and open, the only company being the occasional headlights of passing cars. The soft hum of the van's engine mixed with the quiet music playing on the radio, a low background noise that neither of them was really paying attention to.

Dakota glanced at Lane, gripping the wheel with one hand. "Pull up everything you can on Hollow Park," he said. "If we're doing this, I want to know exactly what we're walking into."

Lane nodded, grabbing his phone and opening up Google. A few quick searches brought up article after article, and he tapped the most detailed-looking one.

"Hollow Park," Lane read aloud, "located in the quaint city of Hollow Creek, officially opened in March 1999. It didn't really take off until June of 2000, when the founder, Jason Langston, launched a half-price summer sale. The park was overrun with guests, the reviews exploded, and soon, everyone wanted to visit."

Dakota smirked slightly. "Classic move. Make it affordable, get 'em hooked, jack up the prices later."

Lane continued, "But it wasn't just about the rides and water parks. This place had everything—a safari zone where people could walk through jungle-like environments and see different types of animals, boat rides with animatronic creatures and guides telling stories about them, a fantasy land filled with characters and movie-based attractions…" He shook his head. "Basically, Hollow Park was a bit of everything"

Dakota exhaled. "Makes sense why it was so huge."

Lane scrolled further. "Yeah, well… didn't stay that way."

Dakota arched an eyebrow. "Why?"

Lane sighed, eyes scanning the screen. "First big scandal was 2001. Park got hit with animal neglect accusations. Fined a few grand." He looked up. "Langston made some changes, fixed the exhibits, and the whole thing blew over."

Dakota hummed. "Typical. Money talks."

Lane scrolled further, and his face darkened slightly.

"But then… 2010 happened."

Dakota flicked his eyes toward him before turning back to the road. "What about it?"

Lane shifted in his seat. "Ride malfunctions. And not just little ones. Like, major screw-ups. Some wouldn't shut down, trapping passengers on them. Others wouldn't start at all. Staff would show up in the morning, and some rides were already running."

Dakota furrowed his brows. "Weird."

"Yeah. They hired one of the best engineering teams in the country, had them check every inch of the park's systems. Weeks of inspections, and they came back with nothing. No faulty wiring, no electrical failures, nothing."

Dakota's fingers drummed against the wheel. "And then what? The rides just started working again?"

Lane nodded. "Like nothing ever happened."

Silence settled between them for a moment. Dakota focused on the road, but he could feel the weight of the conversation pressing down on them.

"That wasn't the worst of it," Lane added.

Dakota shot him a glance. "Oh?"

Lane's voice lowered slightly, as if reading the next part made him uneasy.

"2011. Rumors start spreading that kids were going missing inside the park."

Dakota's grip on the wheel tightened slightly.

Lane continued, "No evidence. No reports. Just parents swearing their kids vanished. But no one could prove anything. Then, in 2012, it happens again—but this time, adults supposedly disappeared." He glanced at Dakota. "Same deal—no evidence. Just stories."

Dakota let out a slow breath.

"Jason Langston denied everything," Lane said. "Had an interview saying no one ever went missing under his watch. He swore the park had top-tier security, cameras everywhere, and wristband tracking for every guest entering and exiting."

Lane finally set his phone down and exhaled. "Man… that's some bad luck."

Dakota didn't respond immediately. His mind was turning, piecing everything together.

Malfunctioning rides. Missing people. An amusement park shutting down under strange circumstances.

It was a lot of coincidences.

Too many.

And they were about to walk straight into it.

For a few moments, they drove in silence. The road stretched ahead, dark and empty, the only sounds being the quiet hum of the van's engine and the faint murmur of the radio.

Then, Lane let out a light chuckle, shaking his head as he stared at his phone screen. "Dude, listen to this," he said, his voice laced with amusement. "I found a list of **conspiracy theories** about Hollow Park."

Dakota glanced at him briefly before focusing back on the road. "Oh, this should be good."

Lane cleared his throat, scrolling. "Alright, first up—Jason Langston **kidnapped** those missing people and did **experiments on them in a secret lab** hidden somewhere in the park."

Dakota snorted. "Classic. Nothing like a good old-fashioned **mad scientist trope.**"

"Oh, it gets better." Lane smirked, still reading. "Theory number two: **The missing people never actually left.**"

Dakota frowned slightly. "What? Like… they **live there now?**"

Lane wiggled his fingers in mock suspense. "More like—**they were never allowed to leave.** Free admission… *permanently.*"

Dakota groaned. "That's the dumbest thing I've ever heard."

Lane grinned. "Hold that thought. This next one is gold." He scrolled further. "So, apparently, **Jason Langston was losing money and needed a way to make extra cash.** So what did he do? **Started working with the U.S. government.**"

Dakota rolled his eyes. "Of course he did."

Lane nodded dramatically. "Yep. And together, they built a **secret underground lab** in the park where they were creating some kind of **hybrid animal.**"

Dakota let out a loud laugh. "What, like Jurassic Park? We're talking **genetically modified roller coasters now?**"

Lane grinned. "I'm just saying, man. Maybe the rides weren't **malfunctioning**—maybe they were being *sabotaged* by an escaped government experiment."

Dakota shook his head, laughing. "God, people are **insane**."

Lane held up a hand. "Wait, wait, wait. The last one is **actually** the craziest—and honestly, the **only one that sounds remotely believable**."

"Oh, this I gotta hear."

Lane cleared his throat dramatically before reading. "It says: **Jason Langston knew everything. He knew what was happening. But instead of telling people, he covered it up with the gas leak story.**"

Dakota raised an eyebrow but said nothing as Lane continued.

"The theory claims that **the ghosts of the missing people roam the park at night.** That Jason didn't shut the park down because he ran out of money—**he shut it down to stop whatever is inside from feeding again.**"

Dakota's smirk faltered just slightly as Lane read the last part:

"There's something in that park. And if it finds you… you vanish too."

Silence settled for a moment.

Then, as if on cue, Dakota and Lane turned to look at each other—eyes wide, faces blank.

And then—

They **burst out laughing.**

Dakota shook his head, gripping the steering wheel tighter as he wheezed. "That is the **stupidest** thing I've ever heard in my entire life."

Lane was laughing so hard he had to wipe his eyes. "Ghosts? **Secret labs?** Bro, who the hell comes up with this stuff?"

Dakota took a deep breath, calming down slightly. "Dude, we've done **a lot** of urban exploring. You know what we've never seen? Ghosts. Monsters. Government freakin' **science projects.**"

Lane snickered. "Oh man, what if we actually **do** find some top-secret hybrid animal?"

Dakota shot him a look. "Then we take it home and make it our **new channel mascot.**"

They laughed again, shaking their heads, the absurdity of the theories lingering between them.

Ghosts. Secret experiments. Creatures lurking in the dark.

It was all ridiculous.

Nothing but stories.

The **motel parking lot** was eerily quiet, the only sounds being the faint hum of streetlights and the distant rush of a passing car on the highway. The glowing **VACANCY** sign buzzed softly in the night, casting a dull red glow across the cracked pavement.

As Dakota pulled into a spot near their room, he glanced at the clock on the dashboard. **10:45 PM.**

"Alright," Dakota muttered, shifting into park. "Go grab the key. I'll start unloading."

Lane unbuckled, stretching slightly before stepping out of the van. Dakota sighed, rolling his shoulders before climbing into the back. The air inside was **warm and slightly stale,** the scent of worn fabric and electronics filling the confined space.

He reached for the **drone case**, placing it neatly in the center of the floor. Then came his laptop, extra batteries, chargers—everything they needed for tomorrow. He moved methodically, lost in thought.

They were **really doing this.**

The **biggest urban exploration of their lives.**

As he reached for another bag, he slid the **side door open.**

His **heart jumped into his throat.**

Lane **was standing right there, holding up the key card.**

Dakota's entire body jolted at the unexpected sight, his breath hitching for just a second. Lane's brow furrowed in confusion.

"Dude," Lane said slowly. "You good?"

Dakota exhaled sharply, shaking his head as his pulse settled. "Yeah, yeah. Just—damn, man, warn a guy next time." He forced a chuckle. "A face like that could scare anyone."

Lane gave an exaggerated sarcastic laugh, tossing the key card onto the **small plastic table outside their room** before reaching into the van. "Hilarious. Truly. You should quit YouTube and do stand-up."

Dakota smirked as he grabbed the **two duffel bags** filled with clothes and necessities. Lane hauled the **equipment cases,** balancing them carefully as they made their way to the **motel room.**

The door creaked as Dakota pushed it open, stepping inside.

It wasn't **the worst place they had ever stayed in.**

The **walls weren't peeling,** the **sheets didn't smell weird,** and—most importantly—it didn't look like a place where you'd wake up covered in bedbug bites. A **cheap wooden desk and chair sat against the wall,** and a small TV was mounted above it, stuck on a channel playing some late-night infomercial.

Dakota **tossed the duffel bags onto one of the beds** while Lane set the **equipment cases down on the desk.**

For a brief moment, they both just stood there, scanning the room.

"It… decent," Lane admitted.

Dakota shrugged. "Could be worse."

They spent the next few minutes **plugging in chargers, double-checking batteries, making sure everything was ready** for tomorrow. It was all routine—steps they had done a hundred times before—but this time felt different.

Because tomorrow wasn't just another **abandoned house or forgotten warehouse.**

Tomorrow was **Hollow Park.**

Eventually, they changed into comfortable clothes and **turned off the lights.** Dakota lay on one bed, staring up at the ceiling as the room settled into silence. The **faint hum of the motel AC unit** filled the air, rhythmic and soothing.

But his mind wouldn't let him rest.

What would they find?

Would they even be able to get in?

Were any of those stories true?

People **disappearing.** A **gas leak that made people hallucinate.** Ghosts. Creatures. Secret government experiments.

It was just **rumors.**

Right?

Dakota exhaled slowly, rolling onto his side, forcing himself to push the thoughts away. **One step at a time.** First, they'd scope out the place. **See if it's even worth the risk.**

He closed his eyes.

It took a while, but eventually—he drifted off to sleep.

The next morning

Dakota was pulled from sleep **abruptly**, his body jolting as Lane **shook his shoulder.**

"Wake up, dude. **Wake up.** You have to see this."

Dakota shot up, **heart pounding,** his mind struggling to catch up. The room was still **dim**, only lit by the faint morning sun filtering through the cheap motel curtains. The air was **stale**, carrying the faint scent of dust and whatever cleaning product the motel had halfheartedly used.

He rubbed the **sleep from his eyes**, blinking rapidly as his brain tried to **process the urgency in Lane's voice.**

Still groggy, he muttered, **"What's the deal?"**

Lane didn't answer. He just pointed at the **TV.**

Dakota **followed his gesture**, his gaze landing on the **glowing screen.** The news was on. The red **"Breaking Story"** banner scrolled across the bottom, and a **serious-looking reporter** sat at her desk, flipping through a stack of documents.

Dakota tried to **comprehend what he was seeing.**

"We're following breaking news this morning regarding the death of Jason Langston, former owner of Hollow Park. Authorities have released very few details, but here's what we know so far..."

Dakota sat up straighter, his **exhaustion fading.**

*"Early this morning, Langston was found in his home by a family member. The police have not given a cause of death at this time, but the Chief of Police has stated that it is **believed to be a suicide**. However, foul play has **not** been ruled out."*

The reporter adjusted the papers in front of her, **her voice steady, but the weight of the news was undeniable.**

"At this time, the investigation is ongoing, and we will provide more details as they become available."

The news cut to **footage of Langston's house**, **police tape** stretched across the driveway, officers standing near the entrance while a few reporters hovered outside the gates.

Dakota and Lane **shared a glance.**

"Dude," Dakota muttered, **shaking his head.** "That's crazy."

Lane exhaled, rubbing his jaw. "Yeah. I mean… **damn.**"

Neither of them really knew **what to say.**

Dakota leaned forward, **resting his elbows on his knees.** "I mean, things happen, right? He lost everything he worked for. The park shut down, the lawsuits, **all the rumors…** No matter what he did, it all just kept going **wrong.**"

Lane nodded slowly, but then, with a **half-smirk**, he said, "Man, the **conspiracy theories** that are gonna come out of *this* one."

Dakota let out a breath—**not quite a laugh, but close.** "No kidding."

It didn't take much to imagine. **The same people who swore the park was cursed, who believed in secret labs and government cover-ups?** They were **about to go wild with this.**

Lane smirked. **"Bet you someone's already saying 'he knew too much.'"**

Dakota chuckled, but the **weight of the situation still lingered.**

Enough of that.

He **grabbed the remote, clicking the TV off,** the screen fading to black.

Swinging his **legs over the edge of the bed,** he stood up, running a hand through his **messy hair.** "I'm gonna grab a quick shower. Need to wake up before we head out. **Make sure the drone is good to go.**"

Lane threw him a thumbs-up, already making his way to the **desk.** "On it."

Dakota **headed for the bathroom,** but even as the door clicked shut behind him, the news report **lingered in his mind.**

Jason Langston.

Gone.

And now, they were about to step into the **ruins of the empire he left behind.**

Chapter Four

The **sun beat down on the van,** turning the metal into an oven as it sat parked on the **overgrown service road** behind **Hollow Park.** The once-maintained path was now **cracked and lined with weeds,** nature slowly reclaiming the forgotten land.

Inside the van, **Dakota and Lane were busy at work.**

Dakota **knelt on the floor,** laptop open, fingers moving quickly across the keyboard as he pulled up the **live feed software.** His eyes flicked between **the screen and the map of Hollow Park** taped to the wall beside him.

Lane, sitting cross-legged, **was setting up the drone,** checking the **battery levels, signal strength, and camera stabilization.** The faint hum of the cooling fans inside the van mixed with the occasional chirp of cicadas outside.

Dakota exhaled, stretching his arms before standing. He reached for the **tripod,** extending its legs before **mounting the camera** on top. With a **click,** he switched it on, adjusting the focus before hitting **record.**

"What's up, guys?" Dakota started, standing in the cramped space with **Lane visible in the background.** "We're finally here. **Hollow Park.** We're on the back road, just outside the property, getting **our first aerial look** before we go in."

Lane gave the camera a quick nod before focusing back on the **drone controller.**

Dakota turned to him. "Alright, let's get this in the air."

He **shut off the camera,** then dropped back down to his laptop as Lane **opened the side door.** A burst of **warm air** filled the van as Lane placed the **drone on the edge,** its **propellers spinning to life** with a high-pitched whir.

With a **small adjustment on the controls,** the drone **lifted off,** hovering for a moment before Lane guided it up and over the **fence surrounding Hollow Park.**

Dakota **watched the feed,** the **grainy black-and-white view** shifting as the drone soared higher. The park came into full view.

It was a graveyard.

Rust-covered **rides stood motionless,** their once-bright paint faded and peeling. **Vines twisted around roller coaster tracks,** trees had pushed through cracks in the pavement, and **decayed food stands sat untouched,** their menus still visible behind shattered glass.

Dakota leaned closer to the screen. "Damn… You can tell this place wasn't really operational for the last few years before Langston shut it down."

Lane maneuvered the drone **toward the park's center**, sweeping over the **main pathways.**

Dakota suddenly tensed. "Hold up—**security.**"

On the screen, **two guards** walked along a cracked pathway, their **dark uniforms standing out** against the overgrown terrain.

Lane hovered the drone at a safe distance. "Not surprising. They don't want people breaking in."

The drone moved further in, passing over **roller coasters, waterslides, the kiddie ride section, and the jungle-themed safari zone.**

Dakota spotted **more guards.** Some were **on foot,** others **in golf carts, patrolling the perimeter.**

Lane sighed. "This is gonna be a pain in the ass."

Dakota exhaled. "Yeah. Bring it back."

Lane guided the **drone back over the fence**, letting it hover for a second before **landing it safely in the van.** The **propellers powered down,** and Lane reached over, shutting the **side door.**

Without missing a beat, Lane grabbed the **camera, switching it back on.**

Dakota faced it, his expression serious but charged with adrenaline. "Alright, so, we've got **security all over the place,** way more than we expected. Getting inside is gonna be **risky as hell.** But we're here, and we're **not gonna let you guys down.**"

Lane smirked slightly. "We've pulled off worse."

Dakota chuckled but didn't argue. "We'll figure it out."

With that, Lane **cut the camera.**

For a second, neither of them spoke, just sitting there, **letting the reality of what they were about to do sink in.**

Because this wasn't just another **abandoned house or old apartment building.**

This was **Hollow Park.**

And getting in was going to be a **lot harder than they thought.**

Dakota reached into one of the **van's storage compartments,** fingers brushing past coiled cables and extra camera batteries before grabbing **two two-way radios.** He tested the weight in his hand before **tossing one to Lane.**

Lane caught it, arching a brow. "Going old school?"

Dakota smirked. "If we split up, we need a way to communicate without relying on cell service. **Dead zones happen.**" He clipped his own radio to his **belt loop,** adjusting the frequency. "Keep an eye on me with the drone while I check out the service road."

Lane gave a nod, **kneeling by the laptop,** watching the **live feed from the drone.** "Got it."

Dakota **stepped out of the van,** the **heat of the midday sun hitting him immediately.** The air smelled of **dry grass, warm pavement, and something faintly metallic.** He pulled his radio up, clicking the button.

"Check, radio check."

A slight crackle, then Lane's voice came through. "**Working.**"

Dakota glanced up, spotting the **drone hovering overhead,** its faint hum filling the silence. He lifted a hand and gave **a small wave.**

Lane's voice cut through the static again. "So far, so good. **You've got a clear path ahead.**"

Dakota walked further down the **overgrown trail,** his boots crunching against the dirt and gravel. The **trees on either side were dense,** creating a natural tunnel that led toward the back of **Hollow Park's massive chain-link fence.**

He slowed his pace, running his fingers along the **metal links,** searching for **weak spots.**

Anything broken.
 Anything loose.
 A section they could slip through.

Minutes passed in **silence.** He crouched by one area where the **fence looked slightly warped,** running his hand along the bottom, testing for give—

Then the radio crackled to life.

Lane's voice, sharper this time. **Urgent.**

"You've got two guards walking down the service—" A slight pause. Then, "**They spotted the drone. Get back. Now. They're heading right for you. About seventy feet up the way.**"

Dakota **froze.** His heartbeat **kicked up.**

"Shit."

His hand shot up to the radio. "**Bring the drone down. Take it back to the van.**"

Then he **turned and ran.**

The **trail blurred past him,** weeds and loose dirt kicking up under his boots. The drone **buzzed ahead of him,** retreating like a silent scout returning to its base.

The van came into sight.

The drone **darted into the open side door**, its propellers slowing as Lane quickly reached in, **grabbing it and powering it down.**

Dakota **jumped inside,** slamming the side door shut behind him. He barely took a breath before throwing himself into the **driver's seat**, turning the key in the ignition. The van rumbled to life.

Lane was still **shoving the drone into its case,** hastily closing the **laptop** and securing it in its compartment. He kept his balance as Dakota **threw the van into reverse,** backing out of the service road.

Within seconds, they were **back on the main road,** putting distance between themselves and the park.

Only after a few minutes of driving did Dakota finally let out a breath. "That was too close."

Lane, now safely buckled in the passenger seat, let out a **nervous chuckle.** "Yeah. **You think they saw you?**"

Dakota shook his head. "Doubt it. But they're definitely on alert now."

They drove back to the **motel,** the weight of what had just happened sinking in.

The room was **dimly lit,** the curtains drawn to keep the late-afternoon sun from heating the place up. The **air conditioner hummed softly,** filling the quiet as Dakota sank into the **desk chair,** rubbing his face.

Lane sat on the **edge of the bed,** hands resting on his knees. After a beat, he spoke. "**So… what now?**"

Dakota dropped his hands, exhaling. "We go back. **At night.**"

Lane studied him. "**Think it'll be any different?**"

Dakota nodded. "Security works in **shifts.** Day crew might be different from the night crew. **Fewer patrols, maybe fewer guards.** We need to know how the place runs *both* shifts before we try to go in."

Lane considered this, then leaned back on his elbows. "Risky."

Dakota met his gaze. "It was always gonna be."

Lane gave a tired smirk. "Fair point."

Dakota glanced at the **equipment laid out on the desk.** They'd have to be **smarter, faster, more careful.**

Tonight, they'd find out **just how impossible sneaking into Hollow Park was going to be.**

And if it *was* impossible—

They'd have to figure out how to do it anyway.

The room was quiet except for the soft clicking of Dakota's **keyboard and trackpad** as he sifted through the **drone footage** frame by frame. The dim glow from his **laptop screen** cast faint shadows across his face, his focus sharp as he scanned for **anything they might have missed.**

Lane sat on the floor a few feet away, surrounded by **a tangled mess of cables and camera equipment.** He sighed, yanking at a particularly stubborn knot. "Dude, why do we always let this happen?" he muttered.

Dakota, too focused on the footage, barely responded. "Because we never organize anything until it's a problem."

Lane exhaled through his nose. "Yeah. Sounds about right."

Dakota's phone suddenly **buzzed against the desk.**

His eyes flicked toward it, and his brows **knitted together** when he saw the name on the screen. It wasn't exactly **confusion**, more like—**a hesitation.** A feeling of **nostalgia mixed with longing.**

His dad was calling.

Dakota hesitated **only for a second** before picking it up. "Hey, Dad."

Lane glanced up briefly but didn't say anything, returning to his mess of wires.

On the other end, his father's voice was warm but distant, the way it always was when they spoke. "Hey, kid. **I'll be home next week.** Thought maybe we could get together, catch up." A pause. "I found **some cool stuff in Egypt** this time—you might like it."

Dakota's lips twitched into a **small, genuine smile.** "Yeah, that'd be great."

They talked for a few more minutes—brief but comfortable. His father told him about **some of the artifacts he uncovered**, the **heat of the desert**, how he'd been meaning to come home sooner but **kept getting pulled into one project after another.**

It was always like this.

Dakota didn't resent him for it. **He missed him.** And he always wished things were different—wished they had more time. But moments like this, even if fleeting, meant something.

After a few more words, they said their goodbyes, and Dakota set the phone back on the desk.

Lane, who had somehow managed to tie **two separate cords into a worse knot than before,** looked up. "What was that about?"

Dakota leaned back in his chair. "Dad's coming home next week. Wants to meet up. **He found some new artifacts in Egypt.**"

Lane nodded, setting a few cords aside. "That's great. **It's been months since he's been back.**"

Then, with a slight smirk, he added, "You know, it's kinda funny when you think about it. Your dad's out there on actual expeditions, digging up lost civilizations, and we're out here breaking into abandoned buildings. We're basically the **discount version.**"

Dakota shot him a **sarcastic look.** "Okay, that was funny." A pause. "**You're stupid, but funny.**"

Lane grinned. "I'll take it."

Dakota let out a breath, shaking his head slightly before **turning back to his laptop.** His eyes flicked to the **paused drone footage**, Hollow Park's overgrown ruins staring back at him.

Tomorrow, they were **going back in.**

And whatever was waiting for them inside the park—**they were going to find it.**

The sky had deepened to a **murky navy**, the last traces of daylight fading behind the **dense tree line**. The air was different now—**thicker, colder, quieter.**

Dakota drove in **silence**, his hands steady on the wheel as they navigated the dark backroads. The only sound was the faint hum of the **van's tires against cracked asphalt** and the low murmur of the radio playing something neither of them was paying attention to.

Lane sat in the passenger seat, arms crossed, staring out the window at the **twisting branches and overgrown brush** that lined the abandoned road. The headlights carved a path through the darkness, illuminating the faint outlines of **faded street signs** and **weather-worn barriers.**

After a while, he let out a slow breath. "Man, places like this **always** felt weird at night. Even when they were open. You ever notice that?"

Dakota glanced at him briefly before returning his focus to the road. "How do you mean?"

"I don't know," Lane shrugged. "Theme parks, carnivals, even malls after hours. It's like—**when the people are gone, the whole place just… changes.** Like it wasn't meant to exist without crowds and noise."

Dakota hummed in agreement. "Yeah. It's the **uncanny silence.**"

The **van rumbled** as he pulled onto the **overgrown service road.** Tall grass and weeds brushed against the undercarriage as they slowed to a stop. Dakota **killed the engine,** and for a moment, the only sound was the soft ticking of the **cooling motor.**

Lane let out a breath. "Here we go."

Without hesitation, they both **moved to the back,** falling into a **well-practiced routine.**

Dakota **grabbed his laptop,** setting it up on a crate as he booted up the **live feed software.**

Lane **unzipped the drone case,** pulling out the sleek black frame and **powering it on.**

Keys clicked. Motors hummed. Lights flickered to life.

Dakota adjusted the **camera settings, switching to night vision.** "Okay. We're live."

Lane **opened the side door,** and the **drone lifted off, its propellers slicing through the quiet air.**

Dakota **watched the screen,** his eyes narrowing as the **park came into view.**

The **drone glided over Hollow Park,** its camera cutting through the dark with eerie precision. The once-bright attractions now stood **motionless and decayed.**

The **coasters** were covered in rust, their tracks swallowed by vines.

The **carousel** stood eerily intact, the horses frozen in mid-gallop.

The **water slides** were coated in grime, their once-colorful tunnels faded to dull gray.

Lane kept the drone moving, weaving through the remains of the park. "Anything?"

"Nothing," Dakota murmured. "No security."

Lane frowned. "You sure?"

"Keep flying over. Check around."

The drone banked left, sweeping over the **main walkway.** After several minutes of nothing, Dakota finally spotted **movement.**

A lone **security guard** came into frame, walking slowly down the cracked path, flashlight in hand.

"That's the first one I've seen," Dakota muttered.

Lane scoffed. "Just one? You'd think this place would be **locked down** after dark. **That's when the real trouble would start.**"

Dakota nodded, eyes glued to the feed. Then—

Static.

The screen **fuzzed out.**

"Shit—what was that?" Lane asked.

Dakota tapped the keyboard, trying to **recalibrate the signal.**

The **feed cut out completely.**

For a solid five seconds, they were looking at **nothing but black noise.**

Then—

The screen flickered back on.

Dakota and Lane both leaned in.

The **guard was gone.**

Dakota frowned. "Where the hell did he go?"

Lane adjusted the controls, moving the drone slightly. "You think he just walked out of frame?"

"Maybe," Dakota muttered, but something **felt off.** The **guard had been in the middle of the path—there was nowhere for him to disappear that quickly.**

Then, in the lower **left corner of the screen…**

A shadow darted across the camera.

Fast. Almost too fast to process.

"What the hell was that?" Lane whispered.

Dakota didn't answer right away. He swallowed hard, eyes flicking across the feed, scanning every inch of the park.

But there was **nothing.**

Just empty rides. Empty walkways. Empty shadows.

Finally, Dakota exhaled. "Alright. That's enough for now. **Bring it back.**"

Lane hesitated for a second before nodding, guiding the **drone back toward the van.**

The **screen remained clear** the entire flight back. No more interference. No more **shadows.**

But the unease **stayed.**

And they both felt it.

Dakota and Lane **glanced at each other**, the dim glow of the laptop screen reflecting in their eyes. The **unease lingered** between them, stretching out in the silence.

Lane exhaled through his nose. "That was **weird.**" His voice was low, contemplative. "The **interference**—it didn't happen earlier today when we flew the drone."

Dakota **rubbed his jaw,** considering it. "Yeah… **there has to be a logical explanation.**"

Lane raised an eyebrow. "Like what?"

Dakota gestured vaguely at the **laptop.** "I don't know, **a signal surge? Maybe it got too far out of range.**"

Lane frowned, shaking his head. "Even if there was interference, **where the hell did the guard go?** There's no way he disappeared that quick."

Dakota leaned back, tapping his fingers against the side of the **van's storage crate.** "Maybe there was a delay in the footage. **Whatever caused the interference might've made the feed lag.** The guard probably walked off **before** we saw the static."

Lane didn't look convinced.

He'd never been the type to **jump to paranormal conclusions.** Neither of them had. They had spent years exploring **abandoned places, forgotten buildings, dark hallways—and nothing supernatural had ever happened.**

Still…

Something about this **felt different.**

Lane shook the thought from his head. No point in **overthinking it.**

Dakota smirked. "I mean, let's be real—it was **probably** the **hybrid dinosaur monster** they were building under the haunted house."

Lane snorted. "Oh, for sure. That thing's **running loose.** Definitely not a glitch."

Dakota grinned. "Or, hear me out—**it was the ghost of Jason Langston.**"

Lane gasped dramatically, clutching his chest. "Damn. **You cracked the case.**"

Dakota nodded solemnly. "Yep. Security guard? **Ghost the whole time.**"

That finally broke the tension.

The two of them **laughed,** the absurdity of it all melting away the last bit of unease.

Lane **reached for the van's side door,** ready to slide it shut.

But just as his fingers **touched the handle—**

Dakota's hand **shot up.**

"Wait."

Lane froze, his smile fading slightly. "What?"

Dakota's head tilted slightly, his expression shifting to something **uncertain.** "Just… **listen.**"

Lane frowned but **obliged,** standing still.

For a moment, **there was nothing.**

Then—

Something faint, **floating on the wind.**

A sound.

Wheezing.

A slow, **troubled breathing,** distant but unmistakable.

Lane's brow furrowed. His **first instinct was to rationalize it.** "It's the wind," he muttered. "Or, I don't know—**an animal or something.**"

Dakota didn't argue. He wasn't even sure **what he thought it was.**

He finally exhaled and waved for Lane to **close the door.**

Lane **pulled it shut,** the **metallic click of the lock** echoing louder than usual in the **heavy silence.**

Neither of them spoke as Dakota **shut off the laptop screen,** plunging the van's interior into darkness.

And outside, the night stretched on.

Still. Watching. Waiting.

The motel room was **dimly lit,** the glow from Dakota's **laptop screen** casting long shadows across the desk. The **low hum of the air conditioner** filled the silence as Dakota sat forward, watching the **drone footage again.**

Over and over.

Frame by frame.

Slow motion. Full speed. Pausing at just the right moment—**just before the static hit.**

Lane stood next to him, leaning over the desk, arms crossed as he **watched alongside Dakota.** Neither of them spoke, their focus locked on the **grainy, night-vision footage.**

They were looking for **anything.**

Something that explained the **interference.** Something that showed **where the guard went.** Something that made sense of the **random shadow.**

After several minutes, Lane let out a **low sigh** and shrugged. "Honestly, the only thing that makes sense is the **lag.** The interference probably caused a delay, and that shadow? **Could've just been light casting weird shapes or the footage catching up.** Probably just the guard walking away."

Dakota exhaled through his nose, nodding. "Yeah… probably."

Still, he played the video **one last time.**

Lane's brows suddenly furrowed. "**Wait—pause.**"

Dakota's fingers **froze over the keyboard.** He hit the **spacebar,** stopping the video. "What?"

Lane leaned in, pointing at a **darkened area between the stalls.** "There. **Look.**"

Dakota squinted. The silhouette was **barely visible,** blending into the blackness. But it was there.

A **shape. A figure.**

His breath **hitched slightly.**

Lane narrowed his eyes. "That's… the guard, right?"

Dakota **sat up straighter,** nodding quickly. "Yeah. **There—see?** We just missed him. **He turned off his flashlight and was in the dark the whole time.**"

Lane didn't answer immediately.

He **leaned in closer,** his expression tightening. "…Something looks **off.**"

Dakota glanced at him. "What do you mean?"

Lane tilted his head. "**I don't know.** Just… **the way he's standing. The proportions look weird.**"

Dakota let out a breath, waving a hand. "It's the **camera quality.** Night vision always makes things look distorted." "It's nothing."

Lane hesitated for a moment longer, then **shrugged.** "Yeah… **guess you're right.**"

That was **one question answered.**

Or at least, **explained away.**

Dakota stood up, **stretching his arms over his head.** "Alright, let's check on Langston."

Lane moved to sit on the edge of the **bed** while Dakota opened Google, typing **Jason Langston's name** into the search bar.

A **new article popped up.** Dakota clicked on it.

JULY 11, 2015
Jason Langston, former founder of Hollow Park, was found deceased in his home early this morning by a family member.

Dakota kept reading aloud.

*"The official reports have now been released. Langston was discovered unresponsive in the bathroom of his Hollow Creek home. An **empty bottle of sleeping medication** was found beside him. Toxicology reports confirm the presence of the medication in his system, and the case has now been officially **ruled as a suicide."***

"At this time, there are no additional details. No further evidence or notes were left behind. It is unclear what may have led to this decision."

Dakota **stared at the screen for a long moment** before finally closing the page. Then, he shut the **laptop.**

Lane watched him. "Damn."

Dakota shook his head, rubbing his jaw. "What do they mean, **they don't know why?** The guy lost **everything.**" His voice was calm but firm. "What did they **think** was gonna happen?"

Lane didn't answer.

The room felt **heavier now.**

After a beat, Dakota exhaled, **running a hand through his hair.** "Alright, let's get some sleep. **We're going in tomorrow."**

Lane gave a small nod, but as Dakota climbed into bed and **shut off the light,** the last image of the **silhouette on the screen** still lingered in the back of his mind.

And for some reason—**it wouldn't go away.**

Chapter Five

The sky was **still tinted with shades of deep blue**, the first slivers of sunlight creeping over the horizon. The **air was crisp**, carrying the lingering chill of the night as Dakota and Lane worked in **near silence,** loading the equipment into the van.

There was an **unspoken tension** between them. **Not fear—just anticipation.**

They had done **plenty** of urban explorations before.

But **this** one felt different.

Dakota secured the last **equipment case** in place, giving it a quick pat before stepping inside. Lane followed, **pulling the doors shut**, sealing them in the dim glow of the van's interior lights.

Without a word, they **set up the tripod**, clicking the **camera into place.**

Dakota adjusted the focus, then hit **record.**

He took a slow breath, looking into the lens. "**Alright, guys. This is it.**"

Lane stood slightly behind him, arms crossed. "**Today's the day.**"

Dakota nodded, running a hand through his **messy hair.** "**We're heading back to Hollow Park, and if all goes well—**"

"**We get inside,**" Lane finished.

They exchanged a glance before Dakota turned back to the camera.

"But," Lane added, "**we don't know if we'll actually get in today.** It might take another day before we figure out the best way inside."

Dakota smirked, tilting his head slightly. "**Not that it really matters what we say here.**"

Lane raised an eyebrow. "What do you mean?"

Dakota gestured toward the camera. "Because **this video isn't coming out until after we've finished the exploration.**"

Lane chuckled. "True. So technically, if you guys are watching this—**we made it inside.**"

There was a brief pause. Then Lane **grinned, shaking his head.** "Or—**we didn't make it back.**"

Dakota gave him a look. "Dude."

Lane shrugged dramatically. "I mean, **let's be real.** If this video never gets uploaded, then we're probably dead." He pointed at the camera. "And in that case, you guys won't be watching this anyway—unless someone finds the footage and makes a **cheap found-footage horror movie** about us."

Dakota let out a breathy laugh, shaking his head. **"You're such an idiot."**

Lane smirked. "You love it."

Dakota rolled his eyes and **ended the recording.** Lane grabbed the **camera,** tucking it into one of the padded storage cases, while Dakota **collapsed the tripod** and slid it back into its compartment.

Then, they **paused.**

For a moment, neither of them spoke.

Just a brief exchange of glances—one last **silent acknowledgment** of what they were about to do.

Dakota finally asked, **"You ready?"**

Lane gave a single nod.

Without another word, they both **stepped up to the front of the van** and climbed into their seats.

Dakota turned the key, and the **engine rumbled to life,** filling the quiet with a **low hum.** He gripped the steering wheel, eyes locked on the empty road ahead, and slowly pulled out of the parking lot.

Their **final adventure** had officially begun.

And one way or another—**it would be their biggest yet.**

The **van rumbled** as Dakota drove down the cracked, forgotten **service road.** The tires jolted every few seconds, bouncing over patches of **uneven asphalt,** the road long neglected and half-swallowed by nature.

Towering **trees loomed overhead,** their low-hanging branches swaying slightly in the early morning breeze. **Tall weeds brushed against the sides of the van,** half-concealing it as Dakota pulled off onto a **small side road,** tucking the vehicle into the overgrowth.

This would have to do. **They needed to stay hidden.**

Without hesitation, **Lane unbuckled his seatbelt** and pushed himself from his seat. He moved with **practiced efficiency,** stepping into the back of the van and grabbing the **drone case.**

Dakota followed, flipping open one of the **storage compartments** and retrieving his **laptop.** He opened it, the screen **glowing dimly** in the shadowed interior of the van.

"Alright," Dakota murmured, fingers moving swiftly across the **keyboard.** "**Let's get this thing in the air.**"

Lane nodded, **sliding the side door open.** The early morning air swept inside, crisp and cool, carrying the distant scent of **damp earth and rusted metal.**

With a soft **whir,** the **drone powered on.**

Lane guided it into the air, the **propellers slicing through the silence** as it rose above the tree line.

Dakota **pulled up the live feed,** his fingers gliding over the keys—**camera rotation, calibration, stabilization.** Within moments, the **park unfolded on-screen.**

The twisted, abandoned remains of **Hollow Park.**

They both leaned in.

The drone moved smoothly over the **main pathways,** gliding over the rusted coasters and decayed attractions.

For a moment, neither of them spoke.

Then Lane frowned. "**That's weird.**"

Dakota glanced up from the laptop. "What?"

Lane adjusted the drone's altitude, sweeping over another section of the park. "**There's no security.**"

Dakota let out a quiet breath. "Don't get too excited. **We just started.**"

Lane nodded, keeping the drone moving, checking all the major areas they had mapped out.

Still—**nothing.**

Dakota's **brow furrowed.** "Where the hell is everyone?"

Lane hovered the drone over the **carousel, the water park, the jungle cruise ride.** Nothing moved. No sign of **guards, workers—anything.**

"You think… they just left?" Lane asked.

Dakota shook his head. "No way. They wouldn't just abandon this place. **It's still private property.**"

They continued searching **as far as the drone's signal would allow.**

Still, **nothing.**

A silence settled between them.

Finally, Dakota exhaled sharply. "This is our chance."

Lane glanced at him.

"Even if security is patrolling **other areas**, we have the **perfect opportunity to get in.**"

Lane didn't hesitate. He **brought the drone back,** guiding it **carefully into the van.** The **propellers slowed,** and the device touched down with a soft mechanical hum.

They both moved fast.

Dakota **grabbed his bag,** filled with **extra batteries, SD cards, and flashlights.**

Lane grabbed the **camera and radios.**

Dakota clipped one of the **radios to the waist of his pants.**

Their **movements were automatic.** No second-guessing. No hesitation.

This was it.

They stepped out of the van, **closing the door behind them.**

Dakota adjusted the **straps of his bag.** "Alright," he said quietly, glancing toward the **looming fence.** "**Let's find a way in.**"

The **sun had begun to rise**, its golden light filtering through the trees, stretching long shadows across the ground. The **morning air was still cool,** but Dakota knew it wouldn't last.

They didn't need their flashlights—not yet.

They **moved quickly,** walking along the **perimeter fence**, scanning for **the weak spot Dakota had found yesterday.**

There—

A **section where the fence had come loose,** the metal untwisted just enough to create a **gap.**

Dakota grabbed the loose section, **pulling it open.** The **metal groaned softly.**

Lane crouched down and **slipped through first.**

Dakota followed, **ducking under the chain-link,** the cold metal **scraping his backpack.**

As he straightened up on the other side, Lane was already **lifting the camera.**

The lens **blinked to life.**

The **recording light flickered on.**

They were **inside.**

And there was no turning back now.

Lane **swept the camera from left to right,** capturing the **desolate remains of Hollow Park's main plaza.**

"This is it," Dakota murmured as they walked forward, **the crunch of loose gravel under their boots.**

Where they had entered led them **straight into the heart of the park**—the main **starting point** where guests would first arrive.

This was where families had once stood, **scanning maps, planning their day.** Where the smell of **popcorn, funnel cakes, and fried food** had once filled the air.

Now?

Empty stalls lined the pathways, their once-vibrant signage now faded and peeling. The **menu boards were still intact**, though barely legible under layers of dirt and grime. **Torn banners flapped weakly in the breeze.**

"This is where you'd go first," Dakota explained to the camera. "**This is the center of the whole park.** This is where you'd grab snacks, souvenirs… and from here, the pathways lead off to all the different sections."

They stopped at **one of the souvenir stalls**, its **wooden counter warped and cracked.** The remains of Hollow Park merchandise still sat **scattered across the surface—old plush toys, sun-bleached t-shirts, plastic cups.**

Dakota reached for a **folded, weathered piece of paper.**

A **park map.**

He glanced at Lane before unfolding it, carefully spreading it out for the camera.

"Alright," Dakota said, studying the faded details. He looked at the camera and raised a brow. **"Where do you want to start first?"**

Lane leaned over slightly, glancing at the map.

He pointed. "**Toon World.**"

Dakota snorted, looking back at the camera with an amused expression.

"Toon World," he repeated, nodding. "For those of you who don't know, **Toon World is the kiddie section.** That's where you'd take the little ones who couldn't or didn't want to ride the big-kid rides."

Then, with a **mocking smirk,** he added, "Only makes sense why Lane would choose that first. **I guess mental age also counts."**

Lane rolled his eyes but grinned. "Laugh it up, but **you know damn well Toon World has the best abandoned animatronics."**

Dakota chuckled. "Alright, fine. Let's check it out."

He turned, **gesturing for the camera to follow** as they made their way toward the **large, arched entrance to Toon World.**

The **painted sign above it was cracked and chipped,** the cartoon characters once welcoming families now frozen in eerie, **faded grins.**

The entrance loomed ahead.

And beyond it—**the unknown.**

The **once-vibrant walkway** leading into Toon World was **barely recognizable.**

It had once been **brightly colored,** covered in fun patterns meant to excite kids as they ran toward their favorite attractions.

Now, the **paint was cracked and chipped,** long since **faded by time and neglect. Weeds** sprouted through the fractures in the pavement, twisting over the walkway like nature itself was trying to reclaim the park.

Lane kept the **camera rolling,** slowly panning around as they walked.

"This place used to be insane," Dakota murmured, scanning the area.

"There wasn't much to it," Lane added, **gesturing toward the surroundings.** "Just a couple of these **cartoon houses.** Most of them were just props—only a few were actually **accessible."**

The **houses were built with exaggerated, cartoonish features**—slanted roofs, oversized doors, lopsided chimneys. They were designed to look **whimsical and fun,** like something straight out of an old Saturday morning cartoon.

But now?

They looked **wrong.**

Like they had **melted slightly, sagging under the weight of time.**

Dakota and Lane approached the **first house,** its once-bright **red and yellow paint now dull and peeling.**

The **door was slightly ajar.**

Lane aimed the **camera toward the entrance,** giving the viewers a **closer look** before following Dakota inside.

The **interior was eerily intact.**

Dust coated every surface, but everything remained **as it had been left.** The fake **kitchen setup, the oversized plastic furniture,** even the **animatronic characters** that had once greeted children with **bright, cheerful voices.**

Now, they **stood in eerie silence.**

Dakota took a slow step forward, his **boots scuffing against the floor.** He looked at the first **animatronic,** his brow furrowing.

"Damn," he muttered. "They're still here."

The first one was a **blue bear**, its once-vibrant **fur now dulled and discolored**. Its **cartoonishly large eyes stared ahead**, lifeless and blank. The fabric around its **snout and ears was torn,** exposing the plastic beneath.

Lane moved the camera slowly to the next figure.

A **pink mouse**, standing with its hands frozen in an open **welcoming gesture.**

The fabric of its **overalls was tattered**, the fur around its **arms matted and stiff.** The animatronic had a **slight forward hunch,** as if it had been left in the middle of a movement that had never finished.

Dakota moved to the **last animatronic**, standing near the back.

A **green dog,** its cartoonish features still oddly **intact** despite the years. It held a **large cream pie** in one of its outstretched hands—a **towering swirl of fake whipped cream, topped with a bright red cherry.**

Lane finally spoke. "Man… this one was my favorite."

Dakota looked over at him. "Yeah?"

Lane nodded, keeping his **voice low,** as if speaking too loud might **wake something up.** "When I was a kid, they had this **game** here—one of those interactive things where you could throw virtual pies at the characters on a screen."

Dakota glanced back at the **green dog.** "What happened to it?"

Lane shrugged. "**Shut down after a few years.** Guess it just wasn't popular enough."

For a moment, the only sound was the **low hum of the camera.**

Then Dakota let out a quiet breath, looking around. "I don't know, man. Something about these places when they're abandoned… it's just **off.**"

Lane didn't disagree.

He just **kept the camera rolling.**

Because there was something about this place—**something lingering beneath the silence.**

And neither of them could shake the feeling that **they weren't really alone.**

Dakota and Lane continued moving through **Toon World,** their footsteps echoing faintly in the hollow silence.

The **second house** they entered was **completely empty.**

It was strange—**the walls were stripped bare,** the once-vibrant décor missing. The space looked **unfinished, like they had been in the middle of renovating it** before the park shut down.

"Looks like they were trying to redo this one," Dakota muttered, running a hand along the **dusty wall.**

Lane nodded, but neither of them lingered. There wasn't much to see.

Then they reached the **final house.**

And they both **stopped.**

It was **colorless.**

Not just faded like the others—**completely devoid of color.** The walls, the door, the roof—**all dull shades of black, white, and gray.**

Lane stared at it for a moment before his memory **clicked.**

"Oh, man—I remember this one."

Dakota glanced at him. "Yeah?"

Lane nodded. "This was **the villains' house.** That game I was telling you about? This is where the bad guys lived."

He gestured at the **monochrome building.** "Their whole thing was that they hated fun. They wanted to get rid of color, joy, everything. You had to **throw pies at them** to stop them from turning the world gray."

Dakota let out a breath, shaking his head with an amused smirk. "So, basically—**corporate America, the ride.**"

Lane chuckled. "Pretty much."

Dakota motioned to the **open doorway.** "Shall we?"

They **stepped inside.**

The interior was **just as colorless** as the outside. The walls were painted in **muted grays,** the furniture and props designed to look **cold and lifeless.**

Even the lighting had been **dimmed intentionally,** making everything feel strangely **flat and lifeless.**

And then—**the animatronics.**

These weren't like the ones in the other houses.

They were **tall, humanoid robots,** built with **rigid, angular bodies.** Their **metal frames were painted to resemble formal suits**, complete with buttons and ties.

But it was their **faces** that stood out the most.

They were **built into permanent scowls,** their **brows furrowed, their jaws stiff, their hollow eyes locked in an expression of perpetual displeasure.**

Dakota exhaled, shaking his head. "Dude… how did this **not** terrify kids?"

Lane stepped closer, moving the **camera up to one of the faces.**

"They were **less scary when they were moving,**" Lane admitted. "They'd talk, their mouths would move—it wasn't as creepy back then." He paused. "**But I was also a kid.** Probably just blocked out how weird they actually looked."

Dakota studied one of the **lifeless figures.**

Standing still like this, frozen in a **silent, unmoving scowl,** they looked less like **cartoon villains** and more like… something else.

Something that was **never meant to be left alone in the dark.**

Lane and Dakota **stepped out** of the **colorless house,** back into the **soft morning light.** The eerie stillness of the animatronics lingered in their minds, but neither of them commented on it.

Instead, Dakota turned to the **camera,** running a hand through his hair.

"Alright," he sighed, giving the lens a **half-smirk.** "Apologies for the **nightmare fuel.** Hope you guys sleep well tonight."

Lane **snorted,** shaking his head as he gave the camera one last pan of the **bleak house.** "Yeah, if you ever wondered **what pure childhood terror looks like—there you go.**"

Dakota **chuckled,** then pulled out the **map** again as they walked **back toward the main plaza.**

They stopped near one of the **dust-covered souvenir stalls,** Dakota **unfolding the map** while Lane adjusted the camera.

Dakota ran his finger along one of the **faded sections.**

"Alright, next up—we're heading into **Western Wonderland.**"

He looked at the camera. "This section was **designed like an 1800s ghost town.** All wooden buildings, dirt roads, the whole pioneer aesthetic."

Lane nodded. "And the **rollercoaster?**"

Dakota tapped a spot on the map. "Yeah. **Gold Rush.** It was the only coaster in this section—you'd sit in a **minecart** and ride through a **fake mountain,** going in and out of **caves.**"

Lane aimed the camera at Dakota as he continued.

"They even had **statues of miners** inside, like they were trying to dig for gold while you passed by. It was honestly a pretty cool ride."

Lane **flipped the camera around,** filming as they followed the **trail leading into the pioneer section.**

The moment they stepped in, **it was like walking into another world.**

The atmosphere **shifted.**

The buildings were still standing—**weathered but intact.**

The **old saloon** had its **swinging doors frozen mid-motion,** caught in time as if someone had just walked through them decades ago. The **general store's window was shattered,** shelves inside still stocked with **faux goods meant to add to the theme.**

Lane **panned the camera slowly.**

There was a **sheriff's office, a bank, a blacksmith shop.** Signs hung above each door, their **lettering faded and chipped.**

"This actually looks **really cool,**" Lane muttered.

Dakota nodded, running a hand over **a wooden post,** the old texture rough beneath his fingertips. "Yeah, **they really committed** to the ghost town theme."

Then, up ahead—

The mountain.

Lane followed it **all the way up with the camera,** taking in the **massive artificial rock structure** that housed the **Gold Rush coaster.**

The **tracks twisted around the mountain,** disappearing into dark **tunnel openings** meant to resemble **mining shafts.**

Dakota whistled. "Damn. **Still impressive.**"

Lane **lowered the camera slightly** and glanced at him.

"Wanna try and walk the track?"

Dakota didn't even **hesitate.**

"Hell yeah."

Without a second thought, he **started toward the stairs** that led up to the **boarding area** of the coaster.

Lane shook his head with a small chuckle but followed, **keeping the camera steady** as they ascended the **creaking wooden steps.**

As they climbed higher, Dakota glanced back at the mountain.

"…You ever wonder if these things are **actually stable?**"

Lane aimed the camera at him, **grinning.**

"Well, guess we're about to find out."

The **wooden platform creaked** beneath their boots as Dakota and Lane stepped into the **empty boarding area** of Gold Rush.

The **metal air gates stood open, rusted hinges frozen in place.** The loading zone, once filled with excited riders, now sat **silent and abandoned.**

Dakota glanced around, then at the camera. "Man, I remember **this line moving fast.**"

Lane nodded. "Yeah, the ride was **only about two minutes long.** Get in, get out, boom—next group."

Dakota slung his bag off his shoulder, unzipping it and pulling out a **flashlight.**

"The tunnels are gonna be dark," he said, **clicking it on** and testing the beam.

Lane adjusted the **camera settings.** "I'll swap to **night vision** if we need it."

Without another word, they **climbed over the air gates** and stepped down onto the **rollercoaster track.**

The **metal groaned softly** beneath their weight, but it held. Dakota **bounced his weight slightly,** testing the sturdiness.

"Seems solid enough," he muttered.

Lane aimed the **camera at the ride vehicles.**

The **mine carts** still sat on the track, frozen in place. Their **once-bright paint was dulled by rust**, streaks of orange and brown creeping over the metal. **Cobwebs clung to the sides.**

"Man, these things are **rotting in place,**" Lane muttered.

Dakota smirked. "Guess they're not **going anywhere.**"

They started walking, following **the same winding path the carts once took.** The metal beneath their boots let out **soft creaks and groans** with each step.

As they approached the **first tunnel entrance**, Dakota **tightened his grip** on the flashlight.

He flicked it on.

The **beam cut through the darkness.**

Lane adjusted the **camera to night vision.** "Alright, let's see what's in here."

They stepped into the **cave.**

The tunnel was **narrow and eerie,** the walls built to resemble **roughly carved stone.**

Dakota's **flashlight beam scanned the passage,** sweeping over the artificial rock. The air was **cooler in here**, the damp scent of **rotting wood and rust filling the space.**

Then—**movement.**

Lane let out a **sharp gasp.**

Dakota snapped his head toward him, **flashlight jerking in the darkness.** "Dude, what?"

Lane **exhaled**, his camera locked on a **figure lurking just beyond the stone archway.**

It took Dakota a second to process.

Then he **laughed.**

The **statue of a miner** stood partially **hidden behind a rock wall, frozen mid-action.** His **pickaxe was raised, eyes locked in a determined stare.**

Dakota grinned. "What's wrong, Lane? **Scared of a little hard work?**"

Lane let out an **exaggerated, sarcastic laugh.** "Hilarious. Truly. You should be a comedian."

Dakota smirked, sweeping the **flashlight beam** along the tunnel's edge. More **miner statues stood frozen** in different poses—some **swinging pickaxes, some crouched beside mining carts, others holding lanterns.**

They continued forward, but their walk **came to an abrupt end.**

A **steep incline stretched ahead of them**, the track rising sharply toward an **opening at the top of the mountain.**

Dakota stopped, **eyeing the incline.**

He looked at the camera. "Yeah, **this is as far as we go.** No way we're making it up that."

Lane **panned the camera up,** taking in the steep drop-off.

Dakota smirked. "**We're YouTubers, not mountain climbers.**"

With that, they turned back, **re-tracing their steps** through the tunnel.

They climbed back **over the air gates,** stepping onto the platform.

Lane shut off **night vision**, adjusting the camera as they walked down the **wooden stairs** leading back into the ghost town.

Dakota dusted off his **jeans.** "Alright. **Where to next?**"

Lane scanned the buildings ahead before nodding toward the **saloon.**

"That place," he said.

Dakota grinned. "Of course, you pick the bar."

The **saloon was never meant for guests to go inside**—it was **just a decorative set piece**, designed for pictures. The windows showcased **lifelike mannequins dressed as old-west characters**, giving the illusion of a **bustling 1800s tavern.**

Dakota pushed open the **wooden double doors.**

The **inside was dim,** dust particles floating in the morning light. The **mannequins sat frozen,** locked in poses—one **"bartender" stood behind the counter**, his plastic hands resting near old **glass bottles glued to the shelves.**

Dakota and Lane **took a seat at the bar.**

Dakota turned to the camera.

"Alright, we're gonna take a quick break. **We'll see you guys soon.**"

Lane **shut off the camera,** setting it on the **dust-covered counter.**

For the first time since entering Hollow Park, the silence **felt heavier.**

Dakota and Lane **sat at the counter**, the air **thick with dust and silence.** The saloon felt **frozen in time**, the mannequins locked in their rigid, lifeless poses.

For a moment, neither of them spoke, just **glancing around** at the eerie stillness of the room.

Then, Dakota leaned forward, tapping the **wooden bar with his fingers.**

"Hey, barkeep," he said, his voice lighthearted, "**let me get a beer.**"

Lane chuckled, playing along. "**Make it two.**"

The **mannequin behind the bar**, a plastic figure dressed in an old-west vest and hat, **stared ahead blankly,** its painted eyes dull and lifeless.

Dakota smirked, shaking his head. "**Worst service ever.**"

Lane laughed again, then leaned on the counter. "**So, what's next?**"

Dakota pulled out the **map**, spreading it across the **dust-covered surface.** He pointed to the **Western Wonderland section.**

"This is where we are," he said, **tracing his finger along the path.** "If we go **this way**, we'll end up in **Adventure Center.**"

Dakota stood, stretching slightly. "**We should probably get moving.**"

Lane grabbed the **camera, turning it back on,** and hit the **record button.**

The lens flickered to life.

Dakota and Lane **stepped out of the saloon,** the **old wooden doors creaking slightly** as they swung closed behind them.

Dust swirled in the air as Dakota turned to the camera.

"Alright, guys," he said, walking backward for a few steps, "we're heading to our next stop—**Adventure Center.**"

Lane adjusted the **camera angle**, panning across the **empty ghost town** as they walked away, before turning it back toward Dakota.

"So," Dakota continued, "Adventure Center is the part of the park that's all about—**you guessed it—adventure.**"

Lane smirked behind the camera. "**How original.**"

Dakota grinned. "I know, right? **Every ride in this section was based on movies or myths.**"

As they followed the winding **overgrown path**, Dakota began listing off the **main attractions.**

The Jungle River Expedition

"This one was **a boat ride** that took you through the **heart of the jungle,**" Dakota explained. "Your **tour guide** was supposed to be leading an expedition to **find a lost tribe.**"

Lane turned the camera toward him. "Let me guess—they weren't **very welcoming?**"

Dakota **snapped his fingers** at him. "**Exactly.**"

He continued.

"It was actually pretty well done. They had **animatronic monkeys swinging from the trees,** and the lost tribe—**totally fake, of course—would 'attack' the boat.**"

Lane tilted his head. "How'd they do that?"

"There were **spouts under the water** that would make it look like **spears or blow darts were hitting the river.** The guide would **panic, speed up the boat,** and you had to 'escape' before they caught you."

Lane chuckled. "Yeah, that sounds **super intense… for a ten-year-old.**"

Dakota laughed. "Yeah, well, it was more about the atmosphere. **It wasn't supposed to be scary, just fun.**"

The Legend of the Hidden Temple

Dakota **gestured ahead**, excitement creeping into his tone.

"Now this ride? **This one was actually pretty sick.**"

Lane raised an eyebrow. "Oh?"

Dakota nodded. "It was basically a **log ride.** You'd get in the **flume,** and it would take you through a **peaceful jungle setting**—birds chirping, waterfalls, all that."

Lane turned the camera toward Dakota again. "Lemme guess—**things go horribly wrong?**"

"Oh, absolutely."

Dakota grinned, motioning as if **painting a picture in the air.**

"You'd reach the entrance of a **massive temple,** and inside, you'd see **all this treasure—gold, artifacts,** all sorts of cool stuff."

Lane nodded, following along.

"But then," Dakota continued, lowering his voice dramatically, "**you realize you've made a huge mistake.**"

Lane smirked. "Naturally."

Dakota grinned.

"By entering the temple, you've **angered the goddess who sleeps inside.** She wakes up, furious, and tries to **steal your soul.**"

Lane let out a low whistle. "Damn. **High stakes.**"

"Oh yeah."

Dakota pointed ahead as they kept walking.

"By the **end of the ride,** you'd see a **huge animatronic of the goddess herself,** standing right in front of you—**arms outstretched, eyes glowing, mist rolling in.**"

Lane nodded. "And then what?"

Dakota grinned. "Then you **drop.**"

Lane tilted his head.

Dakota gestured with his hands. "At the **last second,** the flume **plunges down a steep drop,** and you **escape—barely.**"

Lane laughed. "Man, that sounds **so cheesy.**"

Dakota smirked. "It was, but **it was fun.**"

They continued walking, the **overgrown trail curving ahead,** leading into the **next section of the park.**

As they stepped forward, the **jungle-themed structures came into view.**

Even from a distance, the **remains of the attractions loomed ahead—**

The **faux temple entrance**, partially collapsed.
The **dilapidated jungle huts**, overgrown with vines.
The **jungle boat ride dock**, its canopy torn and rotting.

Lane turned the camera toward Dakota. "So, what are we checking out first?"

Dakota looked ahead at the **silent, abandoned rides.**

Then he smirked.

"How about we **anger a goddess?**"

Lane and Dakota walked **along the overgrown path,** their boots crunching softly against the cracked pavement as they approached the **entrance to The Legend of the Hidden Temple.**

The **grand temple façade loomed ahead**, its intricate carvings worn down by time. The **once-bright paint** had faded into muted browns and greens, now blending **seamlessly with the encroaching wilderness.**

Dakota reached out and **pushed open the heavy doors.**

A low, **metallic groan** echoed through the **abandoned queue line.**

Inside, the air was **thick and stale,** carrying the scent of **damp wood and decay.**

Lane **panned the camera**, capturing the **dust-covered remnants of the ride's waiting area.**

Old TVs were still mounted on the walls, though the screens were cracked and coated in grime.

Fake vines snaked around the pillars, some of them **hanging loose, swaying slightly in the motionless air.**

Piles of artificial gold and treasure were scattered haphazardly along the walls, once meant to add an air of mystery and excitement.

Intricate carvings lined the walls, their once-detailed etchings now softened by **layers of dust and mold.**

Dakota **clicked on his flashlight,** the **beam cutting through the darkness.**

His light swept over the queue area, and he let out a low breath.

"This actually looks **more realistic now** than it did when the park was open," he muttered.

Lane smirked. "**Guess water damage adds authenticity.**"

The two pressed forward, navigating around the fallen debris and broken railings until they reached the **beginning of the ride.**

The loading platform stretched before them, eerily **silent and lifeless.** The **flume**—once filled with rushing water—was now **bone dry,** the concrete track beneath it cracked and stained.

Dakota **leaned over the edge,** shining his flashlight down the empty channel.

He looked at the camera.

"Should we go in? I don't know what to expect beyond this point."

Lane **shrugged.** "How dangerous could it be?"

Dakota **raised an eyebrow at him.**

Lane **grinned.** "Okay, **famous last words, but still.**"

Dakota let out a small chuckle before **sitting on the edge of the flume, sliding himself down.** His boots **scraped against the dry concrete,** the rough texture making it easy to keep balance.

He reached up, **grabbing the camera from Lane** before holding out the **flashlight to help him down.**

Lane **hopped down into the flume,** taking the camera back as Dakota adjusted his bag.

The silence around them felt **thicker now.**

The real adventure was starting.

They entered the **first portion of the ride—the jungle.**

The area was still **partially outdoors**, the **fake trees and foliage** arching over them like a canopy.

Dakota **clicked off his flashlight,** letting their eyes adjust to the faint daylight that still filtered through the gaps in the overgrowth.

He stopped, gazing up at the **fake trees.**

Lane aimed the **camera upward**, panning slowly across the scene.

"These trees are fake," Lane said, a small note of amusement in his voice. "**It's weird they didn't just use real plants.** Some of these species grow **naturally** around here."

Dakota chuckled, **kicking a loose vine with his boot.**

"It's probably **easier to maintain.**"

Lane nodded, still scanning the **dense, artificial jungle** through the camera lens.

For a moment, it was **easy to imagine** the ride in full operation—**the gentle movement of the flume, the pre-recorded sounds of exotic birds, the occasional mist from hidden sprayers.**

But none of that was here now.

Just the **dead silence.**

They continued down the **dry flume,** following the gradual bends and turns that led toward the next section.

After a few minutes, they reached a set of **massive carved stone doors.**

The entrance to the **temple.**

They were **designed to look like towering slabs of ancient rock,** their surfaces etched with **symbols and hieroglyphs.**

But up close, the illusion shattered.

Beneath the chipped paint and **weathered carvings,** the doors were **stainless steel.**

"Damn," Dakota muttered, running his fingers along the surface. "These were actually **metal?**"

"Guess they needed them to be **sturdy,**" Lane said.

The doors were **stuck open,** likely frozen in place after **years of neglect.**

Beyond them, the **interior of the temple stretched ahead, pitch black.**

Dakota turned his **flashlight back on.**

The **beam illuminated the first few feet** of the corridor ahead—faded murals, dust-covered statues, and **the gaping darkness beyond.**

Lane adjusted the camera.

Dakota took a deep breath.

"Alright," he murmured.

They stepped inside.

And the **temple swallowed them whole.**

Dakota and Lane **continued along the flume,** their **footsteps echoing** in the cavernous temple. The **beams of their flashlight and camera** panned across the space, catching the **faint shimmer of artificial treasure.**

Piles of **gold coins, goblets, and gems** lay scattered around the room, **dust-covered and forgotten.**

As they walked, **Dakota narrated for the camera.**

"This was supposed to be the **treasure chamber,**" he explained, moving the **flashlight across the glittering piles.** "The whole point of the ride was to get here, see all the riches—**and then realize you've pissed off the goddess.**"

Lane **panned the camera over the scene,** capturing the eerie stillness.

They **moved into the next section.**

Here, the **room was empty,** except for a few **worn wall carvings.** The air **felt colder,** the silence **even heavier.**

Dakota frowned. "This section was just **projectors and lights,**" he murmured. "They used it to make it look like **spirits were flying past you.**"

Lane tilted the camera slightly. "**So... just a filler area?**"

"Pretty much," Dakota confirmed.

Lane **glanced at him.** "How long was this ride?"

Dakota squinted ahead. "Not that long. **We should be near the ending any second now.**"

They kept walking, their **footsteps muffled** against the damp concrete. The air was **stale**, the kind of heavy stillness that made everything feel just a little **too quiet.**

Then—

They **turned a corner.**

And the **flashlight beam landed on something massive.**

Dakota and Lane **screamed.**

Lane's grip on the **camera fumbled, almost dropping it.**

Dakota **stumbled back, heart hammering.**

Looming in front of them—

A **face.**

A **huge, grotesque face,** staring straight at them.

Dakota's breathing was **shaky** as he forced himself to **lift the flashlight again.** Lane did the same with the **camera**, though his **hands were visibly trembling.**

The **massive, 12-foot animatronic had collapsed**, its once-commanding figure **fallen onto its knees.**

Its **outstretched arms** were still **holding it up,** as if frozen mid-motion.

But it was the **face** that sent a chill down their spines.

Her **once-glowing red eyes** were now **dull and caked with grime,** the thick dust making them look **fogged over.**

Her **jet-black hair, once flowing and smooth,** was now **a tangled, matted mess.** Strands clung to the **rotting fabric of her robes.**

Her **scowling mouth was gaped wide,** as if frozen in a **silent, eternal scream.**

The sheer **size of her presence**, even in her ruined state, was **unnerving.**

Dakota and Lane **exchanged a look.**

Neither of them spoke for a moment.

Then Lane **broke the silence.**

"I'm not scared of much," he muttered, **his voice lower than usual.** "But I've **always** had a fear of **giant animatronics.**"

Dakota let out a breath. "Dude. **Same.**"

Lane aimed the **camera back at her face,** zooming in on the **damaged features.** "It's not even that they look real… it's just… **something about them.**"

"Yeah," Dakota agreed. "They're **too big.** Too **lifeless**—but at the same time, it's like they're… **waiting.**"

Lane didn't respond.

Dakota swallowed, forcing a **small, nervous chuckle.**

"I always wondered how the **engineers or maintenance people** dealt with it," he said, his voice more thoughtful now. "Like, yeah, they had **lights on** when they worked, but imagine having to be **right next to this thing** while it was **still moving.**"

Lane finally spoke.

"…**Yeah, F** that."

Dakota laughed, but it was **short-lived.**

They both turned back to the **fallen goddess.**

Her **clouded eyes stared blankly ahead, unmoving.**

A presence that once **loomed over riders, terrifying them for fun… now sat here, abandoned, decayed—yet somehow, still just as disturbing.**

They stood in **tense silence.**

Neither of them had noticed the way **the shadows behind the animatronic** seemed to **stretch just a little further** than they should have.

Lane **clicked off the camera**, the small beep of the power-down sequence breaking the silence.

"No point in **wasting battery** on things we've already covered," he muttered.

Dakota nodded in agreement, then let out a **sigh, glancing around the abandoned ride.**

"We've explored **three areas** so far," he said, rubbing the back of his neck. "And we haven't uncovered **anything.**"

Lane **raised an eyebrow.** "What, you expecting to find a **corpse in the break room?**"

Dakota scoffed but didn't smile. "I don't know, man. **Something.** There's been **nothing strange, no signs of missing people,** not even any **off-limits areas** from the supposed gas leaks."

He paused, kicking at a **loose piece of debris on the platform.**

"And honestly?" he continued. "We were kind of **dumb** for thinking the **gas leaks** would still be a problem. The **city wouldn't allow the utilities** to stay on if it posed a risk to the environment or public safety."

Lane **shrugged.** "I mean, yeah. That makes sense."

"But still," Dakota added, **his voice more skeptical now,** "you'd think if there **was** a gas leak, they'd have at least **blocked that area off.** You know? To **keep security safe,** to keep the cops who were investigating **safe.**"

Lane **considered that for a second.**

Then he shrugged again. "**I don't know.**"

He **glanced around the temple, the eerie quiet settling in again.**

"But honestly? **I don't care if we get answers.** I just wanted to explore the park."

Dakota turned his **head toward Lane,** studying him for a second.

Then he let out a small breath, nodding. "I guess you're right. I guess it'd be **better** if we didn't find anything."

He exhaled, shaking his head.

"Because that means **nothing actually happened… right?**"

Lane didn't respond right away.

He just **shrugged again.**

Dakota stared at him for a second before finally **pulling himself onto the platform.**

Once he was up, he **reached a hand down, grabbing Lane's wrist,** and helped him climb up after.

They exited the **queue area,** the temple's looming entrance **fading into the shadows behind them.**

Once they stepped out into the **open air again,** Lane **flipped the camera back on.**

Dakota **glanced at the lens,** rubbing his palms together before addressing their audience.

"Alright, so," he said, "**there's no way we can check out the next ride.** At least… **not without a boat.**"

He gestured behind him toward the **murky, man-made river.**

"You **can't just drain a river,**" he added, smirking slightly.

Lane **chuckled,** panning the camera toward the **dark water.**

"Yeah," he said, "and we don't **know what's in there.** Wouldn't wanna **lose a finger to some alligators.**"

Dakota let out a laugh but **kept his eyes on the water.**

Something about it was unsettling.

The way the surface barely rippled.

The way it stretched into the darkness of the overgrown jungle, disappearing behind the abandoned structures.

For a second, he swore he saw **movement.**

Just a faint **disturbance beneath the water.**

But when he blinked, it was gone.

Shaking it off, he turned back to Lane.

"Alright," he said, **forcing a grin.** "Guess that means we move on."

Lane nodded, turning the camera toward the **next section of the park.**

Without another word, they **started walking.**

And behind them, **the water remained still.**

Dakota **unfolded the map,** his eyes scanning the faded layout of the park.

"Alright," he muttered, running a **finger along the path.** "Looks like we'll have to **head back to the plaza** to get to the next area—**Fantasy Island.**"

Lane **angled the camera** toward the map as Dakota continued.

"**Fantasy Island is where all the magic happens.**"

He tapped a **specific section of the map.**

"It had a **huge castle** as the centerpiece, the **world's tallest rollercoaster**, and a couple of smaller things like a **carousel** and a **slow-spinning cup ride.**"

Lane **tilted his head.** "Wasn't that rollercoaster, like… **record-breaking** at some point?"

"Yeah," Dakota nodded. "I think it was the **tallest and fastest coaster in the country** when it first opened. They hyped it up as the **ultimate thrill ride.**"

Lane smirked. "And now it's just **rotting away.**"

Dakota chuckled. "Yep."

Lane **zoomed the camera in on the map.**

"How many areas are left?"

Dakota scanned the layout again. "After **Fantasy Island**, there's two more:

Isle of Animals—which, obviously, was where all the **animals were housed.** I'm guessing that's where all the **animal neglect allegations** came from.

Future Island—this one was supposed to be their **vision of the future**. A bunch of rides about **history and predictions of what the world would look like**."

Lane raised an eyebrow. "That sounds… **kind of boring**."

Dakota shrugged. "I mean, yeah, but people ate that stuff up back then. Future tech, **flying cars, utopian cities**— all that."

Lane nodded, adjusting the **camera angle.**

"Alright," Dakota said, folding up the map. "Let's keep moving."

The two of them **headed back toward the plaza,** the **faint wind rustling through the overgrown pathways** as the silent rides of Hollow Park **waited for them ahead.**

As they stepped onto the **path leading to Fantasy Island,** everything changed.

The trees weren't just overgrown—**they were exaggerated**, like something out of a **storybook**. Twisted roots curled along the walkway, vines draped like curtains, and thick patches of **moss-covered stone walls** peeked through the foliage. It was as if they had **walked straight into a medieval fantasy**—a world of **knights, dragons, and lost princesses.**

And at the center of it all, **the castle.**

It stood **massive and imposing,** its **stone façade weathered** but still breathtaking. Once, it must have been **bright and whimsical,** a beacon of magic for families visiting Hollow Park. Now, it was just **a dark silhouette against the overcast sky,** its **wooden doors shut tight.**

As Dakota and Lane approached, **Lane turned the camera to face himself.**

"Alright," he said. **"What do you guys think we'll find inside?"**

Dakota smirked, keeping his eyes on the castle. **"Nothing. It's just a giant prop."**

Lane tilted the camera toward him. "You don't think there's anything inside?"

"Nah," Dakota shrugged. **"Probably just a break area. A place for the actors to cool off after sweating in their costumes for hours."** He gestured toward the upper towers. **"At most? Empty storage."**

Lane chuckled. **"That's what Jason *wants* you to think. This is where we'll find his secret government lab."**

They both laughed as they **reached the towering wooden doors.**

Dakota pulled his **flashlight from his bag, clicked it on,** and grabbed the handle. The metal creaked as he **pulled the heavy door open.**

The two stepped inside.

Dakota **froze in place, staring at the camera.**

Then, in a dramatic tone, he announced:

"You won't believe this. Lane is… absolutely wrong. But so am I."

Lane panned the camera around. Instead of **an empty shell**, there were **rooms.** Doors lined the stone walls, and a **set of stairs** spiraled up to the second floor.

Lane whistled. **"Well, damn. Guess they put more effort into this place than we thought."**

They started exploring, going from **room to room.**

The **first door creaked open**, revealing **shelves packed with spare parts, costumes, and park merchandise.** Boxes labeled "Parade Supplies" and "Festival Props" sat stacked in corners.

Dakota **swept the flashlight across the space.** "Storage. Just spare junk."

They moved to the **next door**—a **breakroom kitchen.** A dusty microwave sat on the counter, cabinets half-open, old coffee cups left behind.

Lane opened the **fridge.** The second the door cracked, Dakota **stumbled back, gagging.**

"Oh my God," he groaned, clamping a hand over his nose. **"I forgot how bad a broken fridge smells."**

Lane **laughed, panning the camera over the room.** "Damn, I wish I could bottle this smell and send it to our subscribers."

Dakota shot him a glare. **"You're a sick bastard."**

They reached the **last door.**

Lane tried the handle. **It turned—but the door wouldn't budge.**

"It's not locked," he said, **stepping back.**

Dakota tried it too. **"Must be jammed."**

Lane handed Dakota the camera. **"Watch out."**

Dakota **tilted the camera up**, catching Lane as he **rammed his shoulder against the door.** The wood **groaned**, but didn't move.

Another hit. Still stuck.

With a frustrated growl, Lane **threw his weight into it one last time.**

CRACK.

The door **popped open.**

Dakota handed the camera back as they stepped inside.

The air in here was **different**—**stale**, thick with the **faint hum of electronics.**

Dakota lifted the flashlight, revealing **rows of servers and recording equipment.**

Lane **zoomed in.** "This looks like some kind of **security hub.**"

Dakota's stomach **twisted.** "You think someone's been watching us?"

Lane moved deeper into the room, **panning the camera.** "If they were, the cops would've already found us, right?"

Dakota swallowed. **"Yeah… you'd think so."**

Lane **focused on a set of wires running up the wall.** "These are still connected. This isn't an **off-campus system**—everything was **monitored from inside the park.**"

Dakota **followed the wires with his flashlight.** "You think security stayed in here? **Watched the whole park from this spot?**"

Lane frowned. **"Have you seen a security outpost anywhere?"**

Dakota took a slow step **backward.** Something about this room made his skin **crawl.**

"Let's check upstairs."

The spiraling staircase loomed ahead, its steps coated in a thin layer of dust. Dakota hesitated for just a second before placing his foot down, the old metal groaning under his weight. The air was heavy, thick with the scent of mildew and aged electronics. Lane followed close behind, his breathing steady but quiet, the camera held firmly in his hands.

Dakota glanced over his shoulder, voice low. **"If the cameras are still working, that means there's some kind of power here, right?"** His words lingered in the air, as if spoken too loudly they might wake something up.

They reached the second floor.

The moment they stepped forward, both of them stopped in their tracks. Lane kept the camera rolling, capturing every inch of the room in front of them.

It was **not** what they expected.

Rows of **computers lined the walls**, their blank screens reflecting the beam of Dakota's flashlight. **Wires slithered across the floor and walls**, tangled but intentional, leading up into the ceiling where they disappeared into the shadows. **Massive TV screens hung above them, dark and empty**, their thick frames collecting dust like abandoned relics.

"It may not be a secret lab," Lane muttered, keeping the camera steady. **"But what kind of security setup is this?"**

Dakota took a slow step forward, scanning the room with sharp, uneasy eyes. **"Langston wasn't lying. There's no way anyone would get away with anything in this park."**

But if that were true... **how did people disappear?**

Lane panned the camera over every monitor, every keyboard, recording every inch. Dakota followed the curve of the room, shining the flashlight into the corners, through doorways, trying to find something—**anything**—that would explain why this place still had power.

"Make sure you're recording all of this," Dakota murmured, eyes scanning for a control panel, a switch, **anything to turn the damn lights on.**

Lane gave a silent nod and continued filming, stepping carefully over the tangled cables, tracing the thick power cords back to where they fed into the machines. Some of the computers still had tiny red standby lights blinking faintly—a reminder that something **beneath the dust still lived.**

Dakota turned into a small side room, his flashlight cutting through the darkness. **Metal shelves lined the walls**, some empty, some stacked with old security manuals and discarded equipment. But what caught his attention was the **tall, steel breaker box**, bolted into the wall like a vault.

With a low creak, he **pulled open the metal door**. His flashlight flickered over **rows of switches and levers**, all labeled in peeling white text.

He scanned them quickly, **tracing a finger down the list** until he found what he needed.

SECURITY HUB – MAIN POWER

He hesitated.

Then—**click.**

The switch snapped into place.

A deep hum rumbled through the room, **low and mechanical**, like something ancient waking up. Then, **a blinding white light flooded the second floor**, momentarily stunning Dakota as his eyes adjusted.

For the first time, they saw **everything.**

The security hub looked even more **complex, more advanced** than it had in the dark. The wires weren't just carelessly strewn about—**they were methodically placed, expertly connected**. The computers, now illuminated, looked **too clean for a park that had been abandoned for three years.**

Dakota stepped back into the main room, his heart pounding slightly harder now. **"Keep recording,"** he told Lane.

Lane barely acknowledged him, already focused on the glowing monitors.

Dakota exhaled, moving to one of the terminals. He reached out, his fingers hovering over the keyboard.

"Let's see what Langston was really watching."

The hum of electricity settled into the air, a quiet, almost comforting sound against the eerie silence that had filled the castle moments before. The dim glow of monitors flickered to life, casting **blue-white light against the dust-coated walls.** The massive security hub stretched before Dakota and Lane, a tangled mess of **cables, blinking lights, and darkened monitors now struggling to reboot.**

Dakota leaned over the nearest **dusty keyboard**, brushing it off with his sleeve. Lane, still recording, panned the camera over the room.

"This is insane," Lane muttered, zooming in on one of the **larger screens mounted on the wall.** "I knew security had to be tight, but this? It's overkill."

The **monitors began cycling through feeds**, static distorting the footage before snapping into a grid of camera angles. Dakota furrowed his brow as he scrolled through the system, clicking through old security logs. The **dates flickered on the screen,** the latest entry from **two nights ago—the night they shut the park down.**

Dakota exhaled sharply. "Alright, let's see what's in here."

He clicked on the file.

A **grainy black-and-white video** filled the screen.

The timestamp read **July 11th, 3:07 A.M.**

The feed showed a **wide shot of the main plaza**—rows of food stands, souvenir shops, and empty walkways stretching toward the **carousel at the center.** The lights flickered—**just slightly.** Barely noticeable, but enough to feel **off.**

"Okay," Dakota muttered, leaning in. "Why would anyone be here this late?"

Lane zoomed the camera in on the screen. "Security, maybe?"

The footage continued.

A figure entered the frame.

A **security guard,** moving briskly across the plaza. He kept **glancing over his shoulder,** his posture stiff and hurried. His **radio was in his hand,** his lips moving, but there was no sound—only static.

Then, he **stopped.**

He turned, staring back in the direction he had come from.

For a long moment, he just **stood there.**

Dakota's fingers hovered over the keyboard. "What is he—"

The screen **glitched.**

Just for a second—barely a flicker.

But when it returned, the **security guard was gone.**

A chill ran through Dakota's spine. He clicked the **rewind button**, playing the sequence again.

The guard walked. He stopped. He turned.

Then—**static.**

Gone.

Dakota clenched his jaw. "What the hell?"

Lane adjusted the camera, keeping the footage centered in frame. "Did he—run? Fall?"

"No way," Dakota shook his head. "There's **nowhere** for him to go that fast."

He paused the video, staring at the **empty plaza.** The streetlights hummed softly in the background of the footage. The carousel stood completely still.

Lane looked at Dakota. "Play it forward."

Dakota hit **fast-forward.** The footage blurred as the **hours ticked by.** The sun eventually **rose, casting light over the empty park.** No one entered the frame. No one **found** the missing guard.

It was like he had never been there at all.

Dakota exhaled, sitting back in the chair. "So… the missing people thing wasn't just a rumor."

Lane looked at the monitor, then back at the **dozens of files still left unchecked.**

"If that's what happened to one guy," he said slowly, "what about the rest?"

Dakota hovered his cursor over the next **batch of security footage.**

There were **more.**

More **late-night files.** More **cameras.** More **disappearances.**

A **knot of dread** settled in his stomach.

This was **bigger than they thought.**

Lane glanced at Dakota, the camera still focused on the screen, the grainy image of the empty plaza frozen in place. The silence in the security room felt heavier now, as if the walls themselves knew something they didn't.

Finally, Lane spoke. "There should be reports, right?" His voice was quieter than before, as if saying it too loudly would make the truth worse. "Security guards usually write reports about anything that happens in the park. Maybe there's something about the disappearances."

Dakota nodded, his fingers already gliding across the keyboard. He navigated through the system, clicking through old files and searching for anything labeled **incident report** or **security logs.** The system wasn't exactly user-friendly—menus were a mess, folders scattered without any clear organization.

Then, after a few clicks, a window popped up.

A **password prompt.**

Dakota sighed, rubbing his forehead.

Lane leaned in, tilting his head. "What do you think it is?"

Dakota let out a dry chuckle. "I don't know, **'ILoveMyJob123?'**"

Lane smirked, shaking his head. "Yeah, sure. **Try that.**"

Dakota typed it in. **Incorrect Password.**

They both stared at the screen for a moment before Lane shrugged. "I don't know these people. No clue what they'd use."

Dakota exhaled, glancing around the room. "Maybe it's written down somewhere."

They got up, their flashlights **cutting through the dim, dust-filled air.** The security hub was a **maze of desks, metal cabinets, and old equipment.** Dakota pulled open the nearest drawer—**empty, aside from dust and a few old key tags.**

Lane moved to a **filing cabinet,** tugging at the handle. It **wouldn't budge.**

"Locked," he muttered, testing another one. **Also locked.**

Dakota checked a few desk drawers. **More of the same.** Some old **sticky notes, broken pens, an ancient-looking stapler—but no passwords.**

Most of the **cabinets were locked.**

Dakota sighed, standing up and dusting off his hands. "Well, I think we need the crowbar."

Lane groaned. "Yeah, figures."

Just then, a **sharp beep** echoed through the room.

Lane checked the camera screen—it was flashing **low battery.**

"Damn," he muttered. "This thing's about to die."

Dakota slung his backpack off his shoulder, **digging around** until his fingers found a fresh battery pack. He handed it over, watching as Lane swapped out the drained one, clicking the camera back on. The lens refocused, its small red light flickering back to life.

Lane gave Dakota a nod. "Alright." He adjusted his grip on the camera, stepping toward the door. "Let's go back to the van."

Dakota cast one last glance at the **password screen** still glowing on the monitor.

They were **close.**

Now, they just needed a way **in.**

Lane and Dakota rushed back to the plaza, adrenaline coursing through their veins as they sprinted toward the fence. Dakota glanced over at Lane, his voice urgent. "Wait by the fence. I'll grab the crowbar from the van, and we'll get back here as fast as we can."

Lane nodded, his eyes wide with a mix of fear and determination. Dakota darted through the loose piece of fence, his heart pounding. He tore down the service road, careful not to trip over the uneven asphalt that seemed to stretch on forever. The sun hung high, scorching everything beneath it, and the heat seemed to press down, suffocating him. Every breath felt like he was inhaling fire.

When he finally reached the van, the side door slid open with a groan, and the intense heat inside hit him like a wall. It felt like stepping into an oven. Dakota grabbed the crowbar, nearly dropping it in his haste, then slammed the door shut and ran back toward the fence.

But as he slipped under the loose edge, a chilling realization hit him. Lane was gone.

His stomach twisted as he scanned the area, but there was no sign of his friend. Panic crept up his throat, and his heartbeat quickened. He pulled the radio from his waist, his voice shaky. "Lane, Lane, where are you?" His words seemed to hang in the heavy air, stretching into an uncomfortable silence.

Then—he heard it.

His own voice, crackling through the radio just a few feet away.

His eyes locked on Lane's radio, lying abandoned in the dirt, its red light flashing. Dakota's blood ran cold. He snatched it up, his hands trembling, and shoved it back into the bag, his mind racing. Where the hell had Lane gone?

The fear gnawed at him, but he couldn't stop now. He couldn't afford to be weak. He had to find answers—had to understand what was happening here.

"What the fuck is wrong with this park?" Dakota muttered under his breath, his voice barely more than a whisper. He started walking toward Fantasy Island, each step feeling heavier, like the ground beneath him was sinking with every footfall.

When he reached the castle, he ran inside and up the stairs. Something froze him in place.

At the top of the stairs, through the dim light, he saw it. There, sitting at one of the computers, was Lane.

But it wasn't right.

Lane wasn't supposed to be here.

Dakota's breath caught in his throat. His mind raced with questions, with fear. What the hell was going on? Had it all been some twisted trick, or was this something worse? He couldn't understand it.

Chapter Six

Dakota hesitated at the top of the stairs, his breath shallow. Lane sat at one of the computers, illuminated by the weak glow of the screen. Something about the scene felt... off.

Then Lane glanced over. His face lit up.

"Dude, you made it!" He stood from the chair, his voice casual, as if nothing had happened.

Dakota remained frozen, his grip tightening around the crowbar. His mind raced. **This isn't right.** He never believed in supernatural bullshit, but after everything they'd seen in this park, his gut screamed at him that something was wrong.

Lane's brow furrowed. "You good, man?" He took a step closer.

Dakota instinctively stepped back. His pulse hammered in his ears. Lane noticed and hesitated, concern flickering across his face.

"I heard something," Lane explained. "I didn't know what it was. I tried calling you, but I dropped the radio. Figured I'd just come back here. I knew you'd show up sooner or later."

Dakota exhaled, his grip on the crowbar loosening slightly. "I thought you disappeared," he admitted. He felt ridiculous now—his nerves had gotten the best of him. "Guess I jumped to conclusions."

Lane smirked. "Yeah, you do that a lot."

Rolling his eyes, Dakota shook off the lingering unease. "Let's just get this over with."

Lane still held the camera as he followed Dakota deeper into the office, past the dusty desks and overturned chairs, toward the file room. The air was thick with stale paper and mildew. Rows of filing cabinets stood in the dim light, their metal bodies rusted and dented.

Dakota turned to the camera. "This is why you don't listen to stupid rumors. They'll mess with your head."

Lane let out a sarcastic chuckle. "What, worried about me?"

Dakota shot him a look. "No. Just didn't want to make the six-hour drive back alone."

Lane snorted but didn't push it further.

Dakota wedged the crowbar into the edge of a locked cabinet, his muscles tensing as he pried at the metal. With a firm yank, the drawer finally gave way, sliding open with a screech.

Lane tilted the camera downward, catching the mess of old files and scattered papers as Dakota started rifling through them. Dust floated in the air like ghosts of the past.

They had come here looking for answers.

But neither of them was ready for what they were about to find.

Dakota flipped through the first few pages, his brow furrowing. "Looks like basic financial records."

Lane leaned in, adjusting the camera to focus on the papers. "Exciting," he muttered sarcastically.

Dakota ignored him and read aloud:

Expense Report – Q1 2009
Summary of maintenance costs for rides and attractions. Notable increase in repair costs for the carousel and Jungle River Adventure. Engineers note repeated electrical failures despite replacing wiring.

He frowned, setting that one aside before pulling up another.

Purchase Order – March 2010
New animatronic parts ordered for Fantasy Island. Special request for additional silicone molds, 'hyper-realistic' eye mechanisms.

Lane raised an eyebrow. "Hyper-realistic? That's weirdly specific."

Dakota hummed in agreement, flipping through more pages. Then, he found something a little different.

Internal Memo – June 2010
"Staff reports an increase in ride malfunctions. Engineers cleared all systems last month, yet issues persist. Park management advises ride operators to perform manual shutdowns if necessary. If problem continues, consider bringing in third-party inspectors."

Lane tilted his head. "Did they ever bring in inspectors?"

Dakota flipped through more pages, skimming the text. "Yeah, but there's nothing about what they found."

Then, something caught his eye.

Incident Report – September 2010
"Multiple guests report hearing the Ferris wheel operating overnight despite power being cut. Security footage reviewed—wheel is stationary in footage, but staff present on-site swore they saw it moving. Engineering team confirms no power anomalies. No further action taken."

Dakota exhaled sharply. "Okay… that's weird."

Lane smirked. "Now we're getting somewhere."

Dakota pulled out another document, this one more hurriedly written.

Employee Complaint – March 2011
"Night shift janitor (name redacted) refused to return to work after claiming he saw someone inside the mascot storage. Security sweep found no intruders. Employee terminated for failing to show up for scheduled shifts."

Lane snorted. "They fired the guy instead of looking into it?"

Dakota shook his head and grabbed another.

Lost and Found Log – July 2011
"Several reports of lost items: sunglasses, hats, a child's stuffed rabbit. Parents later reported child refused to leave without it, saying 'the man in the ride has it.' Staff could not locate stuffed rabbit, despite extensive search."

Lane shifted in his seat. "That's… unsettling."

Dakota hesitated before pulling out the last document in the pile.

Security Log – October 2011
"2:37 AM: Motion sensor triggered near Fantasy Island.
2:40 AM: Security dispatched, no signs of entry.
3:12 AM: Sensor triggered again. Camera feed showed nothing.
3:30 AM: Security reports hearing faint music from abandoned ride speakers. Logs confirm all audio systems are offline. No further action taken."

Dakota and Lane exchanged a look.

Lane broke the silence first. "Okay. What the fuck?"

Dakota tapped the page, his expression unreadable. "This park was already shutting down by 2012. But people kept reporting weird shit. And no one did anything about it."

He glanced at the filing cabinet. "Let's see what's in the next drawer."

Dakota wedged the crowbar into the next drawer and pried it open. The metal groaned, resisting for a moment before giving way. Dust rose from the files as he pulled out another stack of papers. Lane adjusted the camera, zooming in.

"Alright," Dakota muttered, thumbing through the documents. "Let's see what else they ignored."

Internal Memo – March 2012
"Staff should refrain from discussing 'ghost stories' or unexplained incidents with guests. Management is aware of the rumors and assures all employees that Hollow Park is a safe and family-friendly environment. Any concerns should be reported directly to supervisors, not spread amongst staff."

Lane scoffed. "Translation: 'Shut up and don't scare the customers.'"

Dakota shook his head and kept going.

Security Log – May 2012
"1:15 AM – Motion sensors triggered near Isle of Animals.
1:22 AM – Security dispatched, no visual contact with intruder.
1:40 AM – Patrol reports strange noises near defunct animal enclosures. Described as 'low breathing' and 'scratching.'
1:45 AM – Patrol reports feeling watched. No movement detected.
2:10 AM – Patrol terminated search after hearing loud snapping sound from foliage. No sign of disturbance. No further action taken."

Dakota glanced at Lane. "Scratching?"

Lane exhaled through his nose. "And breathing. That's new."

Dakota flipped to another page, its corners slightly crumpled, as if someone had handled it nervously.

Employee Complaint – June 2012
"Maintenance worker (name redacted) refuses to return to Isle of Animals after closing. Claims he heard someone whispering near the aviary exhibit. Security sweep found no one. Worker insists he saw movement inside an empty enclosure. Management dismissed complaint."

Lane raised an eyebrow. "Empty enclosures don't move."

Dakota didn't answer. He was already pulling out the next sheet.

Security Log – July 2012
"3:00 AM – Unscheduled ride activation reported at Safari Tram station. Ride has been non-operational for three months.
3:07 AM – Security patrol arrived on scene. Tram was still. No power to station.
3:10 AM – Patrol reported hearing footsteps circling the tram, but no movement detected.
3:12 AM – Patrol retreated to main plaza after hearing what was described as 'a sharp inhale, like someone gasping right behind me.' No further action taken."

Dakota clenched his jaw. "No further action taken," he repeated, voice dripping with disbelief. "Are you kidding me?"

Lane sat back, keeping the camera steady. "Man, how many times did people hear shit and just leave?"

Dakota kept going, pulling another memo from the pile.

Internal Memo – August 2012
"Reminder: Employees should avoid discussing personal experiences regarding strange noises or sightings at the park. If any team members feel uncomfortable working certain shifts, they may submit a request to management. However, repeated refusal to work designated areas will result in disciplinary action."

Dakota exhaled sharply. "They were forcing people to work places they didn't feel safe."

Lane whistled low. "So what do you think happened? They knew something was off, but instead of shutting down, they just told everyone to deal with it?"

Dakota didn't answer right away. He set the memo aside and grabbed the next report. This one was short—hastily written, as if someone had scribbled it down in a hurry.

Security Log – September 2012
"4:45 AM – Last sweep of the park before closing. Two security guards confirm all clear.
4:50 AM – Guard at front gate hears something moving near Isle of Animals. Describes it as 'something big, walking slow.'
4:52 AM – Guard refuses to investigate alone. Second guard called to assist.
4:55 AM – Both guards report heavy breathing sound.
4:57 AM – Guards retreat to main plaza after 'loud thud' and sound of something scraping against metal.
5:00 AM – Guards leave for the night. No further action taken."

Dakota stared at the page. The hairs on his arms stood up.

Lane swallowed. "Dude… what the hell was in there?"

Dakota flipped through the remaining pages, but none of them offered an answer—only more reports of strange noises, shadows moving where they shouldn't be, and security refusing to investigate certain areas alone.

Finally, he sat back, shaking his head.

"They knew," Dakota muttered. "They fucking knew something was here."

Lane nodded slowly. "And they never did anything about it."

For a moment, neither of them spoke. The only sound was the quiet hum of the camera recording.

Then Dakota set the papers aside and reached for the last drawer.

"Let's see what else they were hiding."

Dakota set the previous stack of papers aside and turned to the last drawer. The handle was rusted, and when he pulled, it barely budged. He gritted his teeth, wedged the crowbar into the gap, and yanked. The metal shrieked, and with a final snap, the drawer slid open.

Inside, the papers were in worse shape—some were stained, edges crumpled, ink smudged like they'd been handled with sweaty hands. Dakota grabbed the first file.

Financial Report – October 2012
*"Purchase orders approved for security upgrades:

- 12 additional high-powered flashlights
- 10 new night-vision cameras for main areas of concern
- 8 reinforced security doors for maintenance tunnels
- 6 high-voltage stun guns
- 20 sets of industrial-grade ear protection
- Miscellaneous (see attached receipts)"*

Lane frowned. "Why the hell would a theme park need stun guns?"

Dakota flipped to the attached receipts, skimming through lists of purchased items. Most were normal—cameras, radios, batteries—but then his eyes landed on the oddities.

- **Reinforced steel plating** (custom order)
- **Soundproofed helmets** (military surplus)
- **Heavy-duty floodlights** (custom specs, highest lumens available)

- **Tranquilizer darts** (no supplier listed)

Dakota tapped the paper. "These aren't for stopping rowdy guests."

Lane shifted uncomfortably, angling the camera. "They were trying to stop something else."

Dakota set the reports aside and pulled the next file—a security log, the handwriting messy, as if written in a rush.

Security Log – November 2012
"2:35 AM – Security patrol near Isle of Animals reports movement inside an abandoned enclosure. Describes it as 'tall, wrong proportions, hunched over.'
2:37 AM – Patrol requests backup. Second team arrives. No sign of intruder.
2:41 AM – Security reports hearing deep breathing from the shadows. Smell of decay noted.
2:45 AM – Flashlights catch movement—something 'crawling' but too fast to track.
2:48 AM – Both teams retreat to security office. No pursuit. No further action taken."

Lane exhaled sharply. "They saw it."

Dakota flipped through more pages, heart pounding. Each log got worse.

Security Log – December 2012
"4:12 AM – Patrol reports figure standing near old safari entrance. Describes it as 'tall, thin, bones visible under skin.'
4:15 AM – Figure vanishes when light is shined directly at it.
4:18 AM – Security guard claims to hear voice 'mimicking' his own. Other guards hear nothing.
4:20 AM – Patrol retreats after loud snapping noise from trees. No further action taken."

Security Log – January 2013
"3:00 AM – Unidentified figure spotted near maintenance tunnels.
3:03 AM – Security reports 'wrong' movement—figure doesn't walk, but shifts like it's gliding.
3:05 AM – Guard reports sudden ear pain, describes pressure change like 'being underwater.'
3:06 AM – All radios fail simultaneously. Static reported.
3:10 AM – Guards return to office. One reports dizziness, says he 'forgot how he got there.' No further action taken."

Dakota felt his stomach twist. These weren't just noises anymore. They saw it. They *felt* it.

Then he found the memo. This one was different. The paper was heavier, more official-looking.

Internal Memo – Jason Langston – February 2013
*"To All Senior Staff,

There will be no further discussions of 'sightings' or 'unexplained events' happening within Hollow Park. Security will continue their patrols, and additional measures have been put in place.

I understand the concerns. I *hear* them. But we must remember that fear is a powerful thing—it makes men see what isn't there. We cannot allow this place to become a victim of paranoia and wild stories.

The park has always been more than just an amusement park. I won't go into detail, but *some things* were here long before we were. Some things shouldn't be disturbed.

We move forward. We do not look back.

This will be my final statement on the matter.

– J.L."*

Lane let out a breath. "Dude."

Dakota swallowed. His fingers felt cold against the paper.

"'Some things were here long before we were,'" he repeated.

Lane nodded. "He knew."

Dakota dug deeper, pulling the last sheet from the drawer. Another memo. This one was handwritten, the ink smudged, as if Langston had hesitated while writing.

Internal Memo – March 2013
*"To whoever finds this—

I tried.

I tried to contain it, to make this place something more, but I was wrong. We should have never built here. I thought we could control it. We couldn't.

If you're reading this, it means you've seen the reports. You know now. I don't have answers. I don't know where it came from, or if it was ever really gone.

I only know one thing.

Do not listen to it.

I'm sorry."*

Dakota's hands trembled slightly as he set the paper down.

Lane sat in stunned silence before muttering, "Jesus Christ."

Dakota didn't respond. His mind raced, piecing it together. The strange purchases. The sighting reports. The warnings. Langston *knew*. He knew something had always been here, and he chose to ignore it.

A heavy silence hung between them.

Then, in the distance, something scraped against metal.

Lane's head snapped toward the doorway. Dakota reached for the flashlight, his pulse hammering in his ears.

Outside, the park was waiting. And somewhere within it, *so was the thing that had never left.*

Lane and Dakota sat in the dimly lit office, the weight of the documents spread before them pressing down like an unseen force. The stale air, thick with dust and time, made every breath feel heavier. Lane absently ran a hand through his hair, his voice forced into a laugh.

"It has to be a misunderstanding, right? Ghosts aren't real. Monsters aren't real."

Dakota exhaled through his nose, trying to ignore the twisting feeling in his stomach. His fingers fidgeted with the edge of a tattered memo. "It's gotta be some kind of animal. That's the only explanation." He tried to sound sure of himself, but the words felt weak in his mouth. "Everyone just got too paranoid. All the ghost stories—people let them get to their heads. You're in this massive park, alone, surrounded by noises and silence at the same time. It can mess with you."

Lane leaned back in his chair, nodding. "Right. The animals, the animatronics—easy to get freaked out."

But just as Dakota finished his sentence, a scream tore through the air.

It was loud, shrill, and unnatural—like metal scraping against metal, yet raw and *alive*. The sound reverberated through the castle walls, rattling the old windows in their frames. It was long, stretching impossibly far, and then it just... stopped. The silence afterward was almost worse.

Lane and Dakota jolted, eyes wide, chests rising and falling in unsteady breaths. They locked eyes, silently asking the same question.

What the hell was that?

Lane swallowed hard, his hand gripping the camera tighter. "This is crazy," he muttered. "This is *all* crazy. Dakota, we've been to so many places, and nothing's ever happened. Why would this park be any different?"

Dakota forced himself to nod, trying to suppress the instinct to run. "You're right. This is crazy. These people just let fear get the best of them."

They glanced down at the reports again, scanning the words but barely processing them. Dakota turned toward the camera, forcing a casual tone despite the tension coiling in his chest.

"Alright, I guess that means we need to get over to the Isle of Animals, right?"

He tried to smirk, tried to act like it was just another investigation, but the way Lane was gripping the camera told him neither of them really believed it.

They stood, Lane adjusting the strap of his bag while Dakota grabbed the crowbar again, just in case. Without another word, they descended the castle stairs, their footsteps echoing in the empty halls.

Then, they stepped outside.

Everything changed.

The second their feet touched the pavement, the air felt different—lighter, *warmer*. The scent of popcorn and sugary treats filled their noses. The sky, once dim and overcast, was now a bright, cloudless blue. Music played all around them, cheerful and inviting. The laughter of children and the chatter of excited park guests blended into a lively symphony.

Dakota blinked. His heartbeat slowed, his body relaxing.

Lane nudged him with his elbow. "Man, this place is packed," he said with an easy grin.

Dakota looked around, feeling a strange warmth settle over him. The idea that the park had ever been abandoned seemed ridiculous now. Of course, it was open—*look at it*. The rides were running, the food stands were bustling, the plaza was full of people.

"Guess we should get moving," Lane said, lifting the camera. "Let's see what the Isle of Animals is all about."

Dakota nodded, and together, they walked forward, completely unaware that just moments ago, they had been standing in a dead, empty park.

Chapter Seven

The sun was bright overhead, filtering through the lush canopy of trees as Dakota and Lane strolled through the **Isle of Animals**. The trail was lined with wooden fences and signs displaying information about the animatronic creatures within each exhibit. The atmosphere was lively—guests laughed, children pointed in awe, and the distant rumble of a jungle-themed ride echoed through the air.

"This is insane," Dakota said, his eyes scanning the enclosures. "Everything looks so *real*."

Lane, grinning, aimed the camera at each animal as they passed. A massive aviary housed colorful birds that flapped their wings and darted between branches. Their calls mixed with the hum of the park's ambiance, filling the air with a lively energy. The detail in their movements, the way they preened and interacted, was astounding.

As they walked deeper into the exhibit, they stopped in front of a **life-sized gorilla animatronic**. It stood frozen in a natural pose, towering over them with a striking level of realism. Its glossy black fur rippled with simulated muscles beneath, and its face bore a stern, intelligent expression.

"Look at this thing," Lane muttered, adjusting the focus on his camera. "You'd swear it was breathing."

Beside it, an **elephant animatronic** slowly moved its trunk, letting out a deep, mechanical rumble that vibrated through the ground. Its ears flapped lazily, mimicking the slow, deliberate movements of a real elephant. Dakota reached out, running his fingers along the wooden railing that separated them from the creatures.

"This is insane," Dakota repeated. "No wonder people love this place."

Lane lifted the camera again, aiming it at the gorilla, and that's when he *saw* it.

The image on the screen wasn't the pristine animatronic standing before him.

The gorilla on the screen was **broken**. Its synthetic skin was **torn in jagged strips**, revealing rusted metal and deteriorating servos underneath. Patches of its fur were **matted, missing in chunks**, exposing dark, rotten padding beneath. Its eyes—once lifelike and intelligent—were now **glassy and sunken**, almost as if they had deflated into the skull. The animatronic stood in the same pose, but it was no longer a marvel. It was *ruined*.

Lane's stomach twisted. He lowered the camera, looking up with wide eyes.

The gorilla was *fine*. **Perfect**.

Its glossy fur caught the sunlight, its massive frame stood tall and unmoving—just as it had before.

Lane's breath caught in his throat. He *knew* what he had seen.

He nudged Dakota. "Dude, look at this."

Dakota turned, glancing at the screen. The gorilla looked **perfectly normal** through the camera. Pristine, just as it was in real life.

Lane blinked, shaking his head. "It—" He hesitated. He had *just* seen it. But now... it was gone?

Dakota gave him a questioning look, and Lane forced a chuckle. "Never mind," he muttered, lowering the camera. "Thought I saw something weird."

Shrugging it off, they continued down the trails, the thick jungle foliage closing in around them. **Exotic birds** perched in the branches overhead, their feathers catching the light in brilliant shades of blue, green, and red. The sound of rustling leaves whispered all around them, blending into the immersive ambiance of the park.

Lane stole one last glance at the gorilla as they walked away.

It hadn't moved.

But for some reason, he couldn't shake the feeling that it was *watching them go*.

Dakota smiled at the camera, his voice filled with enthusiasm. "Alright, guys, check this out! We're walking through **Isle of Animals**, and man, it's even better than we expected. The animatronics here are insane. It's like walking through a real jungle—birds everywhere, towering trees, and just *look* at these enclosures."

He turned, gesturing toward a massive artificial rock formation where a **tiger animatronic** lay stretched out under the shade. Its chest rose and fell in steady, rhythmic movements, as if it were truly breathing. Water trickled down a carefully designed waterfall beside it, feeding into a small, clear pond where robotic fish swam beneath the surface.

Lane aimed the camera at Dakota, then panned across the sights. "This is wild," he said, unable to hide his grin. "I don't even know how they pulled off this level of detail. Like, *look at that*."

He zoomed in on an **animatronic chimpanzee** perched in the branches above, its head tilting side to side, eyes blinking with eerie realism. A group of children giggled as they watched it, pointing excitedly as the chimp reached out, mimicking a motion like it was grabbing fruit.

Dakota turned back to the camera, eyes alight with excitement. "I swear, guys, you *have* to visit this place at least once in your life. Hollow Park is *amazing*."

Lane flipped the camera around, capturing himself in the frame. His smile was wide, genuine—there wasn't a single trace of doubt in his voice.

"I can't wait to share this footage with you all," he said. "Seriously, this park is something else. I know people have talked about all those weird rumors, but trust me—this place is **incredible**. If you've never been here, you're *missing out*. It's got everything. Rides, animals, insane animatronics—just pure magic."

He looked at Dakota, nodding toward the next trail. "Let's keep going, yeah?"

Dakota gave him a thumbs-up. "Absolutely. Let's see what else we can find!"

They continued walking, soaking in the lively atmosphere. Everything was *perfect*. The laughter of guests surrounded them, the scent of warm food drifted through the air, and the sunlight filtering through the trees gave the jungle paths a golden glow.

It was **perfect**.

It was **the best day ever**.

And neither of them thought to question why.

They didn't remember how they got there.

They didn't remember *why* they had come to Hollow Park.

But it didn't matter.

They were here.

And they were having the time of their lives.

Lane and Dakota finally reached the entrance to the **Rain Forest Cruise**. The ride was a slow-moving boat tour that once took guests through a simulated rainforest, complete with misty waterfalls, exotic animatronic animals, and a lively guide narrating fun facts about real jungle wildlife. The boats would float down a man-made river, past submerged hippos, colorful birds, and robotic monkeys swinging between artificial trees.

Dakota ran a hand through his hair and grinned, looking at the faded sign above them. "Man, I remember seeing commercials for this place when I was a kid. They made this ride look *insane*."

Lane raised the camera, panning across the entrance. The artificial jungle setting was as immersive as he had imagined, with thick trees and vines stretching overhead, filtering the golden sunlight. The sounds of chattering guests and distant music still played around them, filling the park with life.

Every few feet, they stopped to admire the animatronic wildlife. Lane pointed the camera toward a family of robotic chimps hanging from a twisted tree, their heads turning, mouths moving as if mid-conversation. A mechanical elephant raised its trunk, spraying mist into the air.

"This is *so* cool," Dakota muttered, genuinely impressed.

Lane turned the camera toward him. "Dude, we *have* to get footage of the ride itself. Imagine getting an entire POV recording of the cruise."

Dakota nodded, taking a step forward—

Then stopped.

That twisting feeling in his stomach returned, stronger this time. His excitement dulled as an overwhelming sense of unease settled over him.

Something felt *off*.

Lane hesitated too, lowering the camera slightly. The park still looked the same—families walking around, employees running the rides, kids eating ice cream—but there was something unnatural lingering in the air.

Then, they saw **her**.

The **ride operator** stood just ahead of them on the dock. A young woman dressed in an old Hollow Park uniform, the colors slightly faded. But something was *wrong* with her.

She wasn't moving.

She was just... *standing there*.

Her posture was stiff, unnatural. Her eyes were locked forward, unblinking.

Then, slowly—too *slowly*—she raised one hand and waved.

The movement was almost mechanical, her wrist bending awkwardly as if it wasn't connected properly.

Lane and Dakota froze. Neither of them spoke. They just stared at the girl, an uneasy silence stretching between them.

Dakota exhaled shakily. "Dude..."

Lane swallowed, lifting the camera with careful hands. The viewfinder flickered as he focused on the operator.

And then—

His **heart sank**.

On the camera screen, the dock was **empty**.

There was **no one standing there**.

Lane's breath hitched. He lowered the camera, looking at the dock with his own eyes.

She was still there.

He lifted the camera again—

Gone.

His hands started to tremble. "Dakota," he whispered.

Dakota hesitated, his skin crawling. Slowly, he leaned over to peek at the screen.

Nothing.

He lowered his gaze, looking at the dock with his own eyes. The girl was still standing there, still waving, still too stiff, too unnatural.

They looked at each other, realization creeping into their expressions.

The illusion shattered.

The warm sunlight disappeared.

The distant laughter and cheerful music **vanished**.

They were **back**.

No more families. No more vibrant colors. No more functioning animatronics.

The **Rain Forest Cruise** entrance stood in front of them, rotting and abandoned. The dock was warped and covered in grime, the water dark and lifeless. The sign overhead, once full of color, was cracked and missing letters.

It was nighttime.

Lane took a shaky breath, his pulse hammering in his ears.

Dakota turned in place, rubbing his arms, his voice tight. "What the *hell* just happened?"

Lane shook his head. He felt sick. "I—I don't know."

Dakota looked around frantically, his breathing uneven. "No, seriously, Lane, what the *hell* just happened? We were just—" He gestured wildly at the ruined park around them. *"The sun was out! The park was open!"*

Lane struggled to swallow the lump in his throat. "The last thing I remember..." He exhaled sharply. "We were in the castle."

Dakota blinked at him. "Yeah." His voice was barely above a whisper. "We walked down the stairs. And now we're here."

They stared at each other, horror dawning on their faces.

It was like they had been *wiped clean.*

Like something had reached into their heads and erased their memories.

Lane's hands felt numb as he scrolled through the camera's footage. He hesitated, his thumb hovering over the **playback** button.

Then—

A **splash** echoed from the river.

Both of them stiffened.

The water, once still, now rippled. Slow, unnatural waves spread outward.

Something had just **moved** beneath the surface.

Dakota's breath hitched. He reached out, gripping Lane's wrist **tight**.

The dock creaked beneath them.

Then—

A **low, rattling groan** rose from the water.

The same sound from the **security reports**.

The same sound from the **logs**.

The same sound of **something that should not exist**.

Dakota's grip tightened.

"Lane... we need to go. **Now.**"

Lane took one last glance back, staring at the half-sunken boat decaying in the water. The warped metal, the moss-covered seats—it felt like it had been sitting there for decades. But they had just been inside it. Right?

He turned back, lifting the camera, following Dakota closely.

They moved quickly, but **not too fast.** Running felt like a mistake. It would make too much noise. It would draw attention.

Dakota reached into his bag, pulling out the **flashlight**, clicking it on. The beam cut through the thick, suffocating dark, illuminating the cracked pavement ahead.

"Lane," Dakota whispered, his voice low but urgent. "Whatever happens, do **not** stop recording. This is the only proof we have of... whatever this thing is. Whatever happened here."

Lane swallowed hard and gave a short nod, tightening his grip on the camera. The lens swept from side to side, capturing the eerie stillness of the abandoned park.

They finally made it back to the **plaza**—the wide-open space just outside the Rain Forest Cruise. The once-grand area now felt like a trap, the emptiness stretching in every direction.

They had to get out of here.

Now.

Just as they were about to move, Lane suddenly froze.

"Wait," he whispered.

Dakota stilled, listening.

Footsteps.

Somewhere **close**.

The slow, deliberate **thump** of heavy boots on pavement.

Lane and Dakota scanned the area, hearts pounding.

Then—

A voice.

"HEY! What are you two doing here? This is private prop—"

The voice **cut off.**

Choked.

Strangled.

The sound of **something heavy being dragged** across the pavement made them both turn.

Lane **lifted the camera** just in time to catch the security guard—a middle-aged man in a faded Hollow Park uniform—**yanked** into the darkness behind one of the buildings.

His **legs kicked.** His arms flailed, reaching for something—**anything.**

Then he was **gone.**

Ripped into the blackness as if he had never been there.

A sickening **crunch** followed. Then, silence.

Dakota took a shaky step back, gripping Lane's arm.

"Lane," Dakota whispered, his voice barely audible. "Did you—?"

"I saw it," Lane muttered, the camera shaking in his hands.

The plaza was **silent.**

But something was **watching.**

A long, low **groan** echoed from the shadows where the guard had vanished.

The camera **glitched.**

For a split second, the plaza flickered, **warping**.

The pristine, colorful world they had been seeing—the illusion—was **gone.**

And in its place—

The real **Hollow Park.**

Abandoned. Rotting. Dead.

The camera screen showed something else.

Something **lurking** in the dark.

A **twisted hand** dragged along the pavement. Fingers **too long.** Skin **too tight.** The nails cracked and jagged.

And beyond that—

Black, **sunken eyes.**

Watching.

Waiting.

A **mouth**, stretched too wide, just barely curled into a sick, broken grin.

The camera **flickered.**

The screen snapped back.

Everything looked normal again.

The plaza was empty.

The shadows were still.

Lane's breath was ragged.

Dakota turned to him, his face pale.

"Lane," he whispered. "We need to **run.**"

They **ran.**

The wind whipped past them as they bolted across the cracked pavement, sneakers slamming against the ground. The heavy, suffocating silence of the park was broken only by their frantic footsteps and the pounding of their hearts.

They **needed to get out.**

Now.

Lane's camera bounced wildly in his grip as he scanned the area, trying to find something—**anything**—that resembled an exit.

They reached the perimeter fence, a towering structure of rusted chain-link. They ran alongside it, searching—desperate.

But the gap they had entered through was gone.

Dakota skidded to a stop, breath hitching as he spun in circles, scanning every inch of the fence.

Nothing.

Just an endless stretch of metal, looming and **unbroken.**

Lane gulped, stepping back. Something about it felt **wrong.**

It was like the fence had **changed**—like it had always been this way.

"Where—where the hell is the opening?" Dakota gasped, his voice cracking.

Lane didn't answer.

He looked up—

Razor wire.

Thick, coiled loops of **barbed steel** wrapped around the top of the fence. That wasn't there before.

Dakota followed his gaze, his chest rising and falling in shallow, panicked breaths.

They weren't getting out that way.

Dakota turned in frantic circles, hands gripping his hair. His breathing was coming faster, too fast.

"Why did we come here?" he demanded, his voice rising. His hands trembled as he grabbed Lane's arm. "Why did we do this? We should've left—why the hell did we stay?"

Lane tried to steady him, gripping his shoulders. "Dakota—stop."

"We're **trapped,** Lane! We're—" Dakota sucked in a sharp breath, shaking his head. His body was **tensing**, his chest rising and falling too quickly.

He was panicking.

Lane sat against the fence, trying to **breathe.** He needed to **think.**

"We have to find a way out," he said, his voice firm but calm. "We can't just sit here—we're screwed if we do."

Dakota pressed his palms to his face, trying to regulate his breathing. He slid down beside Lane, squeezing his eyes shut.

Lane nudged him. "Hey. We've done this **hundreds** of times. We've gotten out of worse."

Dakota let out a weak, shaky laugh. "Not **this** bad."

Lane forced a small grin, though his stomach twisted with unease. "Yeah, well. First time for everything."

For a moment, they just sat there, catching their breath.

But then—

A low **scraping** sound echoed behind them.

Something **moving**.

Lane's camera flickered.

The screen **glitched.**

For a fraction of a second, it showed something standing at the edge of the plaza.

Watching.

A hunched, **impossibly tall** figure, its fingers dragging against the pavement.

The screen cut back.

The plaza was empty.

Dakota slowly turned to Lane, his face pale.

"We **can't** stay here," Lane whispered.

Dakota swallowed hard and nodded.

They pushed themselves up, their bodies tense, and took off **running** again.

Dakota gestures for Lane to keep up, his voice sharp with urgency. **"Get back to the castle! We can hide out in there, and maybe we can use the system to track where this thing is!"**

Lane doesn't argue. His legs are burning, his lungs feel like they're about to collapse, but he forces himself forward. The two of them weave through the abandoned plaza, past crumbling food stalls and overturned benches. Their footsteps echo against the pavement, and every sound feels too loud, like they're calling attention to themselves. The air is thick, humid, heavy with the smell of rot. It clings to their skin, slick with sweat.

The castle finally comes into view, its towering spires stabbing into the night sky like jagged teeth. The fake stone walls are covered in grime, streaked with years of rain and neglect. The grand entrance—meant to be an illusion of some fairytale kingdom—is nothing more than a hollow set piece. No real rooms, no attractions inside. Just an empty shell with a backroom where employees once took their breaks.

Dakota reaches the doors first, yanking them open with a strained grunt. They slip inside, slamming them shut behind them. The moment the doors close, an unsettling silence falls over the space. The overhead lights flicker faintly, casting a dim, buzzing glow over the scuffed floors and abandoned furniture. The room still has the stale scent of dust, plastic, and something else, something sour beneath it all.

Dakota doesn't waste time. He scans the room, his breaths coming fast. His mind is racing—how do they keep it out? His eyes land on a stack of old tables and chairs shoved into the corner.

"Help me," he says, already moving.

Lane doesn't argue. He keeps the camera rolling, propping it up on a ledge for a moment as they work. Together, they drag the furniture across the floor, the legs screeching against the tile as they shove everything they can against the doors. It's not much. The doors are flimsy, not built to withstand anything stronger than a curious trespasser. If that thing out there wanted in, nothing they did would stop it.

Lane steps back, wiping the sweat from his forehead with a shaky breath. He swallows the lump in his throat before muttering, **"Do you think that's going to stop it?"**

Dakota doesn't answer right away. He stares at the barricade, jaw clenched. Finally, he exhales through his nose. **"It has to."**

But they both know better.

After a moment, Dakota shakes it off. **"Come on, we need to get to the control room. If there's anything still working, maybe we can figure out where it is."**

Without waiting, he makes his way toward the stairwell. His body is screaming at him to stop, to rest, but he pushes through the exhaustion. There's no time to be tired.

Lane lingers for a second, gripping the camera tightly. Every instinct tells him to run, to get out while they still can—but there is no way out.

With a deep breath, he lifts the camera and follows Dakota up the stairs.

Dakota's breath came in ragged, uneven bursts as he stormed into the file room. His exhaustion was overwhelming, a lead weight pressing into his muscles, but he refused to stop. He **couldn't** stop. His hands shook, not from fear but from the sheer adrenaline that kept him standing.

With a sharp **grunt**, he grabbed the nearest filing cabinet, yanking the drawers open and rifling through them at lightning speed. Paperwork flew everywhere, scattering across the dusty floor like discarded leaves. The **clatter** of metal drawers hitting the wall echoed through the empty space as Dakota tore them free, tossing them aside when they yielded nothing useful.

His frustration mounted. He ran a hand through his damp hair, his breathing heavy, before **grabbing the crowbar** from where it rested against the wall. His grip was tight, his knuckles white as he **stormed back into the room.**

Lane stood at the doorway, camera still rolling, watching in tense silence as Dakota **jammed the crowbar into the seams of locked cabinets**. With a forceful **snap**, he wrenched one open. The metal groaned in protest before giving way, the drawer flying open with the momentum.

Still, nothing.

Another cabinet. **Pry. Snap. Crash.**

Lane swallowed hard, the tension in the air thick enough to choke on. He didn't say a word, didn't dare break the moment. He had never seen Dakota like this before—so **frantic, so desperate**.

Finally, Dakota **let the crowbar drop** with a loud **clang**, the sound ringing through the room like a gunshot. He crouched down, hands shaking as he **gathered the scattered files**. His fingers sifted through them with a feverish urgency, flipping pages, scanning documents. He barely noticed the fine layer of dust clinging to his skin, the old paper leaving smudges of grime on his fingertips.

Lane kept the camera trained on him, zooming in as Dakota stormed back to the main floor with **a thick stack of folders and papers in his arms.**

He **dropped them onto the desk** with a heavy **thud**, sending a cloud of dust into the air. The two of them stood there, breathing hard. Dakota didn't look up, just started flipping through the documents one by one, his fingers moving fast.

Lane finally spoke, his voice low, uncertain. **"What... what exactly are we looking for?"**

Dakota exhaled sharply, barely glancing up. **"Anything. A password. A log. Something that proves what the hell happened here."**

Lane nodded, swallowing back the unease curling in his gut. The way Dakota was acting… it was like something inside him had snapped.

He lifted the camera again, watching through the lens as Dakota **dug through the files,** his exhaustion momentarily forgotten.

Dakota's fingers moved quickly, his eyes scanning every page with a sharp intensity. The first few files were mundane—**financial reports**, budget cuts, attendance numbers. He muttered under his breath, flipping through them rapidly. Nothing unusual. Nothing that explained the **horrors** lurking in this park.

Then, something **odd**.

A **guest complaint** from 2010:

"My daughter said she saw a man standing inside one of the animal enclosures. But when I looked, there was no one there. I figured it was just a trick of the light, but she kept crying about it all night. She said he was 'too tall' and 'didn't have a face.' Please make sure your actors aren't sneaking into the exhibits to scare the kids. It's not funny."

Dakota frowned. His stomach twisted, but he shook it off and kept reading.

Another complaint, **2011**:

"Something is wrong with your animatronics. The gorilla in the Isle of Animals wasn't moving right. It was twitching—like, really jerky, almost like it was broken—but when I mentioned it to

an employee, they just laughed and said it wasn't even turned on. Maybe check your mechanics before someone gets hurt."

Dakota felt a chill creep up his spine, but he pushed forward.

A **security log** from late 2011:

"Patrol heard something moving near the Jungle Cruise at approximately 2:30 AM. No intruders were found, but one of the boats was halfway submerged in the water, even though it was dry at closing. Reviewed footage from the night before—nothing on tape."

The further he read, the **worse** the reports became.

Employee complaints about **horrible smells** near the back of the park.

Security logs describing **rides turning on by themselves** in the middle of the night.

A maintenance request from 2012:

*"Something's wrong with the security feeds. Cameras keep glitching, showing static, or worse—showing **people in the park after hours when no one's there.** I checked the tapes, but they don't match up with what's on the monitor. This has been happening for weeks now. Either someone is breaking in, or the system is completely fried. We need this fixed ASAP."*

Another **guest complaint**, early 2012:

"I swear I counted three of us getting on the ride, but when we got off, there were only two. The staff just laughed when I asked where my friend went. They said we must have miscounted. But we didn't. We know we didn't."

Dakota's breathing was shallow now, his hands gripping the paper so tightly that the edges **crinkled** beneath his fingers.

Another **security report**, later that year:

*"A child was reported missing near the entrance of Fantasy Land. Footage was reviewed, but the cameras cut out for exactly **four minutes and seventeen seconds**. When they came back on, there was no sign of the child. No reports were filed with the police. Management advised security to drop the issue."*

Dakota swallowed hard.

Lane hadn't said a word this whole time, just keeping the camera steady as Dakota flipped through the documents, each one **more unsettling** than the last.

Then, finally—**at the bottom of the stack**—a single, typed page.

A **list of passwords.**

Dakota's eyes locked onto it, his heartbeat pounding in his ears.

There it was—the key to the security system. The one thing that could **finally** show them the truth.

He picked up the paper with shaky hands, looking over at Lane.

"We have it."

Dakota's eyes darted across the list, his fingers gripping the paper tightly. The passwords were printed neatly in a single column, each labeled with a different system or access point. His heart pounded as he read them aloud under his breath.

PASSWORD LIST – SECURITY ACCESS

1. **Main Security System Access – H0LL0W2015**
2. **Employee Log Database – STAFFONLY99**
3. **Surveillance Backup Files – EYESEVERYWHERE**
4. **Ride Control Override – G0N3F0R3V3R**
5. **Maintenance Reports – BROKENDREAMS**
6. **Incident Reports (Restricted) – MISSING123**

Dakota swallowed hard, his mind racing.

"Why would an amusement park need restricted access to incident reports?"

He shook off the thought, his fingers brushing over the page. Some of these were expected—employee logs, ride controls—but **Surveillance Backup Files? Restricted Incident Reports?** That wasn't normal.

"Lane," Dakota said, his voice low. "This place was covering up something."

Lane zoomed in on the paper, catching every detail. "We need to see the security footage," he said.

Dakota nodded, flipping through the files on the desk, hoping to find **anything** that could help them log in faster. His eyes landed on an old **security badge**, the plastic faded, the name smudged beyond recognition. He turned it over in his hand.

"Think this'll still work?" he asked.

"Only one way to find out."

The two of them turned toward the **security terminal** across the room, an old computer sitting on a desk covered in dust and loose papers. Dakota wiped the screen with his sleeve, revealing a flickering **login prompt.**

ENTER PASSWORD:

His fingers hovered over the keyboard. He typed in the first one.

H0LL0W2015

The screen flashed.

ACCESS GRANTED

Dakota and Lane exchanged a glance.

They were in.

A list of **camera feeds** popped up, rows of **timestamps** dating back **years.** Dakota scrolled through them, eyes darting across the screen. Most were corrupted, the files broken, but some were still intact.

Lane leaned in. "Go back. Right there—2012. The year people started going missing."

Dakota clicked the file. The screen flickered, static crackling before an image formed—grainy footage of **the park at night.** The timestamp read:

03/17/2012 – 2:46 AM

A security guard walked the empty pathways, his flashlight cutting through the darkness. Dakota and Lane watched in silence. The guard paused near the entrance of the **Isle of Animals,** looking around like he'd heard something.

Then, the screen **glitched.**

For a fraction of a second, something **moved** behind the guard.

Dakota's stomach turned.

"Did you see that?"

Lane rewound the footage. Frame by frame, they watched as the **dark figure** loomed behind the guard. Too **tall**, too **thin**.

The guard turned. His mouth opened to scream.

The feed cut out.

Static.

Then, the next timestamp.

03/17/2012 – 2:50 AM

The guard was gone.

The flashlight lay on the ground, its beam pointing uselessly at the pavement.

The park was **silent.**

Lane cursed under his breath, taking a step back from the screen. Dakota felt his hands trembling as he reached for the next file—**Incident Reports (Restricted).**

He entered the password.

MISSING123

The screen flickered. A new document opened.

INCIDENT REPORT LOG – HOLLOW PARK

DATE: March 17, 2012
REPORT FILED BY: J. Landry (Security Lead)
SUMMARY:

- Security Officer A. Peters last seen patrolling **Isle of Animals** at approximately **2:45 AM**
- Disappeared during routine patrol; last radio transmission unintelligible, described as **"static mixed with breathing"**
- Surveillance footage reviewed – **no clear evidence of departure from the park**
- **No traces of struggle found**

- Uniform **and badge recovered near Jungle Cruise dock**
- No **external breach of park fencing**
- Official Cause of Disappearance: UNKNOWN

RECOMMENDED ACTION: No public statement. No law enforcement involvement. Internal review only.

Dakota's breath hitched. His skin crawled.

"They knew," he whispered. "They knew something was taking people."

Lane swallowed hard, his grip tightening on the camera.

Dakota scrolled further down. There were **more reports.** More **disappearances. Employees. Guests.**

Each one ending the same way:

NO PUBLIC STATEMENT. NO LAW ENFORCEMENT INVOLVEMENT. INTERNAL REVIEW ONLY.

Dakota sat back, the weight of it sinking into his chest. Lane's camera was still rolling, capturing every detail.

"This isn't just some haunted park," Dakota said. "They covered this up. People died here."

Lane looked over at him, his voice low. "And we're still in here with whatever did it."

A loud **thump** echoed from outside the office.

Both of them froze.

Something was moving.

Dakota's fingers hovered over the keyboard, his breath shallow as he typed in the password: **STAFFONLY99**. A moment of silence followed, then the document opened. The title of the memo sent a chill down his spine.

MEMO TO: JASON LANGSTON
FROM: D.P.B.
SUBJECT: RULES

Lane peered over his shoulder, the glow of the screen illuminating both of their tense expressions. "Rules?" he muttered. "For what?"

Dakota swallowed and began reading aloud.

Jason,

This is not a request. This is a warning.

You are making a grave mistake by proceeding with your plans for this park. You bought this land for next to nothing, and you believe that was a lucky break. It wasn't. The land was cheap because no one in their right mind would build here. I assume you ignored the history, and I assume you don't believe in what I'm about to tell you. That's fine. Disbelief doesn't make it any less real.

There is something here. Something old. Something unnatural. It doesn't belong to any classification we know of. It has no true form—only what it chooses to show. We call it the Wraithform. We do not know where it came from, nor do we know if it can be killed. We only know what we have observed, what we have suffered.

Decades ago, we managed to trap it. It was not easy, and it cost lives. The creature does not move in ways we understand. It hunts, but not for food. It stalks for the thrill of it. It enjoys the fear. It bends reality, distorts perception, makes you believe in things that aren't there while hiding the things that are. But it follows rules. Rules that we discovered over years of loss.

Dakota's voice trailed off, his grip tightening on the edge of the desk. "Holy shit…"

Lane adjusted the camera. "They caught it?" His voice was filled with disbelief, eyes flicking between Dakota and the screen.

Dakota nodded, scrolling further. "They had it contained." He took a breath before continuing.

RULES OF CONTAINMENT:

1. **The Wraithform does not move while being directly watched. Surveillance must be maintained at all times. If left unobserved, it will roam freely.**

2. **It must be confined to a sealed, underground space. Concrete and steel reinforced. The more barriers, the better.**
3. **Do not speak to it. It understands. It listens. It remembers. If it learns your voice, it will use it against you.**
4. **Do not acknowledge illusions. No matter what you see, what you hear, what you think is happening—it is not real. If you react, it knows its tricks are working.**
5. **Never, under any circumstances, let it roam at night. The dark is its domain.**

Dakota let out a breath he didn't realize he was holding. Lane wiped his hand across his face. "Jesus Christ… They built the park **on top** of this thing?"

Dakota clicked to the next section.

Jason, I know you won't listen. You're blinded by profit. You don't care what this land was before, but that's exactly why you should be afraid. This thing—it will wait. It will bide its time. And if you disturb it, you will regret it. We kept it locked away for a reason. We followed the rules. But if you break them, you'll be condemning everyone who sets foot on this land.

Do not build your park here. If you insist, then you will need to maintain constant surveillance. Every camera running, every guard on shift. No exceptions. If something happens—if you notice anything out of place—lock everything down immediately. Do not let it spread.

If you fail, if the rules are broken, the only thing you can do is leave. You cannot stop it. You can only escape it.

You won't listen. I know you won't. But when it happens—when you realize what you've done—remember that you were warned.

- D.P.B.

A heavy silence filled the room. Lane let out a shaky laugh, but there was no humor behind it. "Well. Guess we know why he got the land so cheap."

Dakota ran a hand through his hair. "He knew. Langston **knew**."

Lane pointed the camera at Dakota, his voice low. "Then what happened? If they had it locked up, if they had rules to keep it contained… What the hell went wrong?"

Dakota scrolled back up, reading the memo again. "Maybe they didn't follow the rules. Maybe… maybe over time, security got lazy. Maybe cameras weren't checked. Maybe it was an accident, or maybe Langston didn't believe any of this and just let it all go to hell." He looked up, his expression grim. "Or maybe the moment they started building, they broke the first rule."

Lane's stomach twisted. "If it needs constant surveillance, and they were digging, tearing up the ground…"

Dakota finished the thought. "Then they turned their backs on it."

They exchanged a glance, the reality of the situation sinking in.

Lane turned back to the computer. "What now?"

Dakota scrolled further, until the final piece of information appeared:

PASSWORD LIST – SECURITY SYSTEM ACCESS

1. **Main Security Hub – SECUREZONE01**
2. **Surveillance System – ALLSEEINGEYE07**
3. **Maintenance Logs – FIXITFAST22**
4. **Park Emergency Lockdown – REDLIGHTS94**

Dakota exhaled, heart pounding. "We might have just found a way to see what's really going on."

Lane swallowed hard. "Or maybe… we just gave it a reason to notice us."

CHAPTER EIGHT

The smell of bacon and coffee drifted through the air, a comforting warmth pulling Dakota from sleep. His eyes fluttered open, the familiar ceiling of his childhood bedroom greeting him. He blinked, confused for a moment, his mind sluggish as he tried to place where he was. The last thing he remembered was—

He frowned.

What *was* the last thing he remembered?

His body felt heavy, like he hadn't slept in days, yet here he was, tucked into his old bed, the same one he'd slept in through high school. The posters on the walls, the cluttered desk in the corner, even the old alarm clock with the blinking red numbers—it was all the same.

He swallowed down the unease rising in his chest and swung his legs over the edge of the bed, the cool wooden floor grounding him as he stood. His body moved on autopilot, drawn by the sounds of soft conversation and the clinking of silverware.

As he wandered into the kitchen, the scene before him was pulled straight from his memories.

His mom sat at the table, her fork scraping against her plate as she ate. Across from her, his dad was partially hidden behind the morning newspaper, steam curling from the coffee cup in his hand. And at the end of the table, Bryan, his older brother, lazily shoved food into his mouth between scrolling on his phone.

Dakota stood in the doorway, something cold curling around his spine. This felt *wrong*. Not because anything seemed off—if anything, it was too *perfect*.

His dad was the first to notice him. Lowering the newspaper, he offered a warm smile. "Morning, kiddo."

His mom's reaction was different. She barely glanced up from her plate before her brows pulled together in concern. "You okay? You look stressed."

Dakota ran a hand through his messy hair, his skin prickling. He forced himself to shake off the feeling. It was *just* breakfast. "Yeah," he muttered. "I'm fine. Just had a weird dream."

He moved to the table, pulling out a chair and sinking into it, the warmth of the room doing little to ease the strange tightness in his chest.

His dad took a sip of coffee, setting the mug down before looking at him again. "Weird how?"

Dakota hesitated.

His mouth opened, but no words came out.

What *had* he dreamed about?

The details slipped through his fingers like smoke, dissolving the harder he tried to grasp them. He knew it had been something *important*. Something—

His heart thumped painfully in his chest.

He didn't know.

A short, sarcastic laugh broke the silence.

"Lemme guess," Bryan said, barely glancing up from his phone. "You stayed up too late watching those dumb videos again and had a nightmare?"

Dakota frowned at him, the teasing tone feeling distant, unreal. His fingers curled against the table.

Something was *wrong*.

His mind screamed at him to figure it out. To look closer. To *remember*.

But no matter how hard he tried...

He couldn't.

His mother shot Bryan a sharp look, her fork pausing midair. "Be nice," she said, her tone light but firm.

Bryan rolled his eyes, stuffing another bite of food into his mouth.

His dad, still sipping his coffee, chuckled. "First day of summer vacation, and you're already sleeping the day away. If I didn't know any better, I'd say you were hibernating."

Dakota let out a humorless chuckle, rubbing the back of his neck. But inside, the uneasy feeling only grew stronger. There was something *wrong*—he just didn't know what.

Something important.

Something he had to remember, like his life depended on it.

He could feel it, just out of reach. A gnawing urgency clawing at the back of his mind. And it wasn't just about him—someone else was involved. Someone had been with him. But no matter how hard he tried to grasp the thought, it slipped through his fingers like sand.

A sudden knock at the door cut through his thoughts.

His dad pushed his chair back and stood, making his way to the front door. Dakota listened, staring blankly at the half-eaten food on his plate, his mind still wrestling with the emptiness where something *important* should be.

"Lane!" His dad's voice rang through the house, warm and familiar. "Good to see you, kid. Come on in."

"Thanks, Mr. Jones," Lane said politely, though his voice held an odd stiffness to it. "But I actually just came to see if Dakota wanted to go check out the new stuff at the electronics store. They got a bunch of cool new gear in."

At the mention of his name, Dakota's head snapped up.

Lane stood in the doorway, hands shoved in the pockets of his hoodie, his expression unreadable. The feeling of wrongness in Dakota's chest grew heavier. *Something* was off—Lane's posture, his voice, even the way he looked at him. It was like Lane felt it too.

Dakota didn't hesitate. He pushed his chair back and stood, ignoring his mother's questioning look.

"I'll be back later," he mumbled, already heading for the door.

His dad clapped a hand on his shoulder as he passed. "Don't go spending all your money in one place."

Dakota barely acknowledged him as he stepped outside, the warm summer air wrapping around him. Lane fell into step beside him as they made their way down the street, the neighborhood calm and quiet.

For a moment, neither of them spoke.

Then, Lane let out a breath and muttered, "I had a weird dream last night."

Dakota's stomach twisted.

Lane kept his eyes ahead, like he was struggling to find the right words. "I don't know... it's like—I feel like I forgot something. Like there's this huge blank spot in my head where something *important* should be." He hesitated. "And it's not just the dream. Even now, today feels... off."

Dakota swallowed hard.

"I feel the same way."

Dakota's breath caught in his throat. His arm remained outstretched, holding Lane back as if stepping even an inch closer would shatter the fragile, unnatural reality around them.

Lane's brow furrowed. "Dude, what? It's just Mr. Darcy."

Dakota turned to him, his pulse hammering. Lane didn't see it. He didn't *see it*.

His voice was hoarse when he spoke. "Lane… Mr. Darcy moved away before we started high school."

Lane blinked, his lips parting slightly like he was about to argue—but then he looked back at the man. Really *looked*.

The shape of him was *wrong*.

His posture too rigid, his limbs slightly too long, his steps staggered and offbeat like a puppet controlled by clumsy, unseen hands. The lawnmower hummed steadily as he pushed it forward, but Dakota could hear something beneath the mechanical buzz—a faint, uneven clicking sound, like bones grinding against each other.

Lane sucked in a sharp breath.

"What the hell is happening?" he whispered.

Dakota didn't answer. He *couldn't*. He still couldn't remember. Couldn't figure out how they had gotten here, why his gut twisted with a sickening certainty that this wasn't *real*. That something was very, *very* wrong.

Then Mr. Darcy stopped mowing.

Slowly, he turned to face them.

The movement was jerky, unnatural, like a corrupted video file skipping frames. His head tilted too far, his gaze locking onto them with dark, hollow eyes. His lips pulled into something that might have been a smile if it weren't so *strained*.

Then, he raised a hand and *waved*.

A slow, dragging wave, his fingers bending at the wrong angles, swaying like they weren't even attached to muscle and bone.

Dakota felt his stomach churn.

Then Mr. Darcy opened his mouth.

A deep, raspy breath sucked inward, rattling and uneven, like air scraping through collapsed lungs. Another breath followed. Then another. But no words ever came.

The world around them *flickered.*

Dakota barely had time to process it before Mr. Darcy *convulsed.*

His limbs jerked violently, his shoulders snapping back as though yanked by invisible strings. His jaw unhinged too wide, his fingers twitching and curling. Then, in slow, melting horror, his skin *began to slip.*

It peeled from his arms first, sloughing away in thick, wet chunks, pooling at his feet. His face sagged, flesh pulling downward in viscous drips like wax under an open flame. His hollow gaze remained fixed on them, even as his features distorted and liquefied.

Lane gasped, stumbling back. Dakota couldn't move. Couldn't breathe.

And then—

They jolted.

A sharp inhale.

The hum of the security system filled their ears.

Dakota's eyes snapped back into focus. His hands trembled against the desk.

They were still in the castle.

Still staring blankly at the security screen.

The stale, dusty air of the abandoned building pressed in around them. No breakfast. No sunlight filtering through the kitchen window.

Just them.

And the realization that something was *toying* with them.

Dakota and Lane sucked in air like drowning men breaking the surface. Their chests heaved as they frantically scanned the room. Nothing. No shadow lurking in the corners. No unnatural presence looming over them. Just the cold, dimly lit castle, the hum of the security system pressing down on them.

Dakota swallowed, his throat dry. He turned to Lane, his voice unsteady. "Check the footage."

Lane hesitated, his hands trembling as he reached for the camera sitting on the desk. His fingers fumbled over the buttons, stopping the recording. With a shaky breath, he pulled up the most recent file and played it.

They both leaned in.

The footage was normal at first. It showed them sitting in front of the computer, scrolling through the files. But then—*they stopped.*

Their bodies went unnaturally still, their faces blank, eyes unfocused as they stared at the screen. Neither of them moved. Neither of them blinked.

Then the sound started.

A low, raspy breath. Forced. Strained. Like something struggling to *breathe.*

Lane's grip on the camera tightened.

Suddenly, something shifted on the screen.

A sliver of pale skin came into frame, blocking part of the lens. It was too close. Too still. Dakota's stomach clenched as he realized—*it was standing right next to them.*

The breathing grew louder. Slow, dragging inhales followed by wet, rattling exhales.

And for fifteen full minutes, *it just stood there.*

Watching.

Waiting.

Dakota and Lane remained locked in place on the screen, only moving in brief, unsettling twitches—small convulsions that sent jolts through their limbs. Puppets with their strings tangled.

Lane's breath hitched.

Then, as suddenly as it had appeared, the thing moved.

It walked out of frame.

A few more seconds passed, and then—*they jolted awake.*

The footage ended.

The silence in the room was suffocating.

Dakota slowly turned to Lane, his voice barely above a whisper. "It was here." His hands curled into fists, his entire body tense. "It was *playing* with us."

Lane swallowed hard, staring at the now-black screen. His voice was hollow when he spoke.

"Like puppets."

For a moment, Lane sat there, contemplating the next move. Finally, his shaky fingers hovered over the buttons again, starting another recording.

The footage of the park—when it was still open, when they saw it open and running—played back on the screen.

Dakota and Lane sat in tense silence, watching themselves walk through the park, admiring the rides, the exhibits, the animals. But something was *wrong*. What they had seen with their own eyes wasn't what was on the screen.

Lane swallowed hard as the video played.

The moment they had stopped in front of the gorilla animatronic appeared on the screen. He remembered standing there, fascinated, thinking it looked so lifelike—so well-maintained. But on camera, it was a ruined husk.

The fur was matted, clumped together with filth. The synthetic skin was torn and tattered, exposing the mechanical insides. Rusted metal glinted under the dim light from the camera. It wasn't moving. It wasn't lifelike.

It was *rotting*.

Lane's stomach twisted. His grip tightened on the camera as they continued watching.

The footage jumped to the dock.

This was where they had seen the guests. The ride operator. The friendly waves. The boat full of people.

But on the screen, there was nothing. No guests. No ride operator. No boat.

Only *it*.

The Wraithform.

It was hunched over, staring at them through the screen. Its arm was raised, waving—mimicking what they had seen before.

Dakota sucked in a breath. His entire body tensed.

The Wraithform turned away and began walking—slowly, deliberately—toward the water.

Then, just as it reached the edge, it disappeared beneath the surface.

Lane's hands were ice cold. He knew what came next.

The splash.

The moment they had *come to*.

On screen, the water rippled violently as something disturbed it. Then—nothing. The moment the splash echoed through the speakers, the footage ended.

Lane stopped the video.

For a long moment, neither of them spoke. The air in the room felt too heavy to breathe.

Finally, Lane turned to Dakota.

"…It was never real."

Dakota didn't answer right away. He was still staring at the dark screen, like if he looked long enough, the footage would start playing again.

Then, finally, his voice came, quiet and shaken.

"But it *was*."

Neither of them spoke.

Lane's fingers hovered over the pause button, his grip on the camera tightening. His throat felt tight, his breath shallow. He looked at Dakota, eyes wide, heart hammering in his chest.

Dakota didn't move. His jaw was clenched so hard it ached, his hands curled into white-knuckled fists on the desk. His mind was racing, replaying the footage over and over in his head. What they *thought* they saw. What was really there. The gut-wrenching difference between the two.

The park wasn't alive. It wasn't *open*.

It was a rotting corpse, its magic stripped away, leaving behind rusted bones and decayed remnants of something that *should* have been gone.

And the people—no, the illusions—had been nothing but a lie.

Dakota exhaled sharply through his nose, shaking his head. "It was never real," he muttered, voice hoarse. "None of it."

Lane swallowed hard. He felt sick. His stomach twisted violently as his eyes flicked back to the last frozen frame on the camera screen. The Wraithform. Its massive, hunched form. The unnatural way it *stared* at them. The *wave*.

Lane clenched his jaw and set the camera down like it had burned him. He dragged his hands down his face. "Jesus Christ." His voice was barely above a whisper.

Dakota's mind was still racing, pieces clicking together. His pulse pounded in his ears. "That's what made the splash," he said, his voice distant, detached. "When we came to... when we snapped out of it... we *heard* it." His eyes flicked to Lane. "It was *there* with us the whole time."

Lane sucked in a breath through his teeth. His hands were still shaking. "It let us see what it wanted us to see," he said bitterly. "It made us believe we were safe." He let out a humorless chuckle, but it was hollow. Shaky. "It was probably laughing at us the whole damn time."

Dakota's stomach churned. The memory of how *real* it had felt made his skin crawl. The warm summer air. The smell of popcorn and fresh-cut grass. The distant laughter of kids. The illusion had been perfect. Seamless.

And underneath it all, they had been wandering a graveyard.

Lane ran a hand through his hair. "We should've known something was off."

Dakota exhaled through gritted teeth. "We *did* know." He looked at Lane, eyes dark with realization. "But it didn't let us remember."

The weight of that truth sank between them.

The Wraithform wasn't just hunting them.

It was *toying* with them.

Dakota and Lane stood in the dim glow of the security monitors, their breathing still uneven, their bodies tense. Every shadow felt heavier now. Every sound, no matter how small, sent a spike of adrenaline through their veins. They weren't alone in this park. They knew that now.

"We have to get out of here," Dakota muttered, rubbing a hand over his face. "We know it's real. We know it's here. We just have to make it until sunrise."

Lane exhaled sharply, gripping the camera so tight his knuckles turned white. "Screw that. Let's burn this place down."

Dakota shot him a look. "And what? Hope it just *dies*?"

"Yes!" Lane snapped. "We don't know what it is, but we *do* know fire kills *everything*. If we set this whole place on fire—"

"It won't work," Dakota cut him off. His voice was low but firm. "You saw the memo. Fire might slow it down, maybe even drive it back, but it won't kill it." He shook his head, jaw clenched. "We don't even know *if* it can die."

Lane let out a frustrated breath, turning in a slow circle as if looking for an answer in the darkness. The air was thick with tension. The idea of waiting until sunrise felt impossible, like forcing themselves to stay still while something hunted them in the dark.

Finally, Lane broke the silence. "Future Island."

Dakota frowned. "What?"

"We haven't been there yet," Lane said, adjusting the camera strap over his shoulder. "It's the only place left."

Dakota hesitated. The idea of *voluntarily* going somewhere they hadn't checked yet felt like walking straight into a trap. But at the same time, if they were stuck here until sunrise, knowing more about the park—about *it*—might give them an edge.

He let out a slow breath, nodding. "Fine. Future Island."

Lane lifted the camera, hitting record again.

Then, together, they stepped out of the castle and back into the night.

The night pressed in around them as Dakota and Lane moved through the park, their footsteps muffled against the cracked pavement. The air was heavy, thick with the scent of mildew and stagnant water from the overgrown foliage reclaiming the paths. The distant groan of rusting metal echoed somewhere deep in the park, but whether it was the wind or something else, neither of them wanted to find out.

Lane kept the camera running, the red recording light flickering in his unsteady grip. "This place feels different," he muttered.

Dakota nodded. He couldn't put his finger on it, but Future Island loomed ahead of them like something waiting. The entrance was marked by a towering, rusted archway that once gleamed silver but now flaked with corrosion. The words *Welcome to the Future* were barely legible beneath years of grime and neglect.

Stepping through, they were met with a sight both mesmerizing and unsettling. Future Island was designed to be Hollow Park's vision of tomorrow—a retro-futuristic utopia of domed buildings, sleek metallic structures, and glass walkways that once shimmered under neon lights. But now, the future was dead.

The sleek silver paint peeled from the walls, revealing warped metal beneath. Towering fiberglass statues of astronauts and androids stood at odd angles, some missing limbs, their blank eyes reflecting the dim light of Dakota's flashlight. The monorail, which once carried guests above the island in a smooth loop, sagged on its rusted track, threatening to collapse at any moment.

Lane swallowed hard. "You ever notice how theme parks at night feel totally different? Like, during the day, it's all fun and exciting, but at night…" His voice trailed off as he swept the camera across the ruined landscape.

"They feel empty," Dakota finished. "Like a skeleton of something that used to be alive."

They passed what was once the *Tomorrow Theater*, its holographic sign long since shattered. The glass doors had been left ajar, swaying slightly with the wind, revealing rows of dust-covered seats inside. A flickering emergency light cast long, twitching shadows against the walls.

Lane pointed the camera inside. "Nope. Not going in there."

Dakota didn't argue.

Further down, they reached *The Future of Energy*, a once-interactive exhibit showcasing renewable energy sources with massive, now-defunct solar panels and wind turbines. The main attraction had been a glowing sphere at the center of the exhibit, demonstrating artificial lightning. The sphere now sat dark and shattered, its wires spilling onto the floor like severed veins.

Lane let out a breath. "We should check the control center. Maybe we can find something useful. A map, security footage—hell, even a working radio."

Dakota nodded. "Where is it?"

Lane turned in a slow circle before spotting a sign barely hanging onto its last bolt: *Future Island Operations – Staff Only*.

The door was rusted, the keypad beside it broken beyond repair, but the wood had softened from years of exposure. Dakota pressed his shoulder against it, and after a few shoves, the door groaned open.

Inside, the air was thick with dust and something else—something sour. The remains of office chairs lay overturned, papers scattered across the floor. The walls were lined with old monitors, long dead, their screens cracked or flickering with static. A thick, sticky residue covered parts of the floor, and Dakota had no intention of finding out what it was.

Lane stepped carefully over the mess, his camera light bouncing off a row of file cabinets. "Maybe there's something in here," he said, tugging one open.

Dakota moved toward a desk covered in old maps and logs, flipping through them. Most were standard maintenance records, detailing repairs on rides and scheduling for janitorial staff. But one document caught his eye—it was a report from 2012.

Incident Report – Staff Member Missing

His stomach twisted. Before he could read further, Lane sucked in a sharp breath. Dakota turned just as Lane yanked open another drawer and recoiled.

Inside, there was a **jawbone.**

Not an animal's. Not fake. A human jawbone, the teeth still intact, resting on a pile of old security tapes.

Lane slammed the drawer shut. "Nope. Nope. Nope."

Dakota's fingers clenched around the report, heart pounding. This place was more than just abandoned. It had a **history**, and that history was soaked in something far worse than poor management and financial ruin.

Then, from somewhere outside, the sound of slow, deliberate footsteps echoed through the empty streets of Future Island.

Lane shut off the camera light immediately.

Neither of them moved. Neither of them breathed.

The footsteps dragged, the weight of something unnatural pressing against the pavement. Then came the sound of **breathing**—uneven, labored, as if the thing outside wasn't used to air moving through its lungs.

Dakota and Lane locked eyes.

They were not alone in Future Island.

They didn't move.

The slow, uneven footsteps dragged across the pavement just outside the operations building, a sickening shuffle of something that didn't quite know how to walk like a person. The breathing was worse—labored, rasping, as if each inhale was a struggle, each exhale forced through lungs that shouldn't be working.

Lane's grip on the camera tightened. Dakota pressed his back against the filing cabinet, his heart hammering so loud he swore the thing outside could hear it.

The footsteps paused just outside the doorway.

Dakota's breath hitched. The door was still slightly open, just enough for whatever was out there to see inside if it wanted to. He slowly reached forward, his fingers trembling as he pushed the door closed—just an inch, just enough.

The breathing continued.

A shadow passed by the narrow window in the door.

Lane squeezed his eyes shut. The camera was still recording, but he didn't dare lift it to look.

For what felt like an eternity, the thing just stood there. It didn't sniff, didn't groan, didn't tap against the door. It just **breathed**.

Then, just as suddenly as it had come, the footsteps began again, shuffling away, the sound gradually fading into the distance.

Lane exhaled first, quietly, shaking his head. Dakota didn't speak. He wasn't even sure he could. His whole body was locked up, adrenaline burning through his veins.

They waited.

Five minutes. Ten.

Nothing.

Finally, Dakota moved first. He reached out, turning the knob **as slowly as possible**, opening the door just enough to peer outside.

Future Island was silent.

The pathway was empty. The air was still. But something had changed.

Lane stepped out behind him, and they both **felt it**—an absence. Like the entire park had been holding its breath, just waiting for them to move.

Dakota motioned toward the street, and they started walking again, this time slower, more aware of every sound, every shift in the air.

They followed the cracked pavement deeper into Future Island, passing under the skeletal remains of a **defunct ride**. The neon signs were long dead, but the words still lingered in rusted lettering:

"COSMIC DROP – EXPERIENCE ZERO GRAVITY!"

Lane glanced up at the towering frame of the ride. The seats still hung from the top, swaying slightly in the breeze. Or at least, he **thought** it was the breeze.

They kept moving.

Then, up ahead, Dakota saw something. He grabbed Lane's arm and yanked him down behind an overturned bench.

Lane nearly yelped but bit his tongue, looking in the direction Dakota was staring.

And that's when they **saw it.**

The Wraithform.

It stood in the middle of the walkway, hunched over, its impossibly long arms hanging at its sides, clawed fingertips nearly scraping the ground.

Even from here, Dakota could **see the details**. The way its sickly, yellowish-gray skin stretched too tight over its bones. The patches of decay along its ribs, the blackened flesh peeling away in places to reveal the sharp outlines of bone underneath.

But the **worst** part was its face.

Its head was bald, the skin cracked and uneven. Its eyes were **empty black pits**, sunken deep into its skull. Its mouth hung slightly open, revealing a **normal** set of teeth—normal until the jaw **unhinged slightly**, stretching a little too wide, just enough to be unnatural.

Lane barely breathed. The camera was still rolling, the red light glowing faintly in the dark, but neither of them moved to turn it off.

The Wraithform didn't move. It **stood** there, as if waiting, as if listening.

Then, as if sensing them, its head **jerked** slightly.

Dakota's stomach dropped. Lane's breath caught in his throat.

It was looking for them.

They weren't hidden well enough.

Lane instinctively raised the camera, his fingers shaking so badly he could barely keep the lens focused on the thing standing in the middle of the walkway. Dakota didn't stop him—he was too frozen, his body locked in place as he stared at the Wraithform. The thing hadn't moved yet, but the air felt heavy, like something was pressing down on them, **waiting** for something to happen.

Then, without warning, the Wraithform's **jaw began to unhinge**.

The skin around its mouth stretched, cracking as it opened **too wide**, the lower half of its face pulling down in a sickening, unnatural motion. The deep, hollow pits where its eyes should be seemed to **stare through them**, and then—

It inhaled.

A deep, **labored gasp**, like it was sucking in every ounce of air around it. The sound was **horrific**, rattling, like lungs that had long since stopped functioning were being forced to work again. Lane barely had time to react, barely had time to even **breathe**, before—

The scream.

It **shook the world.**

The sheer force of it sent **shockwaves through their bodies**, like something was clawing through their skulls, **trying to break them from the inside out**. Lane and Dakota **collapsed behind the bench**, clutching their heads, their hands pressing **tight** over their ears, but it did nothing—**nothing** to block out the sound.

The very air around them **vibrated**, the pavement beneath them trembled, cracks spiderwebbing through the old concrete. It was like the entire park was **alive**, reacting to the thing's rage, the weight of its scream threatening to **pull them apart**.

Dakota couldn't think. Couldn't move.

His vision blurred, his brain screamed at him to run, to do **anything**—but his body refused.

It wasn't just **sound**.

It was **inside him**.

Lane was shaking, his breath coming in short, broken gasps as he pressed himself flat against the pavement, eyes squeezed shut, the camera abandoned on the ground beside him, still recording.

And then—

Silence.

The scream **stopped**.

For a moment, neither of them moved, the ringing in their ears the only thing filling the suffocating stillness. Dakota's entire body trembled, his fingers twitching against the rough ground as he forced himself to **breathe**.

Lane dared to open his eyes.

The Wraithform **wasn't looking at them anymore**.

It had turned away, its head tilted slightly downward, as if the scream had drained it.

Then, slowly, it **walked away**.

Not in a rush, not with any sense of urgency—just **drifting** into the darkness, its grotesque limbs carrying it further into the depths of Future Island.

Neither of them moved until it was completely gone.

Lane swallowed hard, his throat raw, voice barely above a whisper.

"… What the **fuck** was that?"

Dakota's breathing was ragged, his body still trembling from the aftershock of the scream. His ears rang so loudly he could barely think, his pulse a relentless hammer against his skull. Lane sat beside him, hunched over, his hands gripping his knees like he was trying to steady himself, to **keep himself from falling apart**.

For a long moment, neither of them spoke.

Then Dakota exhaled sharply, running a hand through his hair before pressing his palms into his face. "Holy shit…" His voice was hoarse, barely more than a whisper. "Holy **shit**."

Lane let out a dry, humorless chuckle, shaking his head. "Yeah. That's one way to put it."

Dakota looked at him, his expression dark, exhausted. "It was **right there**. It was standing over us for who knows how long, and we couldn't even move." His jaw clenched. "We can't keep doing this, Lane. We have to get out of here."

Lane's eyes flickered to the camera lying on the ground between them. Slowly, he reached for it, checking the screen. The footage was still there—**it was all still there**. The thing. The scream. Their complete and utter helplessness.

"We need to burn this place to the ground," Lane muttered, barely audible. "We need to kill it—**whatever it is**."

Dakota's head snapped toward him, eyes narrowing. "Yeah? And how exactly do you plan on doing that? You think a few matches and some lighter fluid are gonna do the trick?" He scoffed, shaking his head. "That thing **isn't normal**, Lane. Fire won't kill it."

Lane huffed, shoving the camera into his bag. "I don't see you coming up with any better ideas."

"Because we don't **have** any better ideas!" Dakota snapped, his voice sharper than intended. "We don't even know what we're dealing with! We don't know how it works, what it wants—hell, we don't even know if it can **die**."

Lane glared at him, standing up abruptly, slinging his bag over his shoulder. "So what, Dakota? We just sit here and wait to die? You wanna just let it **pick us off**?"

"I never said that," Dakota shot back, getting to his feet. His hands curled into fists at his sides, frustration burning hot in his chest. "But running around like idiots, making a bunch of noise, **isn't helping either**."

Lane let out a dry laugh, shaking his head. "Right. Because hiding has been working out **so well** for us."

Dakota exhaled sharply through his nose, forcing himself to take a step back, to **breathe**. This wasn't helping. **None of this was helping.**

They stood there for a long moment, neither of them saying anything, just **staring** at each other, the tension thick enough to suffocate.

Finally, Dakota let out a breath, scrubbing a hand down his face. His voice was quieter now, more controlled. "We need to keep moving."

Lane looked like he wanted to argue, but instead, he just exhaled and turned away. "Yeah. Whatever."

They started walking, the silence between them heavy, neither willing to say what they were really thinking.

They couldn't do this much longer.

Something had to give.

Lane pulled the camera from his bag, still recording despite the shaking in his hands. The night vision cast the world in eerie green hues, distorting the twisted wreckage of **Future Island** into something even more alien. He let out a breathy chuckle, dry and humorless.

"Well, at least we'll have proof for when they find our bodies."

Dakota didn't answer.

He shot Lane a look instead, sharp and **exhausted**, the kind that spoke louder than words. **Shut up and keep moving.**

Lane didn't push it. He lowered the camera slightly, but he kept it rolling.

They pressed on, navigating through the crumbling remains of what was once **a glimpse into the future**. Rusted hovercraft ride vehicles sat still on cracked tracks, their sleek designs dulled by time and decay. The neon glow of old signs flickered weakly, their messages unreadable through layers of grime. A massive dome-like structure loomed ahead—the centerpiece of Future Island—its metallic surface dented and corroded, gaping holes where glass once shone.

This wasn't an exploration anymore.

It wasn't about the thrill of sneaking into abandoned places, about capturing something cool for their collection of urban adventures.

This was about survival.

They had to get out.

Had to find a way before they **ended up like the others—like whatever happened to the missing guests, the missing employees, the people who just disappeared without a trace.**

Every step felt heavier, the weight of their own growing frustration pressing down on them. The tension between them crackled like static in the air, unspoken but suffocating.

They were running out of time.

Chapter Nine

The massive dome loomed over them, a skeletal husk of what once stood as Hollow Park's vision of the future. Now, it was nothing more than a **rotting corpse** of shattered glass, rusted metal, and ideas that never came to be. Dakota and Lane hesitated at the entrance, their breath heavy in the silence.

Neither of them spoke, but they both felt it—that pressure in the air, the unshakable feeling that if they stopped moving, even for a second, **it would find them.**

They stepped inside.

The interior was vast, almost overwhelming in its emptiness. The air was thick with dust, the faint scent of mildew and rust lingering beneath the decay. **A museum**, or what remained of it. Rows of **shattered display cases** lined the room, the glass cracked or missing entirely. Their contents, relics of an imagined future, lay discarded on the floor or remained half-propped in place.

Phones of the future—**bulky, strange-looking slabs of plastic** with odd button placements and holographic projections that never came to be.

Futuristic cars—**sleek, chrome-like models with bubble-shaped windshields**, their tires long gone, their metallic frames rusting where the paint had peeled away.

Jets—**crafts that looked straight out of a sci-fi movie**, some still hanging from the ceiling by frayed cables, swaying slightly in the stale air.

Murals stretched across the curved walls, depicting **bright, clean, utopian cities**—skylines with impossibly tall towers, flying vehicles weaving between them, robotic citizens moving in perfect harmony. **A dream of the future, now nothing but a broken fantasy.**

Lined along one wall stood **robot maids**, their humanoid forms frozen in place. Their plastic faces were chipped, their eyes **dark and hollow**, their once-pristine uniforms now tattered and stained.

The quiet between them wasn't comfortable anymore.

They tried to be civil, tried to remind themselves **why they did this in the first place.** The excitement, the thrill of urban exploration, the love for discovering lost places and piecing together their history.

But that **wasn't what this was anymore.**

This wasn't a game. This wasn't an adventure.

This was survival.

Lane kicked at a broken piece of glass, the sound sharp in the silence. "You think this place ever actually worked?" His voice was forced, trying to sound casual, but the edge was there.

Dakota shrugged, stepping around an overturned display case. "Doubt it. Just a bunch of gimmicks. Nothing real."

Lane huffed a small laugh, shaking his head. "Figures."

They weren't arguing. Not yet.

But the weight of **everything** was pressing down on them, squeezing their patience thin. **They were exhausted, on edge, barely keeping it together.** Neither of them wanted to blame the other, but the tension was creeping in, settling into their bones.

Every little thing—**a step too loud, a breath too sharp, a glance held too long**—felt like a **spark ready to ignite.**

They kept moving.

Because stopping wasn't an option.

They moved in silence now, both knowing better than to let their voices carry in the vast, empty dome. Dakota's flashlight swept across the floor, illuminating shattered glass and broken displays, before landing on something that made him stop dead in his tracks.

A door.

It was different from the others—**a rusted metal slab**, bolted into the floor, tucked away in the farthest corner of the room. Almost like it wasn't meant to be found.

Lane glanced at Dakota. Neither of them said it out loud, but they both knew what this meant. If something in Hollow Park had been kept hidden, it **wasn't** going to be good.

Without a word, Dakota stepped forward and grabbed the handle. It was ice-cold to the touch. The hinges groaned loudly as he pulled, the sound splitting the heavy silence like a scream. Dust spilled into the air, and a stairway revealed itself—**a dark, yawning throat leading down into the unknown.**

Lane raised the camera, the red light blinking as he hit record. "This feels like a mistake," he muttered.

Dakota exhaled, gripping the flashlight tighter. "Everything about tonight is a mistake."

Then, they stepped inside.

The air **changed** the moment they entered the stairwell. It was thick, damp, **wrong**. The walls were lined with corroded pipes, some still leaking a black, sludge-like substance that smelled **foul**. The deeper they went, the colder it got, and by the time they reached the bottom, their breath was visible in the dim glow of the flashlight.

The basement was larger than they expected, stretching out into **a cavernous space** filled with old, discarded **things**.

And at first, it was just that—**things**.

Scattered across the floor were **toys**, their bright colors faded and warped, their once-soft fur **matted with filth**. Stuffed animals sat slumped against the walls, their plastic eyes clouded over, their fabric **rotting** from years of exposure to damp air. Dolls lay half-buried in the dirt, their porcelain faces cracked, some missing limbs entirely.

Lane swallowed hard. **These weren't just any toys.**

They recognized them.

From the guest complaints. From the lists of **missing items**.

From the children who had lost them.

A damp, heavy silence settled over them as Dakota crouched down, nudging one of the stuffed bears with the tip of his boot. The thing **squished. Wet. Soggy.** Dakota's stomach **churned**.

Lane's breathing picked up. "What is this?"

Dakota didn't answer.

Because suddenly, he wasn't looking at the toys anymore.

His light had moved, and now it shined on something else. Something **pale**, something **smooth**, something that **gleamed in the dim light like polished stone.**

Something **human**.

Bones.

Scattered across the floor. **Dozens of them.**

Skulls, femurs, ribs—some large, some **small**.

They had been **picked clean**.

And for the first time since stepping foot in Hollow Park, Dakota and Lane realized something—

The Wraithform had been **feeding**.

The underground space stretched farther than they expected, its ceiling low and uneven, as if it had been carved out rather than built. The walls were **damp, slick**, the smell of mildew and something **rotting** thick in the air. Dakota kept the flashlight trained ahead, his grip tight enough that his knuckles turned white. Lane followed closely behind, the camera still recording, though he wasn't sure why anymore. Maybe out of habit. Maybe because part of him still thought proof would matter.

Then, they heard it.

A slow, dragging inhale.

Wet. Strained. Shuddering.

And then, beneath it, something worse—**a sickening, tearing sound.**

Lane stopped moving. "Tell me you hear that."

Dakota nodded once, eyes locked on the darkness ahead. The sound wasn't close—**not yet**—but it was there, **just beyond the veil of shadows.**

They pressed forward, moving carefully, their footsteps muffled against the **grimy**, uneven floor. The deeper they went, the stronger the scent became—**iron, rot, decay.** It was almost suffocating now.

Then Dakota's light hit **something new.**

At first, it looked like **a pile of discarded rags, soaked through with something dark.** But as they moved closer, details became clearer. **Cloth. Flesh. Bone.**

Lane exhaled sharply. **A body.**

Or at least, **what was left of one.**

The torso had been **ripped open**, the ribcage **splayed apart like a broken cage.** The limbs were **wrong**, stretched in directions they shouldn't be, flesh hanging in **torn ribbons.** But it wasn't just the sight that made Dakota's stomach churn—**it was the smell.** A heavy, **coppery stench**, thick enough to coat his tongue.

Lane covered his mouth, swallowing hard. "Jesus…"

And then—

That sound again.

The **breath.**

Labored. Close.

Too close.

Dakota's light swung upward.

At first, there was nothing. Just the long, yawning dark.

But then, movement.

Something **stirring** at the far end of the corridor, **just barely visible beyond the light's reach.**

A shape. **Tall. Unnaturally thin.**

And then—

It **turned.**

Lane barely stifled a gasp. The camera trembled in his hands as the lens tried to focus.

The Wraithform **was there.**

Not an illusion. Not a trick of the mind.

The Wraithform **rose.**

It unfolded itself from the shadows, its **emaciated frame stretching upward**, limbs too long, spine protruding like jagged ridges along its back. The **black voids where its eyes should have been** locked onto them, unreadable, yet entirely focused.

Blood—**thick, dark, fresh**—dripped from its elongated fingers, pooling onto the floor beneath its feet. The stench of **iron, decay, death** thickened in the air.

Dakota couldn't move.

Neither could Lane.

They just stood there, **staring up, frozen in pure shock, in horror.**

It was real.

Not some fleeting glimpse on a screen, not a hallucination, not a story.

It **was right in front of them.**

The Wraithform didn't lunge. It didn't swipe at them.

It just stood there. Watching. Waiting.

A **drop of blood** splattered onto the floor.

The sound snapped them back to reality.

They ran.

Dakota turned first, yanking Lane by the arm as they tore back through the underground chamber. Lane barely managed to keep the camera steady as he stumbled after him, **boots slipping against the slick, filth-covered floor.**

Behind them—**slow, deliberate movement.**

The Wraithform **followed.**

It didn't rush. It didn't need to.

Every step it took **echoed,** heavy against the stone, but it didn't sound hurried. It **wasn't hunting.** It was **waiting.**

They reached the stairs.

Dakota took them **two at a time,** nearly tripping in his panic. Lane scrambled behind him, the camera bouncing wildly.

At the top, Dakota **threw himself against the door,** shoving it open. The second Lane cleared it, Dakota slammed it shut, **bracing his shoulder against the metal.**

Lane grabbed at the nearest thing he could—a rusted metal shelf, half-collapsed with age. Together, they pushed it over, sending a **deafening crash** through the room as it barricaded the door.

Silence.

For a second, all they could hear was their **ragged breathing.**

Then—

A deep, shuddering inhale.

The air **thickened.**

And then—

The scream.

It tore through the air like **a shockwave,** the sheer force rattling the walls.

The windows behind them **shattered, glass exploding outward** as the piercing wail ripped through the structure.

Dakota and Lane **ran.**

They didn't look back.

The scream **followed them,** shaking the very ground beneath their feet as they tore out of the building, sprinting into the night.

Dakota and Lane **stumbled into Toon World,** their steps frantic, their lungs burning with every breath.

The empty cartoon house loomed ahead, its **once-cheerful colors now muted and peeling, its hollow windows black and lifeless.** Dakota didn't hesitate—he **slammed the door shut behind them,** twisting the rusted knob and pressing his weight against it for a moment, as if that alone could keep the nightmare outside.

The house was **silent.** No music. No laughter. Just the distant hum of the park, the ever-present feeling of something **watching.**

They moved toward the **darkest corner,** past the overturned plastic furniture, past the faded murals of grinning cartoon animals, until their backs pressed against the cold, grimy wall.

They slid down, collapsing onto the floor.

Lane reached into his bag, his movements **slow, shaky.** He pulled out the camera and lifted it, **turning the lens on them.**

The screen flickered, illuminating their faces in the dim light.

They looked like **hell.**

Dakota's shirt, **once gray, was now stained with grime, sweat, and streaks of something darker.** It clung to him, **damp and tattered, the fabric torn near the shoulder where he must have snagged it on something.** His arms were **smeared with dust and dirt,** bruises beginning to form along his elbows.

Lane didn't look much better. His shirt was originally black, but now it was **stiff with sweat, dust, and filth,** the edges fraying, a tear across the stomach revealing a glimpse of skin beneath. His knuckles were raw, his palms coated in a thin layer of **dirt and dried blood.** His face was **pale, streaked with sweat,** his dark hair sticking to his forehead in damp clumps.

Their eyes…

Dark circles hollowed them out.

Bloodshot veins traced through the whites, a mixture of exhaustion, stress, and the sheer mental toll of the night.

Lane adjusted the camera, letting it capture both of them in frame.

For a long moment, neither spoke.

Their chests rose and fell, their breathing uneven. The only sounds in the room were the **quiet hum of the camera, the distant creak of the old house settling, and their own ragged gasps.**

Finally, Dakota swallowed hard, his throat **dry, cracked.** He turned his head slightly, looking at Lane.

Lane didn't meet his eyes.

Instead, he just exhaled sharply, a bitter, breathless laugh escaping him as he leaned his head back against the wall.

"…We look like shit."

Dakota huffed, barely a chuckle. "**Yeah.**"

Under different circumstances, they might've laughed. But now?

Now, there was **nothing funny about it.**

Lane adjusted the camera one last time, the lens capturing both of them in frame. **This wasn't for the views anymore. This wasn't for the thrill of the adventure.**

This was their **last message.**

His fingers trembled as he pressed record.

Dakota took a slow, steady breath before speaking.

"If you're watching this... we didn't make it out."

The weight of his own words hit him immediately, **his throat tightening.**

"We just want to say thank you," Lane added, voice raw. "For watching, for supporting us through all of this. For being part of our journey."

Dakota swallowed hard, his fingers **digging into his knees.** "If anyone finds this camera, if you see this video... **get out.** Don't come looking for us. Don't try to be a hero. **Just leave.**"

A silence stretched between them, **heavy, suffocating.**

Then, **Lane broke first.** A breathy, tired laugh. "Damn, man. This is so messed up."

Dakota let out a weak chuckle, shaking his head. "Yeah... yeah, it is."

They sat there for a moment, both staring at the lens, their expressions unreadable.

Then, **they started reminiscing.**

"Remember our first trip?" Lane asked, glancing at Dakota. "That abandoned hotel?"

Dakota scoffed. "Dude, we thought that place was haunted just because the wind knocked over a chair."

Lane grinned, shaking his head. "And the asylum? We swore we heard whispers in that place."

"Turns out it was just a raccoon in the vents," Dakota muttered, a smirk pulling at his lips.

Lane exhaled through his nose, staring at the ceiling for a moment. His voice was quieter when he spoke next. **"This wasn't how it was supposed to go."**

Dakota didn't respond to that. Because what could he say?

He exhaled sharply, rubbing his hands over his face before lowering them. **This was the hardest part.**

"Mom, Dad…" Dakota started, his voice cracking slightly. "I love you guys. I'm sorry. I—I never meant for this to happen." He hesitated, his jaw clenching. "Bryan… look after them, okay?"

Lane swallowed. "Mom, Dad… I know I always said this was stupid, and that we had everything under control." His fingers curled into a fist in his lap. "Guess I was wrong." He huffed out a humorless laugh. "I love you guys. **I'm sorry.**"

For a moment, neither spoke.

Then Lane reached out, shutting off the camera. He set it beside him, the small red light flickering off.

The room felt **quieter.**

They leaned their heads back against the cold wall, **eyes closed.**

The silence stretched, unbroken—until Dakota spoke.

"…Hey." His voice was soft, almost hesitant. "I'm sorry. For snapping at you earlier. I just…" He trailed off, shaking his head. "You've always been my best friend."

Lane sighed, turning his head slightly toward Dakota. "Yeah. **Same.**" A pause. "I'm sorry, too. I always come up with stupid ideas."

Dakota let out a dry chuckle. "**Your ideas weren't stupid.**" He exhaled, shaking his head. "We just have no idea what we're dealing with."

Lane smirked weakly. "Fire's always the best route, right?"

A **hoarse, tired laugh** left Dakota's throat. "Damn right."

They sat there, letting exhaustion pull at them, **letting the moment settle.**

After a moment, Dakota **rummaged through his bag,** fingers blindly searching for anything useful. His fingertips brushed against plastic.

A **water bottle.**

Half-empty. Warm. But it was something.

He pulled it out, unscrewing the cap before handing it to Lane.

Lane took a few sips, the water barely quenching his parched throat, then passed it back.

Dakota finished off the last bit before **chucking the bottle to the side,** the empty plastic hitting the floor with a dull thud.

And for a few moments, **they just sat there.**

Waiting.

Dakota glances over at Lane. "What was your favorite one?" He asked.

Lane let his head lull to the side, eyes heavy with exhaustion as he glanced at Dakota. "Favorite what?"

Dakota gave a small shrug. "Out of all the places we explored... which one was your favorite?"

Lane was quiet for a moment, thinking. It felt strange to reflect on something so **normal** while they were stuck in a nightmare. But maybe that's why Dakota asked—**to remember something good.** Something that didn't involve running for their lives.

A slow smirk tugged at Lane's lips. "Probably the waterpark."

Dakota huffed a tired chuckle. "Dude, you almost broke your leg falling down that busted-ass slide."

"Yeah, but it was fun as hell." Lane grinned, nudging Dakota's shoulder with his own. "Tell me that wasn't the best one."

Dakota shook his head, smiling faintly. "I dunno, man. I still think the mall was better."

Lane raised a brow. "The one with the flooded food court?"

"Yeah. I mean, c'mon—it was eerie as hell. And that massive skylight? The way the light shined through all the overgrown plants? That place looked like something out of a movie."

Lane tilted his head, considering it. "Okay, yeah. That one was pretty cool."

The conversation **shouldn't have felt so easy.** It shouldn't have been this simple to **slip back** into old habits—talking about their adventures like they weren't trapped in an abandoned theme park with something hunting them.

But for a few seconds, **they weren't here.**

They were back in the mall, trudging through knee-high water, laughing as Lane almost slipped on algae-covered tile.

They were at the waterpark, standing at the top of the slide, daring each other to go first.

They were anywhere but here.

But then reality sank its claws back in.

The distant sound of **dripping water.** The cold, stale air pressing in around them.

They weren't in some forgotten mall or busted-up waterpark.

They were in Hollow Park.

And the Wraithform was still out there.

Chapter Ten

The scent of damp concrete and chlorine still clung to Dakota's memory. **That waterpark.** It had been one of their best—and most reckless—explorations.

Back then, the stakes were different.

No monsters. No running for their lives.

Just two idiots sneaking into a decaying waterpark, chasing that rush, that thrill of discovery.

The fence wasn't much of an obstacle. A section of the chain-link had already been peeled back, likely by other urban explorers before them. Dakota crouched and slipped through first, brushing dirt off his jeans as Lane followed.

They stood in silence for a moment, **taking it in.**

The waterpark stretched out before them, a skeleton of what it once was. Massive slides twisted through the air like the bones of some long-dead creature. The lazy river was nothing but cracked concrete, choked with weeds and murky rainwater. The main pool—once the heart of the park—was a gaping, empty basin littered with debris.

"Man..." Lane exhaled, pulling out his camera. "This is **insane.**"

Dakota smirked. "Told you it'd be worth it."

Lane panned the camera across the ruins, stepping forward with a boyish excitement. "Think any of the slides are still climbable?"

"Only one way to find out."

They picked their way through the wreckage, boots crunching over broken tiles and soggy brochures that had long since faded. Signs still clung to the fences, their bold, bright letters sun-bleached and peeling.

"Welcome to Aqua Paradise!"

The irony wasn't lost on either of them.

They reached the slide tower—a massive structure of rusted steel, its stairs still intact but covered in layers of grime.

"You going up first?" Lane asked, motioning toward the stairs with a grin.

Dakota gave him a look. "What, so you can record me falling through and use it for views?"

"Absolutely."

Dakota rolled his eyes but started climbing anyway. Each step groaned beneath his weight, but they held. Lane followed, camera rolling, narrating their ascent like some low-budget documentary.

"Here we have Dakota Jones, professional dumbass, risking his life for the shot."

"Shut up and keep climbing."

When they finally reached the top, the view was **unreal.** The entire park stretched out around them, bathed in the glow of the setting sun. In the distance, they could see the city skyline, just barely visible through the trees.

For a moment, neither of them spoke.

Then Lane stepped forward, peering down the mouth of the tallest slide. "So... you thinking what I'm thinking?"

Dakota scoffed. "Hell no."

Lane shot him a mischievous grin. "C'mon, dude. How many people get to say they went down a **dead** water slide?"

"A lot, probably. And they all broke their legs doing it."

Lane waved off his concern. "We'll just go one at a time. If I die, you can put it in the thumbnail."

Before Dakota could protest, Lane **sat down and pushed off.**

"Lane, you—!"

Too late.

The slide had been dry for **years,** but Lane still managed to pick up speed, his whooping laughter echoing through the empty park. Dakota rushed to the edge, gripping the railing as Lane's voice faded into the distance.

Then—**a loud thud.**

Silence.

Dakota's stomach **dropped.**

He bolted down the stairs, taking them two at a time. His boots slammed against the concrete as he sprinted toward the bottom of the slide, breath ragged with panic.

"Lane?"

Silence.

Then—**laughter.**

Dakota skidded to a stop, chest heaving. Lane was on his back in a shallow puddle, laughing so hard he could barely breathe.

"You—" Dakota pointed at him, rage and relief battling for dominance. "You're a fucking **moron.**"

Lane only grinned, still catching his breath. "That... was **awesome.**"

Dakota exhaled sharply, shaking his head as he extended a hand. "C'mon, dumbass."

Lane took it, hauling himself to his feet, soaked and grinning. "You gonna try it now?"

"Not a chance."

"Fair enough."

They stood there for a moment, the adrenaline still pumping through their veins.

Back then, it had been about **the adventure.** The rush of exploring places that time had forgotten.

They never imagined they'd end up in a place like **Hollow Park.**

Never imagined they'd be **running for their lives.**

But in that moment—laughing like idiots in the ruins of a waterpark—it was **simple.**

And they'd give anything to go back.

The air inside the abandoned mall had been **humid**, thick with the scent of standing water and rotting wood. It had been one of their **most exciting explorations yet**—an entire shopping center left to decay.

Getting in had been the hard part.

They had circled the perimeter for nearly an hour, finding every entrance **boarded up or welded shut.** It was clear that whoever owned the place didn't want anyone inside. But that had never stopped them before.

Their way in had been through a **partially collapsed loading dock**, where rain and time had warped the metal doors enough for them to squeeze through.

"This feels illegal," Lane had whispered as he ducked under the bent doorframe.

"Because it is," Dakota had muttered, sliding in after him.

Inside, the air had been **stagnant**, filled with the scent of **mildew, rust, and earth.**

The first thing they had seen?

The food court.

Or at least—what was **left** of it.

Nature had reclaimed it.

The ceiling had **partially collapsed**, allowing rainwater to flood the tiled floors. What had once been a bustling place of greasy burgers and overpriced coffee had become something else entirely—**a swamp.**

Weeds had burst through the cracks, vines crawling up shattered pillars. Tables and chairs had been **half-submerged** in the murky water, some flipped over, others barely standing. The neon signs of fast-food chains had faded, their letters barely legible. **"BURGER KING"** was missing half its lights, leaving only "B__GER __NG."

Lane had taken out his camera, panning across the scene.

"Alright, this is **insane.**"

Dakota had agreed. "I've never seen anything like this before."

The roof had gaped open above them, exposing the gray sky. Sunlight streamed through in patches, casting reflections over the water. Dragonflies and mosquitoes hovered in the damp air, the occasional frog croaking somewhere in the distance.

A full-on ecosystem inside a dead mall.

Lane had grinned, stepping carefully across the damp floor. "Dude, imagine camping here."

Dakota had snorted. "Yeah, until you get eaten alive by swamp mosquitos."

They had moved deeper, their boots sloshing through the shallow water, careful of broken glass and fallen debris.

Lane, always the first to test his luck, had stepped onto a **patch of algae-covered tiles.**

And promptly **slipped.**

His arms had flailed, the camera jerking wildly in his grip as he struggled to stay upright.

"Dude—**dude!**" His voice had pitched as he skidded, desperately grabbing at Dakota's arm.

Dakota, instead of helping, had **stepped back.**

With a smirk.

"Don't you—**don't you dare let me fall!**"

Dakota had simply **watched** as Lane had **floundered,** slipping back and forth like a cartoon character on ice.

It had lasted a good five seconds.

Then—**Lane had caught his balance.**

He had straightened, brushing himself off, before glaring at Dakota.

"You're a terrible friend."

Dakota had only shrugged. "I was ready to film you hitting the ground. That would've been great content."

Lane had rolled his eyes, but a grin had tugged at his lips. "Next time, you're going first."

They had continued on, making their way toward the mall's **centerpiece**—the old **carousel.**

It had sat at the heart of the mall, once the pride of the entire place.

The colors had faded, the once-glossy horses **cracked and peeling.** Some were missing **eyes,** others had been covered in graffiti.

The metal poles had rusted, corroded by time and weather. The platform itself had **tilted slightly**, like it could collapse at any moment.

Dakota had walked up to one of the horses, brushing dust from its chipped surface. "Man, this must've been something back in the day."

Lane had set up his camera on a **makeshift tripod**, stepping onto the carousel's creaking floor.

"I wonder if it still works," he had muttered, pressing his hand against the ride's central column.

Dakota had raised a brow. "You wanna turn it on?"

Lane had grinned. "No. I wanna **spin it manually.**"

Dakota had blinked. "That's—okay, that's actually kinda genius."

And so they had tried.

With both of them **pushing**, the carousel had **groaned** under their weight, the rusted gears resisting at first. But after a few moments—

It had **moved.**

Slowly.

Creaking and shrieking like something out of a horror movie.

Lane had immediately **jumped onto one of the horses**, raising a triumphant fist. "Hell yeah!"

Dakota had laughed, stepping onto the ride, balancing between two horses as the carousel **dragged itself into motion.**

For a few moments, they had felt like **kids again.**

Lane had stood up, holding onto a rusted pole as the carousel **lurched forward** in slow, groaning circles.

"This is actually kinda cool," Dakota had admitted.

"See? You doubted me!" Lane had shot him a smug grin, adjusting his stance as the ride continued its sluggish rotation.

But then—

A loud snap.

Lane had yelped as the horse he was riding **broke free from its mount, tilting violently forward.**

"Oh—shit, shit, shit—"

He had **jumped off** just before the whole thing had collapsed sideways, hitting the platform with a loud **bang.**

Dust had burst into the air.

Dakota had doubled over **laughing.**

Lane had coughed, waving a hand in front of his face. "Alright, **maybe** that was a bad idea."

"You almost died."

"But it was **so worth it.**"

They had ended their exploration at the old **cinema,** where the floors had been covered in a thick layer of **dust and torn-up carpet.**

The projectors had still been there—massive, ancient things coated in grime.

Lane had stepped onto the **stage beneath the blank screen,** clearing his throat dramatically.

"Dear guests," he had called, voice echoing through the empty space. "Welcome to the world's most **exclusive** movie experience."

Dakota had rolled his eyes, but he had played along.

"What's showing tonight?"

Lane had gestured grandly. "Only the greatest cinematic masterpiece of all time—**Shrek 2.**"

Dakota had **snorted**. "Solid choice."

Lane had then **flopped down into one of the theater seats,** kicking his feet up on the dusty armrest. "Man, I could actually chill here for a while."

Dakota had sat beside him, exhaling as he glanced around the dark, abandoned space.

"You know…" he had murmured. "This one might be my favorite."

Lane had smiled.

"Yeah. **Me too.**"

That had been **one of the best nights of their lives.**

No fear.

No danger.

Just two best friends, exploring the ruins of a world that had been left behind.

Chapter Eleven

The silence sat heavy between them, stretching through the dark corners of the empty house.

The air was **stale**, thick with the lingering scent of old wood and dust. The only sound was their **breathing**—uneven, ragged.

Lane shifted slightly, his shoulder brushing against Dakota's.

"If we make it out of this," Lane murmured, his voice barely above a whisper, "we're going into the film business."

Dakota let out a slow breath, tilting his head back against the cold wall.

A smile threatened to tug at his lips. It was small, barely there—but it was real.

"Found footage?" he asked. His voice was hoarse, his throat raw from running, from screaming.

Lane huffed a quiet laugh, nodding. "Yeah."

A beat of silence. Then another.

For a moment, **they weren't in Hollow Park.**

They weren't being hunted. They weren't sitting in the dark, covered in sweat and dirt and god-knows-what else.

For a moment, it was just the two of them, planning their next big idea.

Just like before.

Dakota swallowed, feeling the exhaustion settle deeper in his bones. He was **so damn tired.**

Not just physically.

His **mind** was tired. His **heart** was tired. The weight of everything pressed on his chest, the fear curling around his ribs like something alive.

He wanted to believe they'd make it out.

But that thing—**the Wraithform**—was still out there.

It was **always out there.**

And even though they had put distance between themselves and that scream, the terror still clung to him, burrowed deep in his skin.

It wasn't just fear. It was **dread**.

Like an invisible hand gripping his spine, whispering that no matter how far they ran, it would **find them again.**

But right now—**right now, he wasn't running.**

Right now, Lane was beside him, talking about movies, talking about the future—like they had one.

"You think we'd be good at it?" Dakota asked, his voice softer now.

Lane leaned his head back, letting out a long breath. "Hell yeah. We've got experience. We know what works. We know what's scary."

Dakota chuckled under his breath. "Yeah. Firsthand."

They both sat in silence for a moment, staring into the darkness ahead of them.

Dakota let his mind drift.

What if they did make it out?

What if, by some miracle, they escaped this nightmare and left Hollow Park behind?

He pictured them in some **tiny, messy apartment,** editing footage, drinking too much coffee, arguing over scripts.

He pictured them on set, directing actors, designing scenes, **bringing their visions to life.**

He could see it.

He could feel it.

And for the first time since stepping foot in Hollow Park, he felt a flicker of **hope.**

"You know," Dakota murmured, shifting slightly, "I always thought you were full of shit when you talked about this stuff."

Lane scoffed. "I am full of shit."

Dakota let out a quiet laugh, shaking his head. "Nah. Not about this."

Lane was quiet for a moment.

Then, he exhaled through his nose, a tired, small smile playing on his lips.

"Guess we just gotta make it out, huh?"

Dakota nodded.

"Yeah," he said. "We do."

They sat there, their bodies **aching**, their nerves **fried**, but for the first time in hours, the fear didn't feel so suffocating.

Because they had a future.

They just had to fight for it.

The two sat there in silence, the weight of the situation pressing down on them. After a beat, Lane broke the silence. "Son of a bitch. Dakota, do you have your phone?"

Dakota perked up, immediately slapping his hands over his face. He was kicking himself inside. Of all the things to forget, he'd left the one thing that could save them.

Lane always left his phone in the van. Not for any real reason—he just never remembered to grab it. Dakota, on the other hand, always kept his phone on him, tucked away in his bag, just in case something went wrong. But now, in the middle of everything, he hadn't even thought about it.

He fumbled through his bag, heart racing. A few seconds later, he pulled it out. He pressed the power button. 10% battery. That spark of hope flickered.

Until he looked at the signal—no bars.

Lane glanced at him, his voice barely audible. "It doesn't matter. 911 always goes through. I don't get how, but it does."

Dakota quickly dialed 911. The line rang twice before the operator's voice crackled through. "911, what's your emergency?"

Without thinking, Dakota blurted out, "We're in Hollow Park. We're being chased. There's something in the park."

"Slow down," the operator said, her voice calm but firm. "Start over. What's going on?"

Dakota sucked in a breath. He knew it sounded insane, but he had no choice now. "We snuck in. We just wanted to see what was left... but we found something. Something... it's hunting us."

He rushed through the details—about the paperwork, the security logs, the monster. "There's something here. A monster. It's after us."

The operator was quiet for a moment, then asked, "Have you taken any drugs or substances today?"

Dakota's temper flared. "What? No! It's real! We've got video—"

"Okay, okay," the operator interrupted, her voice trying to stay calm. "I'm sending units now. They should be there in thirty minutes. Stay on the line."

Before she could say more, the phone went dead.

Dakota **stared at the dead phone** in his hands, his fingers still gripping it like if he held on tight enough, the screen might flicker back to life. But it didn't.

The last thread of connection to the outside world—**gone.**

His stomach twisted. His chest felt tight. They had gotten through. **The cops were coming.** But **thirty minutes?** In this place, **thirty minutes felt like a lifetime.**

"Dakota?" Lane's voice was quiet. Cautious.

Dakota let out a shaky breath and tossed the useless phone onto the ground beside him. He leaned his head back against the cold wall, staring at the ceiling of the abandoned house. "Battery died."

Lane exhaled through his nose. "Of course it did."

They sat in silence for a moment, both of them processing the weight of the situation.

Lane shifted, rubbing a hand down his grimy face before resting his arms on his knees. "Okay," he finally said. "So we just... stay put."

Dakota turned his head slightly to look at him. "You think staying in one place is a good idea?"

Lane shrugged. "Well, **running around hasn't exactly been working out for us, has it?**"

Dakota clenched his jaw but didn't argue. He was **tired.** More tired than he had ever been in his life. His muscles ached, his lungs still burned from running, and his throat felt **raw** from all the dust and dry air. His brain was screaming at him to shut down, to **stop moving** and just let his body rest.

But at the same time… something deep in his gut wouldn't let him relax.

"It knows we're here," Dakota muttered.

Lane didn't respond at first. His gaze was distant, lost in thought. Finally, he spoke. "Yeah. It knows."

Another beat of silence.

Dakota ran a hand through his hair. It was **coated in sweat and grime,** sticking to his forehead in clumps. "We just have to last until the cops get here."

Lane let out a dry, humorless chuckle. "And then what? You think they're gonna roll up in their squad cars, guns blazing, and take this thing out? It **ripped a guy in half, Dakota.** A whole-ass person."

Dakota didn't have an answer for that.

Because Lane was right.

Even if the cops showed up, **what the hell were they supposed to do?**

The thought settled like a heavy weight in Dakota's chest.

"We're getting out of here," he finally said, more to convince himself than anything else. "We just have to be smart about it."

Lane gave him a look, skeptical but not dismissive. "Smart, huh?"

Dakota nodded. "Yeah. We stay quiet. We stay low. **And if it finds us, we run.**"

Lane let out a slow breath before leaning his head back against the wall, staring at the ceiling. "I fucking hate this place."

Dakota let out a small, tired chuckle. "Yeah, me too."

The two sat there, breathing in the stillness of the abandoned house, waiting.

Waiting for help.

Waiting for something to happen.

Waiting for the nightmare to be over.

The air inside the abandoned house was **still.** Stale. The only sounds were the distant creaks of the rotting wood and the soft, uneven breaths of the two sitting against the wall.

Dakota kept his eyes closed, **just for a moment longer.** He could feel the exhaustion pressing down on him like a weight, dragging him deeper into the void of fatigue. His body begged for rest, but his mind wouldn't shut off. His thoughts were racing, tangled in everything they had seen, everything they had done, everything that was still coming.

Then, **he heard it.**

A whisper. **Lane's voice.**

"Daaakotaa…"

It was quiet, drawn out, **unnatural.** The way it carried on the air sent a shiver crawling up Dakota's spine.

He didn't open his eyes. Didn't move. His pulse picked up just a little.

"Why the hell are you saying my name like that?" he muttered, his voice barely above a breath.

Lane didn't respond.

Dakota let the silence stretch for another few seconds before finally cracking his eyelids open. His gaze flickered over to Lane.

Lane was **already staring at him.**

Eyes wide.

Face pale beneath the layers of dirt and sweat.

Something was wrong.

"That wasn't me," Lane whispered.

A chill ran down Dakota's back, but he barely had time to process it before **the voice came again.**

"Dakota…"

It was closer.

His stomach **dropped.**

His breath caught in his throat as his body tensed, his muscles screaming to move, to run—but he couldn't. He was **frozen.**

Lane slowly turned his head toward the door. Dakota followed his gaze, his hands pressing into the floor, every nerve in his body on edge.

Silence.

Then—

Something creaked outside.

A slow, deliberate sound, like weight shifting on an old wooden floor.

Neither of them spoke. **Neither of them breathed.**

The whisper came again, this time from right outside the house.

"Dakota…"

It was his voice now.

Perfectly replicated.

Mocking.

Calling.

The blood drained from Dakota's face. His chest tightened as his heartbeat pounded in his ears.

Lane turned back to him, his voice barely a breath.

"…What the fuck do we do?"

Lane's hands were shaking as he reached for the camera, fingers barely able to grasp it. The weight of it felt different now—**heavier.** Not just the physical weight, but the sheer gravity of what it held. Footage that might be the only proof of what was happening. Footage that, if they didn't make it out, would be the only thing left of them.

Dakota, moving just as carefully, picked up his phone and slipped it back into his bag. **Slow. Deliberate.** Like one wrong move could cost them their lives. Because it **could.**

They didn't speak. Didn't even look at each other. They both knew.

They had to move.

They stood at the same time, cautious, silent. The air was thick, pressing down on them like an invisible weight. The voices in the house hadn't stopped.

They were getting worse.

At first, the whispers were soft, almost lulling—**Dakota… Lane… Come here…**

But now?

Now, they were **furious.**

The words twisted into something **ugly, violent, screaming.**

"DAKOTA!"

"LANE!"

The names were being spat at them, over and over, rattling through the walls, vibrating through the rotted wood.

Lane swallowed hard, his breath hitching as his grip tightened around the camera. Dakota turned his head, his gaze landing on the animatronics in the center of the room. **The cartoon characters.**

Their frozen, wide-eyed faces stared blankly forward, stuck in time, the remnants of something once meant to be **fun.**

Dakota's fingers curled around **the heavy metal pie** clutched in one of their stiff, mechanical hands. The edges were dulled from years of neglect, but the weight? The weight was **real.**

"Help me," he muttered.

Lane rushed over, grabbing the other side. His pulse was hammering against his ribs, adrenaline numbing the sting in his scraped palms.

They yanked.

The rusted bolts groaned, metal bending.

YANK.

A sharp **snap** echoed through the small room as the piece finally **broke free.**

Dakota turned toward the back of the house. The only thing standing between them and an escape was the **plexiglass window.**

Without hesitation, he lifted the metal plate and **hurled** it.

CRASH.

The window **shattered.**

Before they could move, **a shadow fell across the room.**

Both of them snapped their heads toward the front door.

A shape.

Tall.

Wrong.

It peered through the crack in the door, stretching unnaturally, the frame too thin, the angles all **wrong.**

Lane's breath caught in his throat. **It was here.**

No time.

Dakota shoved at the shards still clinging to the edges of the window frame, pushing them away, slicing open his palm in the process. He didn't feel it.

Lane was already moving. **Crawling through first.**

Dakota followed, squeezing through, the jagged plastic digging into his skin as he slipped out **into the back of the house.**

The voices didn't stop.

They **grew.**

And then—

The door creaked open.

They ran.

Their breaths were ragged, chests heaving, legs burning, but they **ran.**

Lane risked a glance over his shoulder.

It was still there.

The Wraithform.

Following them. Moving with that same **unnatural, uneven gait.** Its long, skeletal limbs jerked with each step, as if its body didn't quite understand how to function. But no matter how **slow** it seemed, no matter how **fast** they ran, it never fell far behind.

Every twist. Every turn.

It was **still with them.**

Just **staggering. Watching. Waiting.**

Dakota felt his pulse in his throat, his ears, his skull. He focused on running, on **not looking back.** But even without seeing it, he could **feel it.** That heavy, crushing sense of being **hunted.**

Lane gasped beside him, pointing—**Western Wonderland.**

The faded wooden sign stood crooked, paint peeling, the edges gnawed away by time and rot. It loomed ahead, marking the entrance to the **abandoned Wild West-themed section of the park.**

They bolted past it.

And then—

The Wraithform stopped.

Just like that.

No more uneven movements. No more **staggering.**

It just **stood there.**

Watching them.

Dakota and Lane didn't slow down to question it. They **kept going**, barreling through the dust-covered street, past the broken wagon props and faded storefronts, until they saw it—

The saloon.

The old wooden doors hung crooked on their hinges, swaying slightly as they shoved through, collapsing against the bar inside.

They **gasped for air.**

The room smelled of rotting wood and dust. The floor creaked beneath them, every movement stirring up years of grime.

Dakota finally **looked down**—and noticed the deep **gash** across his palm. Blood had already smeared along his fingers, dark and sticky.

He exhaled through clenched teeth and grabbed the torn sleeve of his already-ruined shirt, ripping it the rest of the way before **wrapping it around his hand.** The fabric stained instantly, but he pulled it tight, securing it the best he could.

Lane just **watched.**

His hands were still trembling. His pulse still hammering. He didn't say anything, but the way he was staring said enough.

What now?

Chapter Twelve

The **crash** behind them was loud, sharp, and wrong.

Dakota and Lane **jolted**, their bodies reacting before their minds could catch up. Their heads snapped toward the source of the noise, eyes landing on—

The bartender.

He wasn't a **mannequin** anymore.

He was **human**. Or at least… he **looked** human.

The glass he had been eternally polishing before now lay in shards at his feet, reflecting the dim, dusty light like tiny knives. His hands—no longer stiff and lifeless—rested on the bar as if he had just set them there.

But something was **wrong**.

His **eyes**.

There was no light in them, no recognition. They were **empty**. Hollow. Staring straight through them like he wasn't really looking at them at all.

And then there was his **smile**.

It stretched too **wide**, the corners of his lips pulling unnaturally. The **teeth** behind them were too **big**, too **white**, too **perfect**, like something carved out of porcelain and jammed into a mouth not meant to hold them.

He didn't **speak**.

He just **stared**.

Dakota's breathing shallowed. Lane clenched his jaw. They both took **one step back**.

The bartender **didn't move**.

Another step.

Still nothing.

Don't turn your back. That's what every instinct was screaming.

They moved **slowly**, never breaking eye contact, retreating toward the saloon doors. Their footsteps were **too loud** against the creaky wood, their own breathing **too sharp** in the silence.

The bartender just kept **smiling.**

Kept **staring.**

Dakota and Lane finally backed outside, their boots hitting the **dirt trail.** They exhaled—

And then **froze.**

There was a **crowd.**

A **gathering of people.**

All dressed in **1800s attire.**

They lined the street, standing outside the old storefronts, on the steps of the sheriff's office, by the broken-down wagons. Their clothes were dusty and tattered, like they had been standing there for **centuries.**

None of them moved.

None of them spoke.

They just **stared.**

Lane and Dakota **glanced at each other.**

Dakota's face was pale, his shoulders sagging. The look in his eyes—**defeat.**

Lane could feel it. **That creeping weight.** The exhaustion. The hopelessness. The idea of just… stopping. Letting it **take them.**

And maybe for a second, he almost gave in to it too.

But they **couldn't.**

They had to get out.

They had to tell people.

They had to bring **closure** to all those families.

Lane **grabbed Dakota's arm**, yanking him out of his daze.

"Come on!"

They ran.

Footsteps pounding. Hearts hammering.

The crowd didn't **chase** them. They didn't **move.**

They just **watched.**

The two of them bolted toward the **Gold Rush roller coaster**, their boots kicking up dust. The wooden tracks twisted above them, faded paint peeling from the supports.

The stairs to the **loading platform** loomed ahead.

Lane took them **two at a time**. Dakota right behind him.

Their **footsteps echoed**, swallowed by the silence.

Dakota and Lane **vaulted** over the air gate, their feet **slamming** onto the wooden coaster track with a hollow *thud*.

Dakota didn't hesitate—his hands **dug into his bag**, fingers fumbling until they closed around the flashlight. He yanked it out, **clicked it on**, and the beam **cut through the darkness.**

They **ran.**

The track was uneven beneath them, warped from time and neglect. The air was thick with dust and the smell of rotting wood. They sprinted toward the **first cave**, the jagged opening swallowing the track in shadow.

Then—

A sound.

Metal clanging.

High-pitched, sharp, **unnerving.**

Dakota and Lane **slowed**, their breaths heaving, eyes darting to each other.

The sound was getting **closer.**

A rhythmic *CLANG. CLANG. CLANG.*

They **crept forward.** Every step was **deliberate**, their bodies tense.

They turned the **first bend.**

Dakota lifted the flashlight—

And **froze.**

The **miners.**

The **statues** that had once stood frozen along the walls, permanently mid-swing with their pickaxes… they were **moving.**

The figures—dressed in old-fashioned mining gear, their faces carved into blank expressions—were **swinging away** at the cave walls, **chipping at nothing.** The sound of metal against rock rang through the tunnel, **sharp and hollow.**

But it wasn't the movement that made Dakota's stomach **drop.**

It was the **eyes.**

Every single one of them had turned their heads. **heads.**

Their dead, **hollow** eyes were locked onto **Dakota and Lane.**

CLANG.

CLANG.

CLANG.

They didn't move toward them. They didn't **chase.**

They just… **watched.**

Dakota swallowed, forcing himself to **breathe.** Lane clenched his fists, shifting uncomfortably. The weight of those **stares** was unbearable, like needles pricking into their skin.

But they had to **keep moving.**

They **walked.**

Slow, deliberate steps.

The miners **kept swinging.** But their **heads** never turned away.

That feeling—the one that had been lingering in their **bones** since this nightmare started—**intensified.**

That overwhelming, suffocating **sensation of being watched.**

They **knew** they were being watched.

Lane let out a breath, shaking his head as he took in the sight of the miners still swinging their pickaxes, their hollow eyes locked onto them. His voice was quieter than usual, but he still tried to keep his usual edge.

"Fire doesn't seem so bad now, does it?"

Dakota didn't answer.

He just **kept moving.**

Lane let out a small huff, but he didn't push it. He knew when Dakota **shut down,** when he was too deep in his own head to respond. That wasn't a good thing. They needed to stay focused, keep their minds sharp. If Dakota was slipping into silence, it meant things were getting worse.

They kept moving **down the track.**

The air inside the cave was heavy, pressing down on them. The sound of their **own breathing** filled the space, mixing with the distant *clang* of pickaxes behind them.

Then, the track opened up.

And Dakota felt his stomach **drop.**

They were **back** where they had stopped hours earlier—right before the **hill.**

A steep incline that loomed above them, the wooden supports **creaking softly** under an invisible weight.

Where could they go?

What could they do?

Dakota turned to Lane, and he could tell by his expression that he was thinking the same thing. They were out of options.

Then, they heard it.

That *sound.*

The low, wheezing **groans.**

The wet, **labored breathing.**

It was **close.**

Dakota barely had time to react before Lane turned to him, **eyes wide.** They didn't need words. There was **no choice.**

Up.

Dakota gave Lane a **subtle nod.** Lane swallowed hard, his Adam's apple bobbing, and then they both **started climbing.**

Each step was agonizing. The incline was **steeper than it looked,** and the coaster track wasn't built to be walked on. Their feet slid against the smooth metal rails, the gaps between the wooden planks making every step feel **precarious.**

But they **kept going.**

The further they climbed, the more the park below seemed to **shrink.**

By the time Dakota reached the top, his head was **spinning.**

He made the mistake of **looking down.**

The world seemed to **tilt beneath him.** The sheer height sent a **wave of dizziness** washing over his body, his stomach twisting into a knot. His fingers instinctively **tightened** around the metal bar at the peak, knuckles going white.

Lane **stood next to him,** his **eyes clenched shut.** His hands were shaking slightly as he gripped the railing.

"You know I hate heights." His voice was tight, strained.

Dakota swallowed, finally forcing himself to tear his eyes away from the **drop below.** He turned to Lane, his own grip **just as tight.**

"Yeah… me too."

He took a breath, forcing himself to **look ahead.**

The drop wasn't as steep as some coasters—it led into a slow, curving descent. But it was still a long way down.

And behind them…

That **thing** was coming.

Dakota and Lane turned back.

And there it was.

The **Wraithform.**

It stood at the **top of the hill**, looming above them, its unnatural frame silhouetted against the faint glow of the moon breaking through the stormy clouds. Its chest **rose and fell heavily**, its entire body moving with each **labored breath**. The sound of it was **loud** in the still air—wet, raspy, almost a *cry*. Like it was in pain.

Or like it was **mourning.**

Dakota and Lane **froze**, staring up at it.

The torn flesh. The unnaturally thin limbs. The deep, hollow **voids** where its eyes should have been.

And yet… behind all of it…

It was *almost* **human**.

That was the worst part.

That nagging question **clawed at their minds**—where did this thing come from? What *happened* for something like this to exist? **What even was it?**

The Wraithform let out another **long, rattling groan.**

Lane **shuddered**, his fingers twitching slightly at his sides.

The thing **inhaled**—a deep, struggling, sucking breath—its whole body expanding as it filled its lungs.

Dakota's blood **ran cold.**

They knew what was coming.

"RUN!"

They didn't hesitate.

They **tore down the track,** their feet slamming against the old wooden planks, rattling the rails beneath them. The descent was **steeper than expected**, their bodies nearly **falling forward** as they fought to stay upright.

Behind them, the Wraithform **moved.**

It didn't run. It **staggered forward**, its uneven steps **slow**, deliberate—yet no matter how fast Dakota and Lane moved, it was never far **behind.**

The track twisted and dipped, stretching endlessly before them. Dakota's eyes **scanned the area**, frantically searching for an exit.

They needed a **low point.**

Somewhere to **jump.**

Somewhere that wouldn't **kill them**—or leave them **too broken** for the Wraithform to **finish them off.**

The sound of its **breathing** was growing closer.

Dakota's lungs burned. Lane **pushed ahead**, his eyes darting wildly.

Then—

"THERE!" Lane shouted.

Dakota followed his gaze.

About **thirty feet ahead**, the track **leveled out** before dipping again. If they could jump **there**—if they landed right—they *might* make it.

They had **no other choice.**

The **shriek** tore through the night, a sound so **inhumanly loud** it felt like the very air around them was **splitting apart.**

The **tracks rattled violently**, vibrating beneath their feet. The entire rollercoaster **groaned**, the rusted metal **screeching** in protest. Dakota and Lane stumbled, nearly **collapsing** under the force of the tremor.

But they couldn't stop.

"GO!" Dakota shouted.

They **jumped**.

The world **blurred** around them as they plummeted, their bodies **slamming** into the overgrown brush below. The wind was **knocked from their lungs**, but they didn't have time to recover.

The **shriek intensified**, growing **louder**—so loud it felt like it was coming from **inside their skulls**.

Then the **rollercoaster shook harder**, its decades-old structure finally **giving in** to the force of the Wraithform's scream.

Metal groaned. Wood cracked.

Then—

A **horrific collapse**.

Dakota and Lane **scrambled away**, forcing their aching bodies to move as the towering coaster **came crashing down**, pieces of metal and wood breaking apart, slamming into the earth with a sound that **echoed for miles**.

And at the center of it all—

The **Wraithform** fell with it.

Dakota turned, heart hammering, just in time to see the **monstrous figure disappear beneath the rubble**.

The dust and debris settled around them, a thick haze in the air.

Silence.

Only the sound of their **ragged breathing** remained.

Dakota and Lane sat there, muscles shaking, lungs burning.

Finally, Lane looked at Dakota. Dakota met his gaze.

No words were spoken.

Just that silent **question** hanging between them.

Was it over?

Was the **nightmare finally over?**

Chapter Thirteen

The night was **still**.

Dakota and Lane stood **motionless**, staring at the mound of **twisted metal and broken wood** that buried the Wraithform. The once towering coaster was now nothing more than **a heap of ruin**, the weight of it crushing whatever had lurked beneath its tracks.

Their bodies were **ragged**, every muscle **aching**, their lungs **burning** from exhaustion. Lane wiped a shaking hand across his sweat-slicked face, while Dakota exhaled slowly, trying to steady his racing heart.

This was it.

It was **finally over**.

Dakota turned to Lane, placing a **heavy, trembling hand** on his shoulder. Lane didn't speak, but the glance they shared was enough—they had survived.

With **slow, unsteady steps**, they **stumbled away** from the wreckage. Every inch of them screamed in protest, but they pushed forward, feet **dragging** through the overgrown pathways of Hollow Park.

Their minds raced, replaying the horrors they had endured. The **twisting corridors of illusions**, the **impossible figures**, the **monstrosity that stalked them through the ruins**. It should have killed them. **It almost did.**

But they had made it out.

They had won.

As they entered the **plaza**, the remnants of the park surrounded them—**lifeless, frozen in time**. The once-vibrant attractions stood **silent**, bathed in the eerie glow of the moon.

Dakota and Lane didn't stop.

They **forced themselves** forward, through the emptiness, towards the **hole in the fence**—their way out.

Lane crouched first, **lifting the broken section** just enough for Dakota to slide beneath. Then Dakota did the same for him.

When they were both on the other side, they hesitated.

Turning back, they took **one last look** at the **graveyard of Hollow Park**.

The decaying rides.
The shattered remnants of what once was.
The **place that nearly consumed them.**

The air was still.

No voices.
No movement.
No sign of life.

Finally, they turned away.

With **staggering steps**, they made their way **down the old service road**, leaving **Hollow Park behind**.

The van sat exactly where they had left it.

Dakota and Lane stood still for a moment, **just staring at it**—this one familiar, grounded piece of their reality. It was **dirty**, splattered with dried mud and leaves from the long-abandoned lot. The windshield was covered in a thin layer of dust, and the once-shiny blue paint was dulled beneath the grime. But it was **there. Real.**

Lane was the first to move. His legs felt like **sandbags**, heavy and sluggish, but he forced himself forward. His fingers fumbled with the handle before he slid the side door open and **hauled himself inside**. He didn't bother finding a seat. Instead, he collapsed against the back wall, letting his **aching body** sink into the hard metal floor. His breathing was unsteady—**not quite a sob, but not far from one either.**

Dakota hesitated, his **tired eyes** sweeping the darkened treeline, as if expecting something to emerge from the shadows. He knew it was over. It had to be. **It was buried.** Yet, some part of him refused to believe it. His fingers twitched against his thigh, waiting for the world to twist around him again, for reality to **fracture** like it had so many times before.

But nothing happened.

Just the **wind**. Just the **distant hoot of an owl**.

He climbed in, shutting the door behind him with **a soft but final thud**. Then he let himself slide down, his back pressed against the cool metal, his legs sprawled out in front of him. He dropped his head back with a heavy **thump**, staring at the ceiling.

For the first time in what felt like **an eternity**, they let out **a long, shaking sigh of relief.**

It was over.

They had survived.

The van smelled like old fast food wrappers and stale air, but it was **safe**. The walls weren't shifting, the ground wasn't falling away beneath them, and there were no dead-eyed figures **watching from the shadows**.

Dakota finally moved, groaning as he pushed himself to his feet. His whole body **protested**, muscles sore from running, from falling, from fighting against something **they never should have found**.

He slid into the **driver's seat**, fingers wrapping around the steering wheel. His knuckles were **raw**, a faint red stain still seeping through the makeshift bandage around his palm. His heart was still pounding, the echoes of adrenaline not yet fading.

The key was still in the ignition.

He turned it.

The engine **roared to life**, cutting through the **oppressive silence**. The sound **grounded him**, reminding him that this—**this moment**—was real. Not an illusion. Not a trick.

Lane let out a **soft, breathless laugh** from the back. **Disbelieving. Relieved.**

Dakota reached for the radio, turning the volume dial up just enough to let **the music fill the van**. The soft hum of a familiar song washed over them, pushing back the lingering echoes of the park's haunting sounds.

Without another word, he put the van into gear, pulling out onto the **service road**. The headlights cut through the night as they drove toward the **main road**, leaving **Hollow Park—and everything inside it—behind.**

The hum of the engine was the only sound Dakota focused on as he pulled onto the **main road**, the wheels leaving the rough service path behind. The instant change in atmosphere was almost **jarring**—the distant glow of streetlights, the rhythmic passing of headlights from other cars, the quiet **hum of civilization**.

They were back.

He didn't even consider going back to the motel. What was the point? **A shower, a bed, a few hours of sleep?** None of that would erase what they had just been through. It wouldn't scrub away the lingering unease that clung to his skin, the feeling that something could still be watching them, waiting for them to **let their guard down**.

They just needed to **get home**.

His hands tightened on the steering wheel, his fingers sore and stiff from the night's events. The faint ache in his bandaged palm pulsed with his heartbeat, but he ignored it. His body was running on **autopilot**, exhausted but refusing to shut down.

A glance in the **rearview mirror** caught his attention.

Lane was slumped against the back of the van, his head tilted at an awkward angle, his mouth slightly open. He was completely **out**, his body finally giving in to the exhaustion that had been **crushing them both for hours**. The slow, steady rise and fall of his chest was **the only reassurance Dakota needed**—they were safe enough now for one of them to let go.

Dakota looked back at the road.

Six hours.

That's how long it would take to get home. But time didn't matter. The sooner they were out of this **godforsaken town**, the better.

His eyes flicked up to the rearview mirror again—this time, at the darkened road behind them. **Nothing but headlights fading in the distance.**

He exhaled, gripping the wheel just a little tighter.

They weren't wasting any time.

The road ahead had stretched endlessly, dark and empty, save for the occasional flash of headlights from passing cars. The hum of the tires against the asphalt had been the only sound filling the silence—until the **radio crackled**.

Dakota barely noticed it at first, static bleeding into the music. He reached forward, twisting the knob to shut it off. **Silence was fine.** After everything, it was welcome.

Then he heard it.

"Dakota."

His grip on the steering wheel tightened. His **own name**, spoken in a voice he knew better than his own.

Lane's voice.

But it hadn't come from the back of the van. It had come from the radio.

"Dakota, please!"

His stomach dropped. His fingers flew to the knob again, turning the radio **off**—but the voice **didn't stop**.

"Dakota, help me!"

The sound grew **louder**, rising in desperation. It was **distorted**, like it was being stretched and torn apart by the static.

Then it turned into a scream.

Dakota's foot **slammed** on the brakes.

The van skidded, tires screeching against the road. His chest **lurched** forward, the seatbelt locking against his body. For a second, his heart pounded so hard it drowned out every other noise.

Then—**silence.**

His hands trembled as he lifted his eyes to the **rearview mirror**.

Lane was gone.

The blood drained from Dakota's face. His breath caught in his throat.

He threw the van into park, nearly tearing the handle off in his rush to get out. The cool night air **slammed** against his skin as he wrenched the door open.

"Lane?" His voice cracked, raw with panic.

Nothing.

He yanked open the side door, searching the back of the van. **Empty.**

"No, no, no—" His pulse **roared** in his ears as he spun, scanning the road, the tree line, the empty stretch of highway. "Lane!"

The only response was the whisper of the wind.

Then—

A **jolt.**

His eyes **snapped open**.

His back was pressed against damp earth. The air was thick, smelling of mildew and rot. The distant creak of Hollow Park's ruins surrounded him.

The **brush.** The overgrown weeds.

He was back.

Dakota's breath hitched. His hands dug into the dirt as he pushed himself up, the world tilting around him.

"Dakota!"

The voice rang out **again**—this time, **not through the radio**.

It was **real**.

Lane was out there. **And he was in trouble.**

Dakota didn't think. He didn't hesitate.

He **ran.**

Dakota's lungs burned, his legs barely keeping up with his own desperation as he **chased the sound** of Lane's cries.

"Dakota! Help me!"

The voice cut through the night, raw and terrified, but then—

Silence.

Dakota skidded to a stop, his breath ragged, heart hammering so hard it shook his ribs. The world around him felt **too still**, like the park itself was holding its breath.

"No, no, no, no—" His voice wavered as he spun in circles, eyes darting through the darkness, searching, **pleading** for any sign of Lane.

But there was nothing. **He was gone.**

Dakota's entire body felt **numb**, but his mind was racing. He knew where Lane was being taken.

Future Island.

It was on the **other side** of the park.

There was no way he'd make it in time.

That thing—**that monster**—was going to kill his friend, and there was nothing he could do to stop it.

His stomach twisted violently, his vision blurring as dread clawed at his chest.

Then, something inside him **snapped**.

His hands dove into his bag, fingers shaking as he grabbed the **camera**. If he couldn't stop it, then at the very least—

The world needed to know.

They needed to see this place for what it really was. **They needed to know the truth.**

Dakota flipped the camera on, the lens flickering to life. His own panicked face reflected in the screen for a split second before he turned it towards the path ahead.

The red **REC** light burned like a warning in the darkness.

With one last deep breath, Dakota **took off running**.

Dakota's breath came in sharp, painful gasps as he stumbled into the **plaza**, his head spinning. His mind was a storm—**he couldn't think straight**—but it didn't matter. He had to keep moving.

The path to **Future Island** stretched ahead, dark and winding, but just as he made his first step—

"Hey, kid! Stop!"

The sudden **shout** sent a jolt through his body. He twisted around, searching for the source.

Then, he saw them.

Red and blue lights cut through the darkness, flashing against the cracked pavement and long-abandoned buildings.

The cops.

Dakota watched in shock as **officers moved to the entrance**, their figures illuminated by the swirling lights. One of them pulled out **bolt cutters**, gripping the chain that sealed the gate shut.

Clang!

The chain hit the ground, uncoiling like a dead snake. The officers wasted no time, rushing in, their voices sharp, commanding.

"Stop! Hands where we can see them!"

But Dakota **couldn't stop.**

Lane was still out there.

A part of him—a small, awful part—thought, *Maybe if the cops go in first, the Wraithform will go after them.*

The thought made his stomach twist in guilt, but he didn't have time to dwell on it.

If the monster was distracted, **maybe—just maybe—Lane would have a chance.**

Dakota turned, **bolting down the path** to Future Island.

"Stop, kid!" one of the officers yelled.

Footsteps pounded behind him.

They were **chasing him.**

But Dakota didn't care.

His eyes locked onto the **Dome building** in the distance, its shadow stretching across the cracked pavement like a gaping maw.

He ran faster.

The officers were shouting behind him, but Dakota didn't stop.

"My friend is in trouble!" he yelled over his shoulder, his voice hoarse, desperate.

The **Dome building** loomed ahead, a hulking silhouette against the night. **Lane was in there.** He had to be.

Dakota **sprinted through the entrance**, barely noticing the cops closing in behind him. His chest burned, but he pushed forward, his heart pounding so hard it was deafening.

Then—he saw it.

The **metal trapdoor.**

It was **bent and warped**, the edges twisted like something had **ripped its way through**. The heavy **metal shelf** they had shoved on top of it earlier was now **mangled**, its legs snapped and crumpled to the side like a crushed insect.

Dakota's stomach dropped.

It got out.

He didn't hesitate. He lunged for the **stairwell**, nearly **tripping** over the uneven steps as he raced downward into the dark, damp space below. The air was thick, humid—it smelled of **mold and something rotten.**

Behind him, **thunderous footsteps** shook the staircase. The officers followed, their **boots clanking** against the metal, their voices sharp.

"Stop! Stop right there!"

"Kid, get back up here!"

Dakota ignored them. **Lane was down here somewhere.** He had to be.

The basement was **larger than he remembered**, stretching into an abyss of shadows. He gripped his **flashlight**, flicking it on, the beam slicing through the dark.

Nothing.

No movement. No sound. Just the distant **drip** of water leaking from overhead pipes.

His pulse **thundered** in his ears.

The officers spread out behind him, their **guns drawn**. Their breathing was heavy, uncertain. Then—

They saw it.

Their movements **slowed**, weapons lowering slightly as they took in the **room around them**.

The **discarded toys**, forgotten and broken, their **plastic faces smeared with something dark**.

The **walls and floor**, coated in dried **blood, thick stains smeared across the concrete** like something had been **dragged across it**.

And then—the **bones**.

Scattered across the floor. Some small. Some **too big to be animal bones**.

The officers didn't speak.

Their **faces paled** in the dim light. One of them **exhaled sharply**, his grip on his gun tightening.

Dakota could feel it—**the air had shifted**.

Like the room itself was **waiting for something**.

The **beam of a flashlight** cut through the dark, landing on Dakota's face.

"What the hell is this?" one of the officers demanded, his voice sharp, edged with something between confusion and fear.

Dakota didn't answer.

He just **kept walking**, stepping deeper into the room, the **stench of iron and decay** thick in the air, coating his throat like something tangible.

He knew.

It was already **too late.**

Then he heard it.

That **sickening sound.**

Ripping. Tearing. Wet, thick, **flesh peeling away** from bone.

Dakota froze. His **breath hitched**. His stomach twisted.

The officers moved in, their **guns steady, flashlights bouncing** off the grimy walls. Their boots crunched over **scattered debris**, shattered plastic, old splintered wood.

"Kid, don't move." One of them ordered, his tone hard but cracking at the edges.

Another officer reached for his **radio**, pressing the button with shaking fingers.

"Dispatch, we need immediate backup at Hollow Park. We have—" He hesitated, glancing at the **bones**, the **blood**. The **impossible nightmare unfolding around them.** *"We have an active crime scene. Requesting additional units, RA, and any available personnel."*

His voice faltered.

Somewhere in the dark—**the tearing sound stopped.**

A wet, heavy sound. Something **slapping against the floor** with a sickening finality.

The officers swung their flashlights **downward**—slowly, cautiously.

And then they saw **him.**

Or **what was left of him.**

Lane.

Dakota's **stomach twisted.** His throat clenched so tight he could barely breathe. **His vision blurred, darkened at the edges.** A scream built in his chest, but it wouldn't come out. His legs felt weak, barely holding him up.

Lane's **body**—if you could still call it that—was **mangled beyond recognition.** Torn flesh, exposed **bone glistening** under the harsh beams of light. His arms lay at unnatural angles, **ripped muscle** hanging in strips, his chest **caved in, hollow, emptied.** His face—his face wasn't even a face anymore, just **a ruined mess of red and bone.**

Dakota's knees nearly **buckled.** His chest heaved, stomach rolling violently. **The world spun.** His skin turned pale, **cold sweat** beading on his forehead. He wanted to look away, **but he couldn't.** He couldn't process what he was seeing.

This was Lane.

His best friend.

The person he had known **since childhood.** The person who had **laughed with him, explored abandoned buildings with him, stood beside him through everything.**

And now—now Lane was **nothing but pieces.**

His insides **churned.** His mouth filled with saliva, warning him he was about to vomit.

This wasn't real.

This couldn't be real.

But it was.

It was **too real.**

The officers reacted first, their training forcing them to **push past their horror.** They raised their guns, their voices sharp and commanding, barking orders into the darkness.

"Police! Show yourself! Hands where we can see them! Walk out slowly, now!"

No response.

Just that **low groaning.** That **horrible, ragged, wheezing breath.**

It came from **everywhere and nowhere all at once.**

Then—**movement.**

From the **shadows,** something **emerged.**

The **flashlights** caught it—illuminating it in jagged, flickering beams.

And the officers hesitated.

Because **they had no idea what they were looking at.**

The **Wraithform** stood **fully upright.** Its massive, skeletal frame **dwarfed them**, its limbs too **long, too thin,** stretching in a way that **wasn't natural, wasn't human.**

It **breathed in, deeply,** its chest expanding, the sound **wet, rattling,** like something **rotting from the inside out.**

Dakota's mind **snapped between emotions.**

Terror. Rage. Disbelief. Loss. Nausea.

Nothing made sense. Nothing felt real. His body was locked in place, trembling, but his blood **boiled** at the same time.

"You..." he choked out, voice barely above a whisper. **A broken, shattered sound.**

The Wraithform's **sunken, black voids** locked onto him.

Dakota didn't feel like a person anymore.

He felt like **prey.**

And this thing—the **thing that had taken Lane, that had ripped him apart and tossed him aside like nothing**—was just standing there. **Watching him.**

His **pulse thundered** in his ears.

This was it.

This was the **truth.**

The monster was **real.**

The legend, the stories, the disappearances—**all of it.**

And now, finally, the world was about to see.

Gunfire **erupted**, the deafening cracks of bullets echoing through the underground chamber.

Dakota flinched at the sound, his breath coming in **ragged, uneven gasps.** The officers' bullets **hit their mark**, tearing **small, wet chunks** from the Wraithform's body—but it **wasn't enough.** The creature barely reacted, only **tilting its head, twitching in that unnatural way**, as if it was more intrigued than harmed.

Dakota's body **moved on its own**, his feet **shuffling backward.** He didn't take his eyes off the thing—not yet.

Not until he saw it **step forward.**

Not until he heard the **sickening crunch** of bones under its feet.

Lane's bones.

A fresh **wave of nausea** hit him, but **he didn't stop moving.** His instincts were screaming, his body begging him to run, to get out, to **survive.**

The officers continued **firing, shouting, cursing.** Then the first **scream** rang out.

Dakota didn't turn back.

Didn't look.

Didn't want to **see** what was happening to them.

Another scream. **Choking. Gurgling.**

Still, Dakota **kept walking.**

The sound of flesh **ripping.**

The echo of bones **snapping**.

His breath caught. **He couldn't stay here.**

His walk became a **jog**.

His jog became a **run**.

He sprinted up the stairs, leaving **the massacre behind him.** The air in the basement had been thick, suffocating, pressing against him like a weight. But as soon as he stepped outside, into the open, he felt the cold night air rush against his sweat-drenched skin. It did little to help the **tightness in his chest**.

His mind was blank—**numb**. His body moved on instinct, legs carrying him back toward the **plaza**.

The **officers had opened the gate**. He could escape. He could **finally leave this nightmare behind**.

His heart hammered as the entrance came into view, as he saw the squad cars parked just outside, the flashing **red and blue lights cutting through the night**.

Then he saw the **gate**.

Closed.

Locked.

The thick chain was **wrapped around the bars once again**, the heavy-duty padlock **snapped shut**.

Dakota **skidded to a stop**.

His breath hitched, his stomach sinking into a **pit of dread**.

"No..." he murmured, barely able to hear his own voice over the sound of his pounding heartbeat.

He stumbled forward, **gripping the metal fence**, rattling it with whatever strength he had left.

Nothing.

The Wraithform must have **locked it behind them**.

His eyes darted past the bars, to the **police cars, the open road just beyond them**.

So **close.**

So goddamn **close.**

Dakota let out a **shaky breath.** A horrible mix of **rage and despair** twisted inside him. His hands balled into **fists.**

The officers were **dead.**

Lane was **dead.**

And now he was **trapped here. Alone.**

Dakota slid down the chain-link gate, his back pressing **hard** against the cold metal. His legs felt like they could barely hold him up anymore—so he let them give out. He slumped against the fence, staring up at the sky.

The **clouds churned**, dark and heavy, rolling over the park like a thick blanket of doom. Then, **thunder cracked**—a deep, hollow sound that rattled in his chest.

Then came the rain.

Soft at first. **Gentle droplets** tapping against his skin, cooling the sweat on his face. But it grew heavier, a relentless downpour washing away the dirt, the blood—**but not the pain.**

Dakota squeezed his eyes shut. **His breath hitched.** The knot in his chest tightened, his ribs aching from the way he held it all in.

Then it **broke.**

A scream **ripped from his throat, raw and guttural, tearing through the storm like a wounded animal.**

"WHY?!"

His voice cracked, hoarse, the sound scratching out from deep inside him. He wasn't even sure who he was screaming at.

The sky?
 The monster?
 Lane?

Himself?

His chest **heaved.** His hands dug into the wet dirt beneath him. He could barely see through the rain streaking down his face, mixing with the hot tears he didn't even remember shedding.

Then—**lightning.**

A blinding **flash,** illuminating the park for just a second.

And in that second, Dakota saw it.

His breath hitched.

The **Fantasy Land castle loomed ahead, its spires stretching toward the sky like jagged teeth.**

But something **was there.**

Hanging **off the side of the tallest tower.**

A **silhouette.**

Large. **Unnatural.**

Even through the storm, Dakota **felt it.**

The weight of its gaze.

Those **cold, dead eyes, buried deep in the shadows. Watching.**

Waiting.

Dakota sat there for a long moment, rain **pounding** against his skin, mixing with the sweat and grime that clung to him like a second layer. His breath came in short, shuddering gasps, his body shaking—not from the cold, not from exhaustion, but from something much deeper.

Something raw.

Something **burning.**

Enough.

Dakota's hands curled into fists against the mud. His fingers dug in, knuckles aching, the cold biting into his skin. His pulse was **thunder** in his ears, louder than the storm overhead, louder than the wind howling through the abandoned park. He felt **sick,** but not with fear. Not anymore.

With rage.

He shoved himself to his feet, his muscles screaming in protest, but he barely noticed. His breathing was ragged, sharp and uneven. His vision tunneled, locking onto the **maintenance building** in the distance.

No more running.
No more hiding.
No more waiting for this **thing** to find him.

If this place was going to bury him, then he was **damn well** going to take it with him.

His boots **slammed** against the wet pavement, splashing through puddles as he trudged forward. His legs were heavy, but they moved with **purpose.** His arms swung at his sides, his hands clenching and unclenching as the fire in his chest burned hotter, hotter. His breath came out in ragged pants, steam curling from his lips.

By the time he reached the maintenance building, he barely slowed. He **kicked the door open**, the **wood splintering** as it swung violently against the wall. The echo barely had time to fade before he stormed inside.

The air was thick with **dust and oil**, the scent of rust clinging to the damp walls. Old tools and equipment were **scattered**, rusting away in the dim light filtering through the broken windows. The flickering **neon sign** above the workbench hummed, barely clinging to life.

Dakota didn't hesitate. His **hands tore through drawers**, his breath coming out sharp and fast as he searched for something—**anything.**

A crowbar. No.
A wrench. No.

Then his hands found it.

A gas can.

It was dented, old—but heavy. Dakota **ripped it from the shelf**, his fingers gripping the handle so tightly his knuckles turned white. He **shook it**—the unmistakable **sloshing** of liquid inside made his heart pound harder.

Yes.

His chest **heaved**, his lips parting as he sucked in a deep breath. His eyes burned. His jaw clenched so tight his teeth ached.

This was it.

No more.

He was going to **burn this place to the ground.**

Dakota's fingers curled tight around the handle of the **blowtorch**, his grip like a vice as he grabbed a bundle of **oil-stained rags** from the shelf. His pulse still pounded in his ears, but it wasn't from fear anymore—it was from **pure, burning resolve.** The storm raged on outside, but inside him, there was a storm of his own, **a fire waiting to be unleashed.**

He stepped out into the night, the weight of the **gas can** swinging at his side, the **rags clenched in his fist.** The rain did nothing to cool the heat rising in his chest, nothing to quiet the **fury** building inside him. Every step was heavy, **purposeful,** crunching against the overgrown pavement as he moved through the ruined park.

The **castle loomed** ahead, its silhouette jagged against the night sky, the towering spires stretching into the darkness. The fake stone was **cracked and weathered**, the large wooden doors swollen from years of abandonment.

Dakota didn't hesitate.

He **pulled the doors open,** the rusted hinges groaning in protest as they gave way to the force of his push. The interior was **dark, cold**, filled with the suffocating scent of mold and rot. The once-grand walls were faded, the murals of fairy tales now nothing more than warped, peeling reminders of what this place used to be.

None of it mattered.

His boots thudded **against the stone steps** as he climbed, the **gasoline sloshing** inside the canister with every movement. The air was thick, still, as if the castle itself was **holding its breath**—as if it knew what was coming.

At the top of the stairs, he reached the **security hub.**

The room was cluttered with **dusty monitors, scattered files, rusted filing cabinets, and broken keyboards.** Dakota could still see the **outlines of papers** beneath layers of dust—**logs, reports, records.** This was where the cover-up had been orchestrated, where **they** had watched everything happen and did **nothing.**

Good.

They could burn with the rest of it.

He **uncapped the gas can** and started pouring. The **thick scent of fuel** filled the air as he **soaked everything**—the desks, the chairs, the computers, the **rotting documents.** The liquid **dripped**

onto the floor, trailing behind him as he moved toward the stairs, leaving a **path of destruction** in his wake.

By the time he reached the **main floor**, he had **one goal left**.

He **lit the blowtorch**, the small **burst of blue flame** flickering to life. His hands were steady. His breathing was slow. He reached for one of the **oil-stained rags**, holding it to the flame.

The fabric ignited instantly.

That's when he heard it.

The groans.

The **labored, wheezing breath.**

The hair on the back of his neck stood up as he instinctively **looked up.**

It was there.

The Wraithform.

Standing at the **railing above him**, its massive frame hunched, its grotesque, **sunken eyes locked onto him.** The shadows clung to its decaying skin, its long **clawed fingers gripping the railing.**

Watching him.

Dakota's chest rose and fell in deep, controlled breaths. His fingers tightened around the burning rag. He could feel the heat licking at his skin, feel the sweat forming on his brow.

He wasn't afraid anymore.

His eyes met the creature's empty, lifeless stare, and for the first time, he didn't feel his stomach drop. He didn't feel his knees shake. There was nothing left to fear.

"I'm not afraid of you anymore."

His voice was steady, firm. **Final.**

And then, without a second thought, he **threw the burning rag onto the trail of gasoline.**

The fire erupted instantly.

Flames **raced up the stairs**, swallowing the security hub in seconds. The **heat exploded outward**, wood and plaster **crackling and splintering** as the old castle **caught fire like kindling.** The walls **glowed orange**, the flames licking their way toward the **ceiling.**

The Wraithform let out a **piercing, guttural shriek,** its form twisting in the light of the growing inferno.

Dakota didn't stay to watch.

He turned and walked through the doors as the flames **devoured** the castle behind him, the **firelight flickering** against the rain-slick pavement.

He didn't stop.

Didn't look back.

Not even as the castle **began to collapse.**

Dakota kept walking, the **heat of the fire** still licking at his back as the castle burned. The flames roared behind him, casting **long, flickering shadows** across the cracked pavement. His body was moving, but his mind felt **numb.** Empty.

Then—

A deafening sound tore through the sky.

A **spotlight blasted down on him**, turning the darkened ruins of Hollow Park into a scene of blinding white light. The wind from the **helicopter's blades** sent dust and ash swirling around him. His eyes squinted against the brightness, but he didn't flinch, didn't react.

Then came the sirens.

The distant **howl of engines** grew into a roar as a **fleet of squad cars rolled in.** Tires screeched, doors flew open. Red and blue lights **flashed wildly** against the crumbling buildings, bouncing off the wet pavement.

Dakota didn't move.

The world around him erupted into **chaos.**

Firefighters rushed past him, dragging thick hoses toward the burning castle. **Paramedics ran forward,** shouting his name, trying to get his attention. Officers poured out of their vehicles, **guns drawn, barking orders.**

"**Get on the ground! Hands where we can see them!**"

Dakota didn't process it all. It felt **distant, muffled**—like he was hearing everything through **water.** His ears still rang from the explosion of heat, from the monster's final, dying shriek.

The air was thick with the smell of **smoke, gasoline, and rain.**

News vans pulled up. **Cameras flashed.** Reporters shouted questions he couldn't make out. The park, **abandoned for years,** was now **alive** with more people than it had seen in years.

Dakota didn't react.

He just **stared at the ground,** his breath shallow, his body suddenly feeling **too heavy.**

His knees buckled.

Slowly, he **sank to the ground,** resting on his knees, his hands lifting behind his head. The asphalt was cold, soaked from the storm. Rain dripped down his face, mixing with the sweat, the dirt, the **blood.**

He barely felt the officers **grab at him.**

One yanked his bag off his shoulders. Another **grabbed his wrists,** twisting them behind his back. The cold bite of metal **snapped around his wrists.**

Click. Click.

The cuffs were tight.

Still, Dakota didn't fight.

Didn't say a word.

Didn't even blink as the park around him **swarmed with life.**

None of it mattered.

Chapter Fourteen

Dakota sat in the interrogation room, silent, unmoving. His wrists throbbed from the tightness of the cuffs, but he didn't care. The room was small, suffocating. The only sound was the hum of the fluorescent light above, flickering slightly. His reflection was faint in the scratched-up metal table in front of him. His clothes were still damp, stained with mud, ash, and blood. His hands trembled, but he curled them into fists, forcing them still.

The door clicked open.

Two detectives walked in. One was older, maybe mid-fifties, bald, sharp eyes, a deep frown permanently set into his face. His badge rested against a wrinkled dress shirt, the sleeves rolled up. The other was younger, mid-thirties, dark hair, tired expression. Neither looked happy to be here. They sat across from him, the older detective setting a manila folder on the table.

For a moment, no one spoke.

The older detective tapped his fingers against the folder before flipping it open. He leaned forward.

"Let's start simple. Why were you at Hollow Park?"

Dakota didn't answer right away. His eyes stayed locked on the table. His voice, when it finally came, was hoarse.

"We… we were investigating it."

The younger detective scoffed, shaking his head.

"Investigating? So what, you're some kind of urban explorer? A ghost hunter?"

Dakota's jaw tensed.

"No. We just wanted to know the truth."

The older detective exchanged a glance with his partner before sighing.

"The truth? About what?"

Dakota finally looked up. His eyes were bloodshot, his face pale and exhausted.

"About what really happened there."

The detectives studied him for a moment. Then, the older one opened the folder, pulling out a stack of black-and-white crime scene photos. He slid them across the table.

"So then, maybe you can tell us what the hell we found at the scene."

Dakota's stomach twisted as he glanced down. The images were gruesome. He didn't need to look long to know what they were—Lane. The officers. What was left of them.

He swallowed hard.

"It wasn't me."

The younger detective let out a dry laugh, sitting back in his chair.

"Yeah? Then who was it?"

Silence.

Dakota could still hear it. The tearing. The screams.

His fingers dug into his palms.

"You wouldn't believe me."

The older detective leaned in, his voice lower.

"Try us."

Dakota's breath was unsteady. His mind screamed at him to tell them the truth—about the Wraithform, about what they saw, what they recorded. But he already knew how this would go. They wouldn't believe him. No one would.

He shook his head.

"I... I don't know."

The older detective sighed, rubbing his temple. The younger one wasn't as patient.

"That's not gonna cut it, kid. We have footage. Your camera? We looked through it. You wanna explain what the hell we saw on there?"

Dakota's chest tightened. They saw it.

Before he could speak, the older detective continued.

"We also found the body cams from the missing officers."

Dakota's stomach dropped.

"We know what happened, Dakota."

A heavy silence filled the room.

Dakota stared at them, his mind racing. If they had seen the footage, then they knew. They knew what was out there.

So why were they still questioning him like this?

The older detective's expression darkened.

"Listen… what's on those recordings?" He shook his head. **"We can't let that get out."**

Dakota blinked, his breath hitching.

"What?"

The younger detective crossed his arms.

"You heard him. We can't risk causing a mass panic."

Dakota's hands tightened into fists.

"People deserve to know the truth."

The older detective closed the folder, resting his hands on top of it.

"This isn't a debate."

"We're confiscating the footage. All of it."

Dakota felt like the air had been knocked out of him.

They were going to bury it.

Just like before. Just like they always did.

Lane died for this. The officers died for this. And they were just going to pretend it never happened?

Dakota's voice was barely above a whisper.

"You knew… didn't you?"

Neither detective answered.

But the look in their eyes told him everything.

The air in the interrogation room felt heavier, the silence stretching. Dakota's fingers twitched against the metal table, his nails pressing into his palms. The older detective kept his hands on the folder, unmoving, while the younger one leaned back, watching Dakota like he was some kid who didn't understand how the world worked.

Dakota's jaw clenched. **"You knew."** His voice was steady now, stronger.

The older detective let out a slow breath. **"Careful, son."**

"Careful of what?" Dakota snapped, shoving the crime scene photos back across the table. They scattered, sliding off the edge. **"You knew something was in that park. You knew people went missing, and you did nothing."**

The younger detective scoffed. **"We don't know shit."**

"Bullshit."

The room went still for a second. Dakota's breathing was shallow, his pulse hammering in his ears. He could feel the weight of their stares, the quiet tension pressing down on him. The older detective's fingers tapped against the table, slow and deliberate.

"You think you're the first idiot to go looking for trouble in Hollow Park?" His voice was calm, but there was something in his tone—something that sent a chill up Dakota's spine. **"You're just the first one we found alive."**

Dakota swallowed hard, but he didn't back down.

"Then why cover it up? Why hide the truth?"

The younger detective gave a dry, humorless laugh. **"Jesus, kid. You really think people could handle knowing there's some... some thing hunting in that park?"** He shook his head. **"You think the world would just accept that and move on?"**

Dakota's hands balled into fists. **"So you just let it keep happening? How many more people have to die before you actually do something?"**

The older detective's expression darkened. **"You think it's that simple?"** He leaned forward, his voice lowering. **"You think we haven't tried? You think we don't have bodies of our own buried under that place?"**

Dakota's breath caught in his throat.

The younger detective rubbed his temple, suddenly looking years older. **"There are things out there that don't make sense, kid. Things we can't stop. So yeah, we keep it quiet. Because the alternative? Is worse."**

Dakota shook his head. **"No. You're just cowards."**

The younger detective slammed his hands on the table, the sound echoing off the walls. **"Watch your mouth."**

"Or what?" Dakota shot back, his voice shaking. **"You'll lock me up? Make me disappear like everyone else?"**

The older detective exhaled sharply, rubbing his temple.

"We're not your enemy, Dakota."

"Yeah?" Dakota's laugh was bitter. **"Because it sure as hell feels like you are."**

The older detective studied him for a long moment. Then, finally, he sat back, folding his hands over the folder again.

"This conversation is over."

Dakota's chest rose and fell, anger and exhaustion fighting for control.

The younger detective stood first, shaking his head. **"Take our advice, kid. Walk away. Forget any of this happened."**

Dakota's glare was ice. **"I'm not forgetting anything."**

Neither detective looked surprised. The older one simply sighed as he stood, picking up the folder.

"Then I hope you're ready for what comes next."

With that, they turned and walked out, leaving Dakota alone in the suffocating silence.

Dakota's fingers trembled as he reached for the scattered photos on the floor. His breath hitched when his eyes landed on **Lane.** The image was grainy, black and white, but it was enough. His chest tightened. He swallowed the lump in his throat and picked it up carefully, his hands dirty, smudging the edges.

That's when he saw it.

Nestled beneath the photo, barely noticeable against the dull concrete floor—**a camera SD card.**

Dakota's pulse jumped. He darted a glance toward the door, listening. Nothing.

Quickly, he scooped up the SD card, shoving it into his pocket along with the photo. He sat back in his chair, forcing his expression blank, his hands resting flat against the table just as the door **creaked** open again.

The younger detective walked back in, a cardboard box tucked under one arm. He looked tired—**like he wanted this to be over just as much as Dakota did.** Setting the box down on the table, he pulled a small key from his pocket and reached forward, unlocking the cuffs around Dakota's wrists.

The metal clinked as the cuffs came off, and Dakota exhaled slowly, rolling his sore wrists. He didn't look up.

The detective didn't sit this time. He just **stood there, watching him.**

"Stay out of trouble." His voice was firm, but there was something else underneath. A warning.

Dakota didn't answer.

The detective sighed, rubbing the back of his neck. **"And stay away from that place."**

This time, Dakota **did** look up. His stare was blank, unreadable.

"Why?"

The detective exhaled sharply, shaking his head. **"Because it's quarantined. Locked down by people way above my pay grade."** His eyes flicked to the door, then back to Dakota. **"That thing won't be hurting anyone else."**

Dakota scoffed, his voice cold. **"I burned it alive."**

The detective gave him a look—somewhere between **pity and disbelief.** Then he chuckled, shaking his head as he grabbed the empty cuffs and shoved them into his pocket.

"Yeah, sure. You're lucky we're even letting you walk. Too much damn paperwork trying to explain that you're crazy and burned down a fake castle trying to slay a dragon."

Dakota's expression didn't change.

224

The detective lingered a second longer before grabbing the box and shoving it toward him. **"Take your stuff and go."**

Dakota reached for the box. The SD card **pressed against his leg in his pocket.**

He still had the truth.

And he wasn't done yet.

The apartment felt **hollow.**

No stupid jokes. No sarcastic remarks. No sounds of Lane raiding the fridge for a midnight snack or scrolling through his phone while humming some random song off-key.

Just **silence.**

Dakota sat on the couch, hunched forward, elbows resting on his knees. The TV cast a dim glow over the room, flickering as the news report played. He wasn't even sure why he left it on—maybe he was hoping, **somehow, some way,** they'd tell the truth. Maybe they'd say Lane's name. Maybe they'd say **anything real.**

But they didn't.

"The fire at Hollow Park was determined to be caused by faulty wiring within the structure."

Dakota's breath hitched, his fingers curling into the fabric of his jeans.

"Due to unauthorized individuals gaining access to the park, power was restored to sections of the property, leading to an electrical malfunction. This, in turn, ignited the fire within the castle."

Bullshit.

His fists clenched. His nails dug into his palms, but he barely felt it.

They weren't just **lying.** They were rewriting the entire thing. Erasing it like it never even happened.

The screen cut to a familiar face—the **older detective.** The same one who had sat across from him in that interrogation room, staring at him like he was some **delusional kid who didn't know what he was talking about.**

"There was no criminal intent," the detective said, his voice calm, smooth, practiced. "**Just a case of reckless trespassing. The park has been officially quarantined, and no further incidents are expected. We strongly advise the public to stay away from the area.**"

Dakota's pulse thundered in his ears.

The **castle. The park. The bodies.**

Gone.

No mention of Lane. No mention of the officers who went in but never came back out. No mention of the thing **that killed them.**

They were covering it up.

They were pretending none of it mattered.

Like **Lane didn't matter.** Like those officers were just **inconveniences.**

Dakota's breath came sharp, ragged. His whole body **tensed, locked up, shaking with something raw, something furious.**

They were going to get away with it.

No.

His fingers twitched against his jeans, brushing against the **small, hidden SD card** in his pocket.

They could erase the news reports. They could lie to the public. They could destroy whatever evidence they wanted.

But they didn't get everything.

His eyes flicked back to the TV. The newscaster had already moved on—some bullshit about a traffic accident on the highway. The Hollow Park story was **done. Closed. Over.**

As if it never even happened.

Dakota exhaled shakily, his jaw tightening.

Not if he had anything to say about it.

Dakota paced the apartment, his mind a storm, thoughts colliding, crashing, spiraling out of control.

How the hell was he supposed to do this?

How could he make them listen? How could he show them the truth when the people in charge had already **decided to bury it?**

His hand curled into a fist before running through his hair, yanking at the strands in frustration. His pulse was racing, his breath uneven. He couldn't just sit here. He couldn't just do nothing.

His fingers brushed against his pocket, and he stopped.

The SD card.

He pulled it out, holding it between his fingers, turning it over, feeling the tiny ridges beneath his thumb. It was so **small,** barely anything, just a stupid piece of plastic and metal.

But it was **everything.**

The only proof he had. The last pieces of **Lane.**

His throat tightened as he walked to his desk, heart hammering as he slid into the chair. His laptop sat open, the screen dimmed from inactivity. He hesitated, the card burning in his hand.

This was it.

He inserted the SD card.

The files loaded. A folder popped up. Dozens of video files, their timestamps marking the hours, minutes, seconds of that night. He clicked on the first one, and the screen filled with a shaky shot of the road—**their journey to Hollow Park.**

A lump formed in his throat as he watched.

They had been **so excited.** Laughing, talking, arguing over music choices. Lane had been cracking jokes, recording dumb commentary about how they were about to uncover some dark, hidden secret, how they'd **become legends in the urban exploration scene.**

If only they had known.

The footage cut to them sneaking in. The way their excitement had **shifted** the deeper they went. How the laughter faded into uneasy whispers. The way the darkness swallowed the park whole, turning every broken ride, every shattered light post into something twisted.

Dakota watched as they **explored, joked, reminisced.** He watched the moment where they thought they were going to die—when they apologized, when they forgave each other, when they talked about **their past, their families, their regrets.**

He heard Lane's voice, raw and shaken.

The way had sat there telling his family that he loved them. The defeated goodbye.

Dakota gripped the edge of the desk, his chest **aching, burning.**

What did Lane's parents know?

Had anyone even told them yet? Were they sitting at home, waiting for a call? Wondering why their son hadn't come back?

Or had the cops already fed them **the same lies?**

His breath came ragged. He could see them in his head—Lane's mom, sitting at the kitchen table, phone clutched in her hands, eyes red and swollen. His dad, stiff, quiet, trying to be strong for her but **just as broken.**

And he was sitting here, watching it happen. Watching **Lane's last moments over and over again.**

His vision blurred. He wiped at his face, **furious at himself** for letting it get to him, for being so damn useless.

But he **wasn't** useless.

Not yet.

He **had this.** He had Lane's last words, their last conversation, the **truth.**

And no matter what those bastards tried to do—

He was going to make sure the world saw it.

Dakota's eyes burned, dry and aching, but he kept them locked on the screen. The glow of the laptop cast deep shadows across his face, the only light in the dark apartment. He hadn't moved from the chair in hours, barely even blinked.

4:23 a.m.

His body was begging for rest, for just a few hours of sleep, but he ignored it. **He wasn't done yet.**

He leaned forward, clicking through files, dragging clips into the editing software. His fingers trembled from exhaustion, but he pushed through it, sorting, cutting, piecing everything together.

Each video had a purpose.

One for Lane's family. **Only the goodbye.** Nothing else. They didn't need to see the fear, the horror, the things that haunted Dakota every time he shut his eyes. They only needed to hear Lane's last words to them—the ones he never got to say in person.

One for his own family. His voice cracking as he spoke to them in the footage, saying the things he never thought he'd have to say. **Just in case.**

A separate video for the news stations. A carefully edited montage of **undeniable proof.** The truth. The things the authorities had covered up, the things people **deserved to know.**

And then—**the full footage.**

Raw. Unedited. The **real** story.

It was already uploading to YouTube, scheduled for release. He had given himself a head start—**enough time to get out of town before it went live.**

By the time anyone saw it, he'd be long gone.

Dakota sat back in his chair, staring at the progress bar on the screen. **Almost done.**

His chest ached, but it wasn't exhaustion. It wasn't even grief.

It was **rage.**

They had **lied.** They had covered it up, swept everything under the rug like Lane, those officers—**like none of them ever mattered.**

He gritted his teeth, shoving himself away from the desk. He grabbed his bag and started packing, moving on autopilot. Clothes, essentials, what little cash he had left. Everything was shoved into a duffel and tossed into the van, one thing after another, until all that was left in the apartment was his laptop, still glowing, waiting.

Dakota stood there for a moment, staring at it.

Then, without hesitation, he grabbed it and **smashed it against the floor.**

The screen cracked, the plastic casing splintered. He stomped down on it once—twice—**until it was nothing but shattered pieces.**

No trails. No way for anyone to track where he was going.

This wasn't over.

But by the time they realized it—

He'd already be gone.

Epilogue

The mountains had a way of swallowing a man whole.

Dakota had been out here for years now, tucked away in a cabin that barely counted as a home. It was small, simple—just enough to survive. A creaky wooden table, a sagging couch, a bed in the corner. No decorations, no photos, nothing personal.

A fire crackled in the stone fireplace, the only sound in the otherwise dead-silent room. No phone. No computer. No connection to the outside world.

No one knew he was here.

He ran a hand over the scruff on his face, staring at the embers glowing beneath the flames.

Every time he went into town, he used a different name. Paid in cash. Kept his head down. The locals barely noticed him, just another quiet man passing through for supplies. It was safer that way. **No questions. No attention.**

But he knew it wouldn't last.

The suits—the ones pulling the strings behind that goddamn cover-up—**they'd find him eventually.** He was living on borrowed time, just waiting for the day when he'd disappear for good.

But that wasn't what mattered.

What mattered was that the truth was out.

Everything they worked so hard to bury had been **dug up, dragged into the light.**

They couldn't erase it. Not completely. It had spread too far, reached too many people. Hollow Park was no longer just some forgotten urban legend.

People **knew.**

And that meant Dakota had already won.

At first, they tried to contain it.

The videos disappeared—one by one, accounts wiped clean as if they never existed. News stations pulled their reports, claiming **"false information"** and **"public misinterpretation."**

Officials denied everything, calling it a hoax, dismissing the footage as doctored, fabricated nonsense.

But it was **too late.**

The internet was relentless. **Too many people had seen it, saved it, reuploaded it.** Every time a video was taken down, five more popped up in its place. Anonymous forums were flooded with discussions, people dissecting the footage frame by frame. Was it real? Was it some kind of elaborate stunt? But the raw terror in Dakota's voice, the sheer **agony** in Lane's final screams—**those couldn't be faked.**

Then came the **panic.**

At first, it was just outrage. People demanding answers, posting and reposting the footage, tagging officials, police departments, news stations. But when silence was the only response, that outrage turned to something **worse.**

Fear.

A fear that spread like an infection.

Talk shows and radio stations picked it up. Paranormal investigators, conspiracy theorists—**even mainstream journalists**—couldn't ignore it anymore. Families of the missing came forward. **Dozens.** Then **hundreds.** They spoke about their loved ones—people who had gone to Hollow Park, never to be seen again. Some of them had been dismissed as runaways, others as tragic accidents or unsolved cases. But **now?** They had proof that something **had been hunting them.**

That's when the protests started.

First, it was just **grieving families** demanding answers outside city halls, police stations, news networks. But as more people saw the footage—**really saw it**—it spread beyond just the families. People filled the streets with signs and banners, screaming at the government, at the police, at anyone who would listen.

"HOW LONG HAVE YOU KNOWN?"
"JUSTICE FOR THE LOST!"
"WHERE ARE THE BODIES?"

Then came the riots.

Mobs broke into government buildings, stormed local police stations. Officers tried to hold the crowds back, but **how do you fight a city full of people who have nothing left to lose?** The families of the victims were joined by angry citizens, by Hollow Park employees who swore they had seen **something** lurking in the dark corners of the park before it shut down.

One night, the Hollow Creek Police Department was **set on fire.** The whole building went up in flames, along with **decades of records.** People swore they saw men in suits—**not officers, not local officials**—arriving before the fire had even started. **Destroying everything.**

Trying to erase the truth again.

But it was **too late.**

Dakota sat in his cabin, watching it all unfold through the grainy signal of his old TV. He barely had service up in the mountains, but it didn't matter—he had **no** intention of reconnecting. No phone. No computer. No way for them to trace him.

He **couldn't** risk it.

His face was everywhere now. News stations used his mugshot from his brief arrest after the fire. Internet sleuths dug up old photos of him and Lane—**smiling, happy, alive.**

They called him a criminal. A hero. A lunatic. A whistleblower.

It didn't matter.

The truth was out.

The footage had reached every corner of the world, burned into the minds of millions. And now, the people weren't **asking** for the truth anymore.

They were demanding it.

Dakota leaned back in his chair, listening to the fire crackle in the fireplace. The heat from the flames didn't touch the cold sinking deep into his bones.

He had done it.

It cost him **everything.** His home. His best friend. **His life.**

But in the end…

He won.

Sleep never came easy.

No matter how much time passed, **it never faded.**

Dakota sat on the edge of his cot, staring at the dying embers in the fireplace. His body was exhausted, aching, pleading for rest—but his mind refused. Every time he closed his eyes, he was **there again.**

Back in that place.

The air thick with the scent of burning wood and charred flesh. The heat licking at his skin. The darkness shifting, twisting, **watching.**

Then—**that scream.**

That same, **soul-ripping, earth-shaking scream.**

It always started the same way. A low, guttural noise, like something scraping against hollow bones. Then came the rattling breath, the inhuman groan as if the thing was **struggling to exist.** And then—

The shriek.

Louder than anything he had ever heard. Loud enough to shake the ground, to make his teeth ache, to set his nerves on fire.

In his dreams, he always turned his head—just in time to see it rise from the darkness. That grotesque, towering **thing,** its jagged limbs moving unnaturally, its gaping mouth unhinging wider than any human jaw should.

But it wasn't just the monster's scream he heard.

It was Lane.

"Dakota! Dakota, help me! Please!"

The raw, **shattered desperation** in his voice cut through him like a blade. The sheer terror, the gut-wrenching pain—**Lane knew.** He **knew** he wasn't getting out of there.

Dakota still saw him, being dragged away, arms outstretched, reaching—**begging.**

And Dakota wasn't fast enough.

He had no choice. **There was no saving him.**

But his nightmares didn't care about that. They replayed it over and over, each time twisting the scene, making it worse. Sometimes he got there in time, grabbing Lane's wrist and pulling with everything he had—only to watch in horror as Lane was **ripped away** from him, his screams cut short in a sickening crunch.

Other times, it wasn't Lane's voice at all.

It was the officers. The men who had risked their lives to save him. He could still hear the chaos—the gunfire, the shouting, the sheer **panic** in their voices.

"Fall back! FALL BACK!"

"Jesus Christ, what IS that thing?!"

"It's still coming! It's STILL COMING!"

And then—**silence.**

Their screams always ended the same way. Cut short. Swallowed by the darkness.

Gone.

Dakota snapped awake, gasping for breath. His body was damp with sweat, his heart hammering against his ribs like it was trying to escape.

He was still in the cabin.

Still alone.

He ran a shaking hand down his face, exhaling slowly, trying to steady himself. But the echoes still lingered in his ears. The screams, the fire, the monster's haunting, ragged breaths.

It never went away.

And deep down, Dakota knew it never would.

Dakota sat on the edge of the cot, his body hunched forward, elbows on his knees, fingers gripping his hair. The fire in the hearth had burned down to embers, casting long shadows that flickered against the cabin walls. The wind howled outside, rattling the windows in their frames.

He had been waiting for this moment.

For **them** to come.

For years, he had lived like a ghost, cut off from the world, always looking over his shoulder. But the waiting was worse than the inevitable. He had nothing left—no family, no friends, no future. Just this cabin and the knowledge that someday, someone would come to make him disappear.

Maybe tonight was that night.

The sound of **footsteps.**

Dakota's entire body went rigid.

Slow. Crunching against the frost-laced ground.

Not an animal.

He had learned to distinguish the sounds out here. He knew the way deer moved, the way branches snapped under their hooves. This was deliberate. **Heavy. Human.**

He didn't move, barely breathed.

The footsteps stopped just outside the door.

A slow, deliberate knock followed.

Dakota's pulse **spiked.** His fingers twitched, itching to reach for the shotgun resting against the wall, but he couldn't move.

Then came a voice.

Soft. Familiar.

"Dakota?"

His chest **seized.**

No.

No, that wasn't possible.

"Come on, man. Open up. It's freezing out here."

He **knew** that voice.

Lane.

Dakota's breath came in short, shallow bursts. His mind scrambled for an explanation, anything that made sense.

Lane was **dead.**

He had watched him die. Had seen the horror in his eyes, had heard the way his screams were swallowed by the darkness. He had lived with that moment replaying in his head for years, echoing in his nightmares.

But now?

"Dakota, please."

His fingers twitched at his sides. It sounded just like him. The same cadence, the same slight rasp at the end of his words. Like they were back in the van, laughing at something stupid, like nothing had ever happened.

A lump formed in Dakota's throat. His heart **pounded.**

This wasn't real. It **couldn't** be real.

He squeezed his eyes shut, willing the voice to go away.

But it didn't.

Another knock.

Softer this time.

"You left me."

Dakota's stomach **dropped.**

The room suddenly felt smaller, the air heavier, pressing down on him like a weight. He swallowed hard, forcing himself to his feet. His legs felt unsteady as he moved toward the door, each step slow and deliberate.

His fingers hovered over the handle.

Silence.

He took a deep breath.

And then—**he yanked it open.**

The cold night air hit him like a slap.

But there was **nothing** there.

Just the endless stretch of snow-covered trees, the wind whistling through the branches.

His breath curled in the air, visible in the moonlight. He stepped forward, scanning the tree line, his heart still **hammering.**

The wind whispered through the trees.

Dakota stood there, staring into the dark, his pulse **thundering** in his ears.

He wasn't alone.

He could feel it.

Something was out there. Watching. Waiting.

A shiver crawled down his spine.

Slowly, he stepped back inside, shutting the door. His hands were shaking. He locked it, took a step back, staring at the wooden surface like it might burst open at any second.

The cabin was silent once more.

Except for his own breathing.

And then—

Another knock.

Soft. Persistent.

"Dakota..."

Dakota stood frozen, staring at the door.

The knock had been softer this time, almost **gentle.**

Like it was waiting.

Like it knew.

His breath came in short, uneven bursts. His body was rigid, muscles coiled tight, ready to **run**—but where? There was nowhere to go. No one left to run to.

His fingers twitched at his sides.

He could ignore it. Pretend it wasn't there. Pretend it was just exhaustion warping his senses, twisting his mind against him.

But he had heard it. **Felt** it.

Lane's voice.

He squeezed his eyes shut.

It wasn't real. It wasn't real. It wasn't real.

"You left me."

Dakota's eyes **snapped open.**

That voice. It wasn't coming from outside anymore.

It was behind him.

A shudder raked through his body. He didn't turn around. He **wouldn't.**

The cabin felt **smaller.** The walls seemed to press in around him, the air thick and suffocating. His own heartbeat pounded in his skull, drowning out everything else.

A shadow flickered in the corner of his vision.

No.

He wouldn't look.

Looking meant acknowledging. Acknowledging meant believing.

And if he **believed**—

A whisper at his ear. Close. Too close.

"Dakota…"

His breath caught. His hands clenched into fists.

Slowly, he turned.

The cabin was empty.

The fire had burned down to nothing but glowing embers, casting long, **twisting** shadows along the walls. The wind howled outside, rattling the windows, but inside, everything was still.

But it didn't **feel** empty.

His gaze swept across the room, searching, waiting—**dreading.**

Nothing.

Just the worn furniture. The cold fireplace. The door, still locked.

And yet…

His skin crawled. The weight of unseen eyes pressed against his back.

Dakota swallowed hard, backing up until he felt the rough wood of the wall against his spine. His breaths were slow, shaky.

It was nothing. **Nothing.**

Just the exhaustion. Just his mind playing tricks on him.

He squeezed his eyes shut. Counted his breaths.

One.

Two.

Three—

A whisper, right at his ear.

"You can't run forever."

Dakota's eyes snapped open.

The cabin was **empty.**

But he knew.

He would never be alone again.

THE END

Printed in Great Britain
by Amazon